KOJO LAING was born in K͏... educated in both Ghana and S͏... Arts degree at Glasgow Univer͏... doing administrative work in th͏... year at the seat of Government ͏... made Secretary to the Institute ͏of African Studies at the University of Ghana. He is currently Chief Executive of a private school, St Anthony's, established by his mother in 1962.

With the publication of his first novel, *Search Sweet Country* (William Heinemann, 1986), Laing established himself as a remarkable writer with a sparkling, ironical and witty style. His second novel, *Woman of the Aeroplanes*, was published in 1988 (William Heinemann), and *Godhorse*, the first published collection of his poems (AWS 1989), reveals Laing's highly inventive poetic style.

Major Gentl and the Achimota Wars is his third novel.

Besides writing, Laing has a penchant for hunting, walking, playing football and planting trees.

KOJO LAING

MAJOR GENTL
AND THE
ACHIMOTA WARS

HEINEMANN

Heinemann International Literature and Textbooks
a division of Heinemann Educational Books Ltd
Halley Court, Jordan Hill, Oxford OX2 8EJ

Heinemann Educational Books Inc
361 Hanover Street, Portsmouth, New Hampshire, 03801, USA

Heinemann Educational Books (Nigeria) Ltd
PMB 5205, Ibadan
Heinemann Kenya Ltd
Kijabe Street, PO Box 45314, Nairobi
Heinemann Educational Boleswa
PO Box 10103, Village Post Office, Gabarone, Botswana

LONDON   EDINBURGH   MADRID
PARIS   ATHENS   BOLOGNA   MELBOURNE
SYDNEY   AUCKLAND   SINGAPORE
TOKYO   HARARE

First published by Heinemann International Literature and Textbooks
in the African Writers Series in 1992

British Library Cataloguing in Publication Data

Laing, B. Kojo, 1946–
Major Gentl and the Achimota wars. – (African writers series)
I. Title II. Series
823[F]

ISBN 0–435–909789

Photoset by Wilmaset Ltd, Birkenhead, Wirral
Printed in Great Britain by
Cox and Wyman Ltd, Reading, Berks

92 93 94 95 10 9 8 7 6 5 4 3 2 1

CONTENTS

AUTHOR'S NOTE ON THE GLOSSARY

The words listed in the glossary at the back of this book are the outcome of the world of *Major Gentl and the Achimota Wars*. The motive behind them is to internationalise the English. I believe that more parochial areas of the world need a broadening of vocabulary – hence many of the words are repeated in my novels and poetry. Some are invented, most are direct translations from Akan and Ga and sometimes Hausa. It is usual in Ghana (with such a cosmopolitan mix of cultures) to intersperse one language with words from another. This ought to be done universally for the idea is to create one gigantic language.

Kojo Laing, 1992

ZONE ONE

War

Major aMofa Gentl was feared in Achimota City for his gentleness, since it was this quality that won the first war for the golden cockroach, the emblem of the city. And this emblem, accompanied by its friend the silver mosquito, would shed its symbolic nature and become a real city cockroach crawling about looking for truth.

The war was won against Torro the Terrible Roman, the only man in the universe who could stand both frontally and sideways at the same time, boof. The major had arranged with the golden crawl to rent two rooms on the moon, rooms that you needed no rocket to reach: he just banged a nail in the nearest airship, under the strange lunar songs, held on tight, and then had access to the deepest craters. From there he would use magic to see far into other countries.

The major's great effort in quiet and cunning during the First War of Existence – like arranging for a million dead flies to climb up the nostrils of half of Torro's army – was rewarded in a desperate manner: since he would not accept promotion or decoration, the military leaders promoted his shadow to the rank of sergeant instead, thus creating substance for Gentl whatever size his shadow was . . . short sergeant, tall sergeant. Atinga, the major's bodyguard, was so jealous of this promotion that he beat the shadow sergeant mercilessly whenever his master was not looking. And the shadow let the blows painfully through.

You had to take time to see the major's height – he was such a calm man. It was known that he was friendly with the gods, and he could thus achieve his own weight in wisdom every few days. But he had no wisdom in love koraa. He had an extraordinarily brown nose up to which the rest of the colour of his face led; a face so small that you had to look twice before you could get enough of it to fill both eyes.

As the major and the golden cockroach had breakfast together, the mist was low enough in the major's raised bamboo house to fill their glasses. Mist in the mouth. They were discussing the Second War of

1

Existence, which was new, and which made it possible for them to meet in the middle of their minds, with all inessentials gone: to win the war, you fought it sideways. When the sun finally came out over their banku and okro stew, with early morning palm-wine, the tangerine shades caught the mango shades, with the green oranges lengthening their shadows to join the shading.

'This city is ripening now,' Mr Cockroach said, taking a long draw from its sikadillo cigar with a small guava stuck at the end of it. It smoked fruit.

The major said nothing, taking hold of his favourite snake and transferring it to his shoulders. What he remembered was the last thing he saw through his magic binoculars: a Europe that had finally given up language and humanity to what it thought were the poor areas of the world, a Europe that had its own secret code of communication, having arrived at that ludicrous point that the major quietly snorted at: purity and exclusiveness in a world that cried for the opposite things. As the golden cockroach usually said, a ripe city was something very modern, for it embraced and did not reject the opportunity to widen humanity.

'It's as if they are saying that only the poor can afford humanity, Major, no?' asked the golden cee, still expecting no answer from the major.

The short grass of the fruit-tree garden housed dragonflies and grasshoppers that darted and jumped cleanly from calabash to calabash. The sun crawled further out of the leaves, its rays stretched elastic as the golden cockroach pulled them and slurped the last of its mist and wine. It got up stylishly to leave on one leg, its tight-round Bonwire hat cocked at the kente sun; but since the major continued to stare into the distance, it stood there thus, suspended in gold. Mr Cee then quickly descended on to its other legs and gave the major's chin a push, saying, 'I am trying to work out to what degree you have to be kind to the enemy before you defeat him . . . last time, in the first war, you almost ruined it koraa by foolishly upgrading your sympathy to empathy for the enemy. Torro the white Roman is a wild man, and if you're not careful he'll win the Second War of Existence . . .'

The major got up at last at the mention of victory for Torro, rubbed the top of his pockets as the snake slid off him, and then said with force, 'You don't build a city like this and then let Torro take it free.'

The golden cockroach just laughed and laughed at the passion of

2

Gentl, some emblematic problem, some problematic emblem, the sun glinting on its nose, whaaaat. After complaining about silver malaria from carrying the mosquito, and pointing sardonically at the small face of the major, the golden cee left the garden in its odd flight: it bit a series of elevating spaces to ascend the sky, this crawler that flew, bite, ka, bite, ka, bite, ka . . .

Over the last two decades, Achimota City's fast new geography had devoured Accra almost completely while at the same time most of the rest of the country had inexplicably vanished, land and all. Thus, by the year 2020 Achimota was a truncated city bursting to survive and to find the rest of its country soon. The three elders of government, each with a beard the shape of X, Y or Z, had shepherded the city over this deep crisis, directing history as if it were mad traffic. They had rules which helped to form the new ways that the century demanded. Fruit was law: every street had to have dwarf banana trees in belts and lines, buckled with close groups of any other fruit trees, so many guavas and oranges. There was fruit in the toilets, fruit in the halls, and fruit in the aeroplanes, so that you could eat the city. Other rules cut across the entire political history, such as the one allowing every adult, and a few children too, the chance to be head of state for months, weeks or even minutes, under the supervision of the elders. The ruled did the ruling, and neither stole nor murdered, nor arrested anybody, for the glare of the new and the glare of the crisis was too much for anybody to cheat under, deebi.

But it was Pogo Alonka Forr the carrot millionaire who spoilt the system of rotating leadership by refusing to hand over power to Abomu Kwame the drunkard. He had insisted that Abomu would rule under the authority of akpeteshie, akpeteshie parliament, akpeteshie law. With Torro's tricks rising in intensity, the elders had agreed to suspend the system temporarily, giving districts to Major Gentl, Nana Mai the Grandmother Bomb, and Pogo Forr himself. The elders were not concerned about losing face at all, for with a true power base there was no face to lose.

aMofa Gentl was born in bits when the whole of the country existed: head on Monday, torso on Thursday, and the popylonkwe on Friday. He could thus be named after his own genitals. Like Torro, the major had manoeuvred to be born at a particular place, leading his mother from the womb to give birth to him among the pendant guinea-corn in the north. He spoke through her beautiful microphonic placenta, which was finally released in the south. As soon as Major Gentl was fully born, he gave an enormous salute which nobody could return. The salute broke a branch. At the age of two, he already had a military face, and six months later, he had shouted, 'The ants have taken over my hands, please free my bitten salute!' At the age of ten, he had exclaimed before the same elders of government, holding their beards at exactly the same angles as when he was two, 'The planet is leaking, get ten thousand chamber-pots to catch the energies of the cities of the world to use against the enemies!' He was thus only ten when he was made a corporal. And his gentleness grew as several small wars came and went, none of them being resolved before the wars of existence. Some small wars passed under the soles of his feet, some passed over his head, some wounded his knees when he was fifteen, and yet others tightened his nose so that that the army didn't smell the same. By the age of seventeen he had appeared so mysterious with his womb power and his oracles that the elders of government had offered him the Ministry of Fruit. He had covered himself in sweetapple and oranges, and then he had refused the fruity ministry, spitting out orange pips at the government. Yet he remained in the army for the next twenty years, quite uncomfortable, but directing things all the same, first as a teenage commander – small boy danger – and then as a moody captain fighting the invisible wars.

These small wars were totally invisible in the sense that you never saw the enemy. There were guns without hands, ships without captains, planes without pilots, and camps without soldiers but with adequate food and weapons; everything was controlled by the bosses abroad. And it was only after the newly promoted captain and Nana Mai the Grandmother Bomb had worked out new strategies that Achimota City won these wars; strategies such as turning the automatic guns back-wards and shooting into nothing – you heard the zero screams – or deserting battlefields and whole areas for weeks at a time to escape the germ warfare, against which Nana Mai had worked out subtle screens. After these small wars came Torro the visible enemy.

It was when Gentl was promoted to major that he left the army, with his shadow still in it. There he was on a cool morning, rushing away from the officers' mess, chattering in anger at the sky; and they had sent a low Air Force plane after him to persaude him to stay, and from an impulse he had spat at the wings, they were so low; and the plane had risen with a roar, carrying his spit back to the military. After analysing his saliva, they knew he was serious about leaving. What did you do with a man who left the army but continued to have a place at the top of its command? After such large gestures, it didn't take the major long to return to the position where others like Pogo and Torro thought they were the better heroes.

Torro, the loser of the First War of Existence, would in fact boast of the following, his bright red tie rolling over the folds of his belly like a second higher popylonkwe; he said he knew that the bosses abroad were working paa on Time, so that twenty-four hours there would not be the same as twenty-four hours here, they would handicap the time just as they had weighted down money in different places, except Achimota City which was fiercely independent. Torro's smile got broader and broader as he continued with utter confidence. He boasted that the gathering of consciousness, of pure cerebral energy, had reached such an advanced stage that all that was needed to burst out of the present galaxy on to others was the consciousness of only two hundred million people from the poorer areas of the world. And Torro was getting excited, with his ever-broadening smile, about what he called essences, the same leaking essences that the major wanted to catch in chamber-pots: they were supposed to negate distance, mass, and even space itself, so that space occupied things as much as the other way round; and if a few million new inventions were made in these rich countries, there would be no difference between one essence and another, there would be no need to move, no need to stay still, and finally there would be no need for existence at all when essences themselves purified each other into nothing. How happy that would be! Torro would enthuse. And he never failed to be sarcastic to Major Gentl about the so-so soul of Achimota City: some soul so full of being that the people of the city would first want to imaginatively EXPERIENCE something like astrophysics before studying it.

'Yes, yes,' Torro would shout at the top of his voice, 'this may keep you at one with the universe, but weel you survive? Hahahaha!' His laugh would alter the shapes of his belly, as it finally pushed his smiling aside. That would be the limit of Torro trying to be philosophical, some head-head man, and he would drop his thoughts and take up his powerful cigars instead, blowing smoke into Gentl's face, for he was annoyed that Gentl believed that true and high intelligence belonged to

5

this unassuming city here, no fears. Very soon, the major would think, Torro would announce that all paradox abroad had been conquered, including the paradox that they couldn't possibly have achieved this.

As he rose from the breakfast table now, it was love that was bothering the major: he had met his wife Ama Three casually at the battlefront holding a gun, and actually fighting for the enemy, Ama fighting for Torro's army! As his head raced round itself, Gentl exercised extreme restraint, caution was for when the heart rose wild. She had greeted her husband among the flying bullets, and apologised for failing to make the breakfast that morning, 'since, my dear husband, I was coming here to be busy with the guns, and I didn't want to hurt you by telling you in advance that I was going to fight for the other side. When I return home to make the lunch, I will explain everything to you.' She had then given his neck a fast embrace, and continued with her shooting, twice aiming at him and missing him narrowly. She had duly returned home at lunch, full of hustle and bustle. Then she had imperiously postponed her explanations to next week, telling him that she loved him just too much. Gentl's soldiers laughed behind his back.

So the Second War of Existence started at the back of a rat, with Torro's third rodent being shot by aMofa Gentl in the Achimota sky. Torro retaliated by shooting at the major's favourite snake, but he missed, and then ran back into his helicopter farting freely in unison with the sikadillo smoke leaving his mouth in angry rings. With his energy-stealing brain machines hidden at various points in the city, Torro had prided himself on being able to manipulate these machines to force the Achimotans to forget the names of the rich cities of the world; primarily so that the locals wouldn't know who their biggest enemies were. But now Torro was confused, shouting out, 'Tell me my name pronto, tell me my name! I am the man who has been able to get your wife fighting against you . . . respect me!'

Torro never failed to want to provoke Gentl beyond the bounds of his legendary patience, a patience that went beyond wives, bosses, rich cities, small wars, first wars of existence, and over-fed rats. The major smiled from the opposite side of Torro's expectations, arranging his big chest hard against Torro's abuses from the helicopter just taking off; and thinking with justice: he who made others forget names would be the first to forget his own name. Torro insulted the major with two fingers and a thumb, by the propellers.

Torro the Roman was an agent of the rich cities abroad, which preferred now to work through such mercenaries and agencies in their relations with the poorer areas of the world; for this kept their codes secret, and made their beloved exclusiveness and wealth easier to guard. The direct relationships of the past were out of date . . . Torro had been fond of the third rat, for apart from sharing the same shape of jaw with it, it would nibble at his toes to calm him down in moments of crisis; and so for the major to shoot it rather than even the first rat was not only an act of war, but also an attack on true rodent love.

This Torro was born in Italy, but arranged through intrigues in the womb to be born again in South Africa, where he had accidentally left one of his favourite shoes. He was therefore known to walk about sometimes with only one shoe in memory of the other shoe. It was rumoured that he had established fast an association of chiropodists for his bare foot. In Rome, his hometown, he would rob banks with style, and give to the poor, after which he would rob the same poor immediately, having a great love for reversed kindness when he was the one doing the reversing, ampa. He thus had a rotten pocket, bulging with cash and betrayal in equal proportions. Torro Too Good!

The elders of government were like eternity compared with the immediate and terrible urges of Torro. Their confidence went beyond wealth, power, and technology. They had wisdom at the end of their gardens, and could thus afford to sanction yet another strange war, though the strangeness never hid the fact that these were all wars of survival, whether big or small. Direct wars too were out of date with the bosses abroad, subtle extinction being preferred . . . to such an extent that for them to enter and win a war with their full might was considered not quite sophisticated enough, except when it came to germ and chemical warfare, or nuclear missiles, or . . . The elders loved Major Gentl even more without than within the army, for he had the strangeness and the gentleness to guide the wars. Also, he knew, unlike the over-confident Pogo Forr, that defeat could be anywhere round any corner any time. Thus he was militarily very supple. In this wisdom, it was decreed that the two armies were to fit into small acres of land, irrespective of their tanks, planes and even ships. Everybody was so packed together that all the bombs had to be shot upwards. For three weeks vast amounts of amunition were shot up into the unwilling sky . . . until Torro the Terrible had the fine idea that his soldiers should shoot straight down. So now while one army shot absolutely up, one shot absolutely down.

And it was in the middle of battle that Abomu Kwame now standing at some akpeteshie angle and bisected into ludicrous shape by his own gun, shouted, 'Is it now time for break? Major, please consult that mad Torro admiring himself in the mirror. The way we're fighting this war, it's very tiring and silly staying alive, even your wife hasn't shot any of us. Can the gari and sardines be brought out? Those of us in the lower ranks have rights too, we can complain if we are not dying enough, we almost shot our own Air Force by mistake with these upward bullets, and do you know sir that six of Torro's soldiers have got wounded toes from their downward shooting? I swear on my late father's adaka that this safe war is a trick!'

'Shut up there Kwame Abomu with your hot and rotten stew! How dare you complain about being alive? Besides aren't you the one who was fighting for the enemy just now, shooting down instead of up just because they offered you some cool odolontous gin of the local! But for me I couldn't care less because you are so useless that you are more useful to the enemy than to us,' growled Atinga standing beside the shadowless major by the banana trees at the command centre, 'and don't you know that the major knows what he's doing? He has won one war already, which has given us another lease to exist, me I say stop your mouth, Allah!'

Abomu gave a scowl worthy of the stew of his name, but refused to be intimidated, saying, 'And how long are we going to take the orders of a golden cockroach? If we had won the first war well enough there would be no need koraa for a second one. Finish . . . but I still don't understand why we must fight them and then sit and drink beer with them later, eh?'

As aMofa was walking up with his crab-shell walk to find out what the problem was, he was told not to mind that Abomu speaking from his fount of molasses. For after all didn't even the children know that the more confused the battle scene, the greater the chance of slipping into victory, especially when dealing with an agent whose masters could ultimately destroy you in a few minutes? And why have a gentle man of oracles with lunar rooms when you were not certain of victory . . .

Surrounding the battlefield with stylish uniforms were the men of Pogo Alonka Forr's peace-keeping force, and around the entire scene were chattering groups of women selling their wares, from dukus to

8

kosee, with a single-mindedness that went beyond bullets and tanks, mammies of the future that existed now. One mammy said to another, 'Sister, will we sell more when they start dying, or are we selling more now? I have ordered my carpenter husband to start making those popular coffins in the shapes of vulture, boat, and trotro. Ei, the world changes–O!'

The peace force was dreamed up by Pogo the carrot millionaire as a means of keeping trade going during difficult times, and it was a fine role its men had: standing there watching the war, listening to radios, and distributing carrots. The head of the peace force was General Jolloff, who often had rice on his epaulettes out of a carelessness that his late wife had encouraged, since she had passionately wanted him to die first, so that she could enjoy the grief of his funeral, for she loved him so mech. The general relished another thing, apart from rice: he loved receiving contradictory commands from the civilians above him, so that he would not have to act at all. He had also kept the peace for the first war, and had grown to admire the seemingly stupid gentleness of Major Gentl. He had a great deal of advice to give to the major, and it all concerned: rice. And he would give this strategic advice while his right hand played uselessly in a plateful of dry gari, making an incredible number of shapes which eventually turned into one thing: rice.

When it was lunch time Ama Three rushed home again and made her food, quarrelling with two of her three children who deplored what she was doing. They hated the teasing and the little backhand laughs of the other children of the district. But the third child supported her.

Now it was evening and Ama had returned to a battle that was not as thick as her nails. Men were drifting off back home in groups of tired marching; the mammies had counted their gains and had gone long ago, followed closely by General Jolloff and his men. The crickets had taken over the battlefield, after the last bugles sounded. And there facing each other in the dusk, with the snakes and rats each in attendance by the appropriate master, stood Major Gentl and Torro, the former with a look of fresh earnestness, and the latter one of exaggerated pain. aMofa's snake crawled protectively around his knees, as two of Torro's beloved rats sat each on its master's shoulders. There was a twitch on Torro's left cheek as he gave a long belch and pointed at his belly and said, 'Mama mia, dear Major, I'm losing my Roman accent, I do not comprehendo. My dear belly is shaped just like one of the eastern hills in your dear city, and I do nothing but let wind escape in any direction. Diavolo! I theeenk I have the serious ulcers, noo!'

As Torro talked he slyly nudged one of the rats, the one on the left shoulder, and it leapt with a quick squeak towards the eyes of Gentl . . . only to end up in the open jaws of the quivering python ever ready to protect its master. There was an eerie pause as aMofa stared dead straight, with Torro looking up with awe and disbelief. He cut the awe from his tongue: 'To continue our grreat friendship I would like you to geev me one of your snakes. You not only shoot my rats but also arrange for my rats to beeee swallowed, shall I say! We are truly at war, no?'

Torro seemed to be reshaping his belly with the agitation of his hands. aMofa looked at him with pity, the type of pity that he kept for the advanced who did not wish to know the limits of their power, kuse-kuse. With lightning speed the python shot from its master and tightened itself round the neck of Torro. Torro gasped with a shortened scream. The squeeze continued as the major kept the earnestness on his face, not moving a single limb. As soon as aMofa raised his right hand the snake slid off Torro's neck, leaving him panting and sputtering, and in a desperate search for his gun as he cursed ten times over.

'The snake has brought your gun to me,' aMofa declared, retaining the same stare on his face. The other rat had rushed into Torro's pocket, and Torro took it out by the tail in anger and tore it to bits with a high growl that seemed to straighten his neck at last.

'The battle is just beginning!' he shouted as he stormed into his helicopter, shaking the sleeping pilot with a curse. aMofa ambled up to the starting propellers, and handed the raging Torro a note which simply said, 'If you are not careful they will replace you.' And then the major went into his jeep as Atinga came out with a a grimace from the bushes: the number of times Atinga wanted to save his major's life, yet found this unnecessary, was getting annoying, ah. The jeep drove off in the smell of torn rat. The snake polished aMofa's knees with some vigorous slithering. The dusk had touched the night long ago, and the major wondered whether that frog that jumped into Torro's armpit as he struggled for breath was still there, amplifying the flesh with some oxter croaking.

The inventors

The golden cockroach with the smallest shoes that couldn't be seen had a red ribbon on its head and a tama round its non-existent waist, and its current Big Wish was to present Pogo Alonka Forr with an impregnable defence that would serve for both enemies and friends. The cockroach and the carrots shared a golden nature, but the minute the mosquito started to shine its silver so fine, Pogo would look twice at it wondering whether the silver would provide more profit after all than the golden. So the cockroach would retain the secrets of its defence, and concentrate on providing rooms in the moon for the major and giving him little tips from a distance towards winning the second war.

Pogo the carrot millionaire had a fast-yard laugh for difficult situations of this nature, a laugh that would blow both his wife and his girls off course if they happened to be standing in roughly the same place. Pogo was kind and cunning to all, amassing his wealth through carrot-inspired intrigues, through wars, delicate helicopters, his own beautiful Kwahu scarp-sharp thighs, and bright eyes that didn't need one beam from anyone else's power. Pogo was rich enough to have his own lights. But his wife Delali, who was growing more and more fond of bananas and less and less of carrots, was getting worried because she often found herself daydreaming about Major Gentl. No reason, just that his gentleness grew beside her breasts; and for this she would often give the sign of the cross in the shape of her husband's pioto. Sometimes Pogo would be so sensitive that all the carrots around him would be sliced with the pervading subtlety; and it was in one of these moods that he had built a beautiful miniature building that he installed in one of the few filthy old-fashioned gutters, so that he would feel the paradox blowing over him with the bad whiff . . . He wore robes around which grew songs of praise, so that you couldn't blame him if he didn't want to listen to his own innate modesty. Horses and helicopters brought his breakfast in the mornings.

11

But this morning he couldn't eat early because one of these breakfast horses had eased itself on a plate in transit to his table. He, Pogo, had the horse's rump massively perfumed out of a revenge that kept the horse smelling backwards for days. And when the clean plates were finally brought by the helicopters, Pogo, the grim godish man, ate alone, slowly, through the memory of horse dung. By his favourite glass window in his mansion of glass and bamboo he stood, his arms raised in salute to the sun. Ever since he had heard that the major had rooms among the lunar craters, he had faithfully cultivated the sun to see whether an arrangement could be worked out there in a serious and solar manner; bamboozle the sun with attention and you could even end up having a hotel in it, burning ambition, he said. Hey, in his postprandial joy Pogo had perfected the long smile for his wife.

She shortened it. 'Papa Pogo my husband with the long chest, the Grandmother Bomb has just called on the telephone to say she's coming over to inspect your latest carrot invention, now . . .'

Pogo with the tintiintin torso and the short thighs stared in fury.

'But this old woman with science for a husband should not come and trouble me this morning–O! I haven't perfected my new invention yet. She is in a hurry as usual. She'll be in a hurry-aaa, then you the slow one you tire–O!' Pogo laughed, offering the sparkle in his eyes to Delali; then he winked but she refused to follow the wink to the bedroom, saying, 'Pogo have you no shame trying to entice your own wife! And don't you know that I have started to daydream again . . .'

'O yes! my dear wife with the misty eyes, I wouldn't be surprised if you have been dreaming about that soft major with the osode eyes . . . and I too will tell you a secret: I have caught his wife eyeing me filifili in the middle of battle among the bullets while I was supervising my reluctant General Jolloff supervising the war. You see we are both odolontous! Come and let me hold your softsoft doona so that you can daydream about my hardness, I am not a millionaire for nothing!'

Then Pogo held the silence at her back, as she half pulled away, and he said, 'Nana Mai the Grandmother Bomb is coming to find out whether I have been able to transform a carrot into a donkey or a donkey into a carrot. Ah, at least I have begun: I feed the donkey with carrots, and then I feed the carrots with donkeys, that's a beginning! . . .' There was a pause, and he added, 'But seriously, my good wife fond of the helicopters, I am trying to breed a round carrot the same shape as the sun . . .'

There was a second pause, one pause equal to each of Delali's breasts, Pogo thought, and just as he was pulling her into the chookoo alligator-decorated bedroom, she asked him, 'Pogo my man of millions, when are you going to promote one of your girlfriends, because excuse me to say you are always talking in your dreams about promoting the one with the very thin waist . . .'

There was a sarcastic shine on her forehead which he dimmed with a caress. 'Ah woman! how dare you listen to my dreams when they are not true! How can a man of carrots dream about the status of girls that are too strong for men these days? I implore you to look at the wealth around you and keep quiet . . .' Laughing and laughing, he rushed the semi-struggling Delali towards the bed . . .

. . . Only to rush back out again because there was a call that the Grandmother Bomb had arrived at his incomparable glass palace with the bamboo holdups.

'Ewurade! This old woman that invented the first African bomb that pours a libation of fire before exploding always arrives at the wrong time . . . I can't even be benevolent together with my wife without meeting her searching and whirlwinding eyes, Allah!'

There was a sudden crash of breaking glass, and Pogo screamed, 'Who is the untutored sakoa nana that is breaking all my glass above my smooth bamboo . . .?'

When Alonka stormed out to see who dared break his glass, he saw Nana Mai the Grandmother Bomb rigid with anger before a broken glass wall, holding a metal walking-stick that told the tale for Pogo. Nana Mai and Alonka Forr both stared incredulously at each other, the old lady with her incomparably beautiful eyes. Not a word was said as she went along to the next pane and broke that too, ostentatiously. Pogo about-turned with his millions angry in his eyes and rushed off.

'Now where is that stupid gari-and-carrot-dominated man going to? Does he not know how to receive his callers . . .' Nana Mai asked imperiously of the confused Delali, and crushed a bit of broken glass with her short heel.

All Delali said was, 'But.' But then at last bursting out of the corner on his favourite white horse was Pogo Forr, riding off his anger and shouting boldly to the Grandmother Bomb, 'Ah, my great mother of

13

science and invention, see me in my glory so that you don't dare break any more of my precious glass . . . It's the sun I'm after now! You lady of science, taste my horse now!'

Nana Mai, with one eye shut, looked contemptuously at the horse with its front hooves raised overseas, and said to Pogo, 'It's your donkey I'm after. Get off that animal now, and show me your new invention, I have no time, and I am suspicious: when did you stop making money and take to ideas?'

Pogo raised his horse again regardless, his robes flowing about him with joy, and said, 'Hail to the finest woman with her scientific district! My carrots have eaten all my donkeys, but I will soon show you the first round carrot in the world . . . But in the meantime I have created some fine diversion for you to use in your district: luxury gutters in the form of a small beauty building put in the gutter a little beyond this house, put there to collect slime and filth as a great duty for the beauty . . . Don't worry Nana Mai, I will soon offer you the most favourable carrot you have ever seen after you've paid for the glass broken out of the anger of waiting. But watch the wind if you eat it too fast, I do not want some hiccup boom from wise old ladies of science in Achimota City . . . !'

Grandmother Bomb said not a word but kept the snarl on her face, then walked into Pogo's sitting-room and sat down disdainfully, while Delali followed her with more than a little trepidation, suddenly dying to daydream again major or minor. Then Nana Mail spoke to Delali's continuing silence.

'I'm allergic to the butterflies on your glass . . . I may break more.

'But the rich don't want to be sophisticated too mech in this city . . .' floated in the voice of Pogo just before he arrived in the sitting-room . . . still on his horse.

There was a duet roar from Grandmother Bomb and Delali, so strong that Pogo had to ride back out snorting as much as his horse, and complaining above the neighing of it that if he really wanted to ride majestically into his own sitting-room, who would dare stop him?

His voice floated in again: 'Would you be satisfied if I entered with the horse riding me instead? . . .' And lo! there was Pogo staggering in with the horse's front legs up on his shoulders and a saddle on his back. And what was the horse wearing? The horse was wearing its master's darkglasses. Ebei and Delali began to weep to make conversation; but Nana Mai had already stormed out saying to her female bodyguard, 'He

14

can let his horse's hooves rise over the rich cities if he likes, but I've wasted my time paa coming here. The man is mad, has been mad, and will always be mad . . .'

The bodyguard suddenly pointed up to her mistress's helicopter. There sitting on the propellers was Pogo the Alonka Forr, holding up an oval carrot in triumph, smoking a cigar and very glad to be a serious cigarist by the oval root of orange. At first he didn't say a word.

He was about to burst in his own silence until the words raced out, 'Yes Grandmother, I agree that you should take a picture of me for eternity. Admit it, you have never seen a carrot like this . . .'

'No I haven't, and I don't care either, not even for all the okros in the world, for how can such inventions help to win the second war . . .' Nana Mai almost spat out these words.

'Patience, siabots at once my grand old lady. I thought your logic was better than that! What are the best types of inventions for a silly war? Kwasia war, kwasia inventions! Silly launches silly! Besides, my inventions are only for the sun, I will soon manage to broaden the oval shape into a circle, just like the sun!'

'Be intelligent,' was all Grandmother Bomb said, as the sudden start of the propellers threw the man of millions to the ground, with Delali rushing down to save him, only to meet his passionate embrace instead, with carrots at the back of his hands.

Pogo burst joyfully out of the bedroom, after the High Life and hugging there had left Delali exhausted, and he was determined to pursue Grandmother Bomb, first to let her change her mind about his latest invention – she had to rethink his carrots – and second, to purchase one of her latest missiles in case he needed it to supervise the war. They thought he was a fool supervising a silly war but they would soon see the wisdom in his pogofoolery, he said to himself aloud.

'Prepare my horses! The old lady has agreed to pay for my broken glass,' he had ordered with an effervescence that was interrupted only by six bites he took from border bananas planted out of a sudden anger for his wife's preference for them . . . dangerous daydreaming bananas; and Delali had been delighted to find secretly that she could still make him jealous.

The two mighty horses were prepared, including the golden one which was a sight to see, provided you could do so when the sun was shining full force 440 on the mane. Pogo was continuing to dress in his white robes. After a slow libation to the gods he ascended the golden horse, and with his bodyguard on the other horse, they attacked the streets and skies with speed. Woman Amina was the bodyguard, called thus by her master in a fit of admiration. But he didn't want to mix her body with her guarding; and besides Amina was not amenable: she had a tiny husband whom she loved passionately, hoping perhaps that the love would make him grow to be at least half her height. She cared less for appearances.

And the city received them, with people pointing, staring, and chattering. Ride on, ride on! There was Aboloo Street with two marble buildings, one of them a big Ghana Commercial Bank, the other a hotel belonging to Pogo. The owner waved to his windows. The street sellers had fine aluminium sieve-sealed trays that kept the angry flies out; you could buy a rockbun without dust and without the touch of flies. The groundnuts lay in packets. The hair of all the women was natural in Egyir Kuma Street, skins a glistening bronze in spite of the war. And that seller with the bell, her sound was programmed to travel only six feet in radius, hurt no ears. By High Street the sea was still trying to conquer its cliffs, which could now be raised with Nana Mai's steelgrid invention.

The most popular activities, apart from FRUIT and computers of the African kind which were soft to touch, were walking, dancing and walking in that order, and then planning ways to make money out of the war. There was a widespread and deep seriousness in the attempts to outwit Torro: some would do the opposite of what they were thinking in case Torro was cheating and had a satellite that took personal pictures for analysis; some created images that couldn't be analysed, like thirty beetles turned into earrings and worn alive to settle family quarrels when no one was looking; yet others photographed clothed adult buttocks of all types, for they boasted that if there was anything that Achimota City had, it had the essence of natural walking.

The buildings were generally small, dwarf bungalows that sometimes disappeared into the ground, but the city had achieved the use of proper space: every house touched every building, whether by the nudge of a window, the slice of a wall, or the jut of a sewerage pipe, and yet there was so much space that the breeze didn't know what to do with it. Pogo helped the wind by suddenly releasing twenty handkerchiefs which the children raced for in wonderfully clean ceramic-street runs. Allah! And

16

in streets like Kojo Thompson Road, great long buildings could move and change direction, could face the sun or back it, with their huge ball bearings under the foundations. Ride on you shoogly horses! Past the house of the adjournable magistrate, who was known to be so confident and yet so short of time that he could adjourn the sun into the time of the moon; and he had imperiously stopped his old friend Pogo, and offered him fresh milk from the Achimota plains plus slices of rich squirrel thigh especially roasted near his court to get the legal flavour.

Pogo and Amina chopped, and as they raced back on to the streets, Pogo said to her, 'My old friend is good–O, he eats my carrots in court; and he has so many cases: nutcases, suitcases and a glasscase of red roses with their thorns carefully cut off, so that his life would be smoother.' And when Amina smiled her boss stuffed a fresh handker-chief into her mouth and then laughed his golden horse on and on.

Did Pogo's horse make golden dung? Walai! that was one secret that the garrulous Pogo never told anybody, not even the stable boys.

The two horses leapt over a sleeping Mercedes Benz simultaneously, and when its driver suddenly blew the horn, they leapt even higher. But not as high as the thousands of delicately crisscrossing baked-mud pipes hanging all over the city, and built to accommodate the voracious wandering of the soldier ants and the termites. Thus ants and fruit were very much a part of the city, in and out of whose pipes dodged aeroplanes and helicopters. And at various points, changing perma-nently the architecture of the city, were vast anthills, orange, brown, and grey. Government House was itself a series of extraordinary anthills joined and reinforced by arcs, arches, gables, rifts, humps and multi-directional walls; and it looked like some gigantic cathedral dedicated to crawling. And Pogo burst into laughter as he caught a glimpse of one of the elders of government holding his grey beard by the oval-shaped windows, waving in the direction of the horses. He laughed because he knew that the old man enjoyed the joy of ruling in very difficult times that needed much fruit and calm in equal quantities . . . O you guava government.

It was only a big sneeze that finally wiped off the fixed smile on Alonka's equestrian face. They were now approaching the mile of absolutely sraight road that led to Grandmother Bomb's district, this bomb who could walk sitting down and crawl standing up all day on Wednesdays. It was a road enlivened by bold cheese sellers and traders of cola that sold in the proverbial two cola colours; and there was cassava-fish and fried octopus; there were dried slices of beef; and there were the roasted ears of wild deer, next to the subtle white meat of the fresh akrantsi. Nana Mai had insisted that the cheese be sold, for it reminded her of the mutability of milk, and it helped her to invent, especially from one form into another.

'What sort of wild market has the old lady encouraged to be built here?' Pogo complained as he jumped over a boy who refused to get out of the way of the horses and was trying wildly to strip the organic gold from his horse. Amina went a few yards ahead to clear the way for her master. She was hungry for deer and bokoboko leaves; but she wasn't worried about the horses' hunger koraa: they could chew guinea grass, drink adoka and gallop at the same time.

When Amina suddenly came to a halt, Pogo almost rode over her, his horse was snorting gold: there at the far end of the market, near the end of the road, sat Nana Mai herself, wearing a wide sunselling straw hat with a glass sieve of simple kosee on her tray for sale. There was a strange still woman sitting by her.

'Ah, by the surprised spirit of my living acestors! I never knew that our woman of advanced wonder would become so human as to sit down and sell. Only your sunselling hat! Allah be good to severe grown ladies of invention! Nana Mai, we are coming to your bombs and missiles at once! Today no helicopter at all, I just wanted the touch of gold between my thighs before I came to you . . .'

'Be quiet, Pogo Forr, leave me alone to sell my last twenty cedis. Go ahead to my house and I'll be with you soon. I warn you not to talk too much or you will disturb my parrot, nor should you ride into my sitting-room . . .', Nana Mai said, not even looking in Pogo's golden direction.

He gave her a long golden smile before cantering off with Amina still in front. Half-way up the strict geometric road Amina stopped abruptly again, making it necessary this time for the golden horse to jump clean over her and her horse.

Woman Amina shouted to the flustered robe-gathering Alonka, 'Yewura Forr, yewura Forr, I have just realised that I saw a ghastly sight . . .'

'Forr what?' asked Pogo with a laugh.

'Sir, I'm serious! There was a dead woman sitting beside the Grandmother Bomb . . .'

18

The two horses had already turned round galloping back.

'Poor poor woman, probably no one has noticed that she is selling her wares dead . . .' shouted Alonka Forr.

True when they reached there, aghast, there was the dead woman sitting quite close to Nana Mai, and propped up with her dead hands on money ready to give change to the living.

'Nana Mai!' screamed Pogo, 'You haven't realised that that woman sitting next to you is dead! kaput! and selling from the nether regions. Haven't you noticed the flies on her wrists . . ?'

Nana Mai looked up slowly, without a single glance at the dead, looked up as high as her head would go, and then said almost inconsequentially more to the golden horse than to Pogo himself. 'Do not defile the dead.'

Then she turned her head tenderly to the dead woman and whispered, 'Aba, Aba, tell them you wrote your will and wanted to sell when you were dead and embalmed, tell them we are carrying out your will for the afternoon . . .'

There was a long silence broken only by the breathing of the horses. A helicopter disappeared behind the clouds with its thinning cuts of sky. An old woman with a faded cloth left the wusa and shrow on her tray and came back to talk and sing to Aba. Alonka dismounted, then went and gave poor dead Aba a long hug, leaving a golden cedi in her hands. He went back on to his horse without a word as the wailing grew.

'Dont go!' Nana Mai shouted after him, 'I want to join your bodyguard on her horse to the house.'

And she beckoned her helicopter to go ahead. Nana Mai sat stiff behind Amina, her sunselling hat still on, and bumping up and down with extrordinary vigour, complaining, 'What do these women want me to do? Leaving my machines to go and minister unto the dead. Did you know I'm qualified to be a fetish priestess . . ? They ask me to stretch the centuries too much. Is that not true, young lady . . ?'

Amina looked behind at her passenger in a startled manner, and was wondering what the old lady was doing, telling her this.

'Yes, Mama Mai,' she answered, and kept quiet.

'Hey Pogo Forr! You are creating too much dust ahead. Only half my road is tarred because I love dust when it's not flying about.'

Pogo riased his horse overseas again, as he was wont to do to the

19

Grandmother Bomb, saluted with a laughing deference while peering back into the market, and saying with surprise, 'They are putting poor Aba in a coffin the shape of corned beef!'

'Yes, yes,' Nana Mai replied impatiently, 'yes, that's precisely what she wanted, and we usually do what the dead want.'

'Nana Mai, I hope it's not corned beef for lunch,' Pogo snorted and rode on.

Nana Mai's house was a short fat bungalow with many cellars for research; and when you leaned on the house to the left it leant with you for four feet, when you leant to the right it leaned with you for three. Roses and zinnia came bursting out of its roof, from flower-pots high. And the sitting room had so many levels that it was often difficult to see the guest who was doing the talking. The grey parrot in this room had no cage, and had been taught to talk science while guarding the windows from no one, with ferocious pecks of glass. The door was two unusual gentlemen, one with a hat that could barely shut: these two men had bullied a market woman, and as their punishment were sentenced to be doors at Nana Mai's house for six months. They were wedged together with bamboo, and stood on small rollers, so that they could be shut and they could be opened. They had chosen to be one door instead of two doors, for they could then chat while they were being pulled or pushed. And most important while they were in the house they could acquire valuable research experience from Nana Mai, being aspiring professors of physics. Only one at a time could eat or go to the toilet, for it was forbidden to go through their two spaces at once, hollow physics.

'$e = eo - vc/c^2$' said the parrot, its beak shortening with great speed, as Pogo passed with a look of scornful pity at the physical door with its double humanity; and this door was asleep with half of it snoring.

'How can you bear so many new things Nana Bomb? . . .' Pogo turned, with vigorously clasped hands, to ask Nana Mai.

She was not there. She was talking to her crows, kept as a foil to the parrot, and chattering into her cornmill.

'I will be with you soon!' she shouted absent-mindedly towards the oblivious Pogo.

Amina was still outside, and she was flustered, for she was desperately trying to push back in her horse's risen penis before Nana Mai could see how ludicrous its length was.

'It's all these carrots!' she said to herself with self-righteous menace.

20

Nana Mai sauntered in covered in corn dust, with scarcely a look at Amina, who was forced into putting the horse's popylonkwe into her pocket hastily to prevent the old lady witnessing it as she passed. Pogo was sitting at such a low level that she couldn't see him.

'OK, OK, Grandmother Bomber!' he shouted, 'I am hiding somewhere in this room, though it's not my fault that you can't see me! I congratulate you on letting your guests speak in hiding . . .'

Nana Mai was looking at him so sternly that he could no longer pretend that she couldn't see him.

'I deplore your supervision of the war,' she said without warning.

Pogo shot up in dismay: he had been sitting on the parrot, rump science. One door went to the toilet and let the harmattan come in free.

'This is one of the disadvantages about using human beings for doors, they leave their spaces free . . .' he said to Grandmother Bomb, ignoring her complaint about the war.

The old lady reset her face, and said again, 'If you didn't hear me, I am telling you again now now that . . .'

'. . . that I don't have to reveal all my plans to you!' Pogo interrupted merrily.

Nana Mai rose and got two glasses of orange juice, without taking her eyes off him. He stared back, and then closed his eyes when his freshly squeezed juice got finished. He kept his eyes closed, saying, 'I don't want to take advantage of you, I need your bombs and missiles small. But don't make me weep by suspecting my motives . . . Torro can only be defeated by the most cunning gari, by a double-sided plate, each side with gari rising on it . . .'

'Then use your gari to defeat him!' Nana Mai said with finality.

There was a pause, with Pogo looking deadly serious in it. He said to himself: how dare people think that me Pogo the man of laughter has no plans to free this land! Pogo rose and stood close to the mathematical parrot.

'Everybody wants to help the major,' he said with annoyance.

'And that is because the major won the first war, and he doesn't have motives polluted by money . . .' Nana Mai answered as she adjusted her duku.

Pogo banged his table with such force that his glass fell and broke. He would pay for the breaking if necessary.

He shouted, 'Now let's get things straight, the bush path can't be

21

bent! . . . Who financed the last war? I will answer that myself: Pogo Alonka Forr, the carrot millionaire, standing before you now and refusing to sit! Who made the necessary compromises with that Torro to soften him for his own defeat? Nana Mai, don't let me talk too mech . . .'

'My dear horseman, you are already doing very well, thank you,' Grandmother Bomb interjected with a high chuckle in her gruff sandpaper voice.

'Yes, yes, and I intend to continue!' Pogo screeched, 'Do you people really know this Torro at all? He does not keep his heart soft among the broken eggs! He has ants and termites that suddenly come around him because they think he may kill something or somebody in the room. It can be rats, it can be a servant from Italy. He has synthetic bombs now, he has unreal weapons that you think are unreal until they kill you, and his brain energy machines are working . . .'

'But you know I have neutralised that . . .' Nana Mai said impatiently.

'No, Nana, No! He told me he has introduced new ones with a higher intellectual suck . . . and you know what his latest plan is? He wants everyone of us here to have a double abroad – imagine that, we still can't remember the names of the cities there, hmmm – and the trouble is that each double there will have all the happiness, and its counterpart here will be left with some massive sadness. They think they have at last separated joy and sorrow, another cheap break of the paradox, and they want to give us the sorrow and monopolise the joy. From what I can see in Torro's talk, everything abroad now is pretty and nothing is beautiful, ha! Do you know what the fool said to me one day? He said that the only reason he tells me so many things is that he knows there's nothing we can do about stopping the onward march of his strategy, and that the more we know of his plans the more interesting and taxing the war becomes, like a game of draughts. The friendly war! He is afraid of the major's gentleness, for he thinks that is a quality he can't always trap. And he admires you enormously even though he feels he can defeat you! Nana Mai, I am prepared to use the sun to defeat Torro if necessary . . .'

'Yes, once you've built your hotel in it,' Nana Bomb replied, using the same chuckle, and then she added quickly before Pogo could react, 'Pogo your order for missiles is ready, and I want to study your oval carrot. I don't want to tell you that though you gave much money towards the first war, you also made a lot from it . . . no, don't talk now! I will always doubt your motives till you prove me otherwise!'

Pogo's eyes were red with anger. 'Alleluya', was all he said as he collected his bombs, making a deep bow to the old lady, who still had a large twinkle in her eye.

Half a door smiled as Alonka Forr went out to Amina, who had now tamed the horsy popylonkwe. The golden horse was neighing to the crows, and the parrot was adjusting the science in its perch.

'One last point, you Pogo,' Nana Mai said, looking more stocky and merry than ever, 'Could you please bury Aba on the way by the nearest neem tree? Her wish was to be buried by the man with the golden horse!'

Pogo stood struck for a full minute, gave a second deep bow, then rode off with the body on the golden horse, with Amina giving furtive glances at the anger of her master.

'This law allowing the dead to make such silly requests should be changed!' he shouted over his shoulder to her, as if the laughter was coming back into his voice.

It wasn't. He insisted on burying Aba himself, but he did nothing but complain as he was doing it. After finishing the rituals, they raced back through the city at such a speed that the magistrate, waiting to give them the choicest goat's balls finely roasted, didn't even see them pass koraa . . .'

ZONE THREE

Strategies

. . . Which goat's balls, darkened further with the essence of deep cola, ended up on the plates of Major Gentl. First of all the major attacked the delicacies with a leap, until he remembered how slow he was, and then left one for his wife. Ama Three was at the same time eating goat's eyes, which she had wanted to pluck live out of the goat's face to make up for the major's gentleness – this gentleness she usually misinterpreted. Even though he could win wars and act decisively – not to mention his celestial rooms and magic binoculars – she felt that she did not have enough adventure in her life. And she thought that the best way to test the very limits of this proverbial gentleness was to do the most outrageous things possible; like fighting on the opposite side of her major in his most important war, or taking second looks at Pogo Forr, look, look.

It was because people knew that Ama and aMofa loved each other so much that they didn't talk too long about Ama's pranks. They just watched in amazement, wondering how far she was going to push the major and whether the major was an eternally pushable man. Hero Gentl's centres of feeling included a good stock of big ice placed strategically against the excesses of Ahomtsew Ama. Poor Gentl: Ama was three troubles one god. But the best thing she did last week was to lick his entire head clean of dust when he returned from an exceptionally hot battlefront through the back door. This included the nape of his neck. He had sat absolutely motionless, allowing the luxury of a little scorn on his lips: Ama had almost shot him again that afternoon, and she had love in her eyes when she shot. Gentl's toes had twitched silently in the presence of the connubial lick; and his snakes, which didn't like his wife very much, lay asleep by his feet; and outside a banana grew through an orange.

It was when the revenge orange pushed aside its slick banana that the three children of aMofa and Ama came to attack their parents.

24

'Two of us don't agree koraa with what Mother has been doing, Papaa, and people tease us about it,' began mMo holding down his anger with a grimace from the latest two of his twelve years.

'I agree with mMo immediately,' declared Aba Y standing there at attention and holding her rifle.

'Do not pay any attention to the two of them, my dear parents,' shouted Adu, who not only preferred the adventure of his mother to the gentleness of his father, but also loved being in opposition to everything that his elder brother and sister did or said.

The parental expressions were bemused and wry, and Ama spoke through her forehead. 'Go and play and come and talk to us later when we have finished eating.'

'No, Mother, the law doesn't allow you to push us aside like this. We children, we have rights . . .' Aba Y ordered, brandishing her rifle with its butt on the nearest dish, and adding, 'And Mother, I speak in the name of the law.'

Ama Three suddenly got up, in consternation, saying, 'O, I will be late for the war! There's an afternoon session . . . O my dear husband, I forgot to tell you! It was a message from General Jolloff. This special session is going to be followed by apapransa and portello, koko dedeede!'

'Sit down Mother immediately! We have decided to be tough with you from now on. Besides, I have now p-e-r-s-o-n-a-l-l-y decided to join the police force. I am the first girl in Achimota City to do so.'

'Now you children . . .' began Mother Ama.

'I believe in what the children are doing,' said Father Gentl with a faraway look in his eyes.

'Please do not include me in what mMo and Aba Y are doing, Father, you have to consult me first. I agree with my mother,' Adu said, going to stand authoritatively near his mother whose long-suffering look up to the sky met a stray hawk.

There was a pause as they all stared at each other in amazement. mMo and Aba Y had blocked the door, and standing holding hands before them were mother-of-war Ama, and Adu. The major was adjusting his snakes.

'Ama, sit down,' he said, with little force, but with authority filling up his small face.

There was a look of defiance on mother Ama's face as she said, 'But the war! . . .' Then she sat down and Adu sat down on her knee. He doubled her defiance with his face.

'But you agreed to give me total freedom when we married,' Ama said to aMofa whose face suddenly took on another sadness.

'Mother, as somebody who is now almost a police recruit, r-e-c-r-u-i-t, I order you to talk sense, Papaa is somebody! He is an original man, o-r-i-g-i-n-a-l, and he deserves more respect from you!'

'Yes,' mMo continued with his hand inconsequentially in his father's pocket. 'Some of us intend to help our father to win the second war . . .'

Ama Three shot up, but she had forgotten that Adu was sitting on her lap; she helped him up from the floor, and said, 'The only way for this family to stay together is for all of us to enjoy as much freedom as possible. Children get less, of course . . .'

'Mother, I am exercising my freedom now by refusing to let you be free to disgrace us! And that's my final word on the matter,' mMo said, suddenly fighting back tears.

When his mother went over to comfort him he pushed her away.

'Do not push your own mother away,' Adu declared threateningly.

But Mother Ama insisted and comforted mMo by force.

'Mother, leave my brother to enjoy his sadness!' shouted Aba Y, also on the verge of tears.

'How do you all know that what I am doing is not the best way to save us . . ?' asked Ama, wiping the reluctant tears of Aba. Then she suddenly brightened: 'We can come to a compromise, c-o-m-p-r-o-m-i-s-e. You can all allow me to go to the battlefront, but I will carry an empty gun, and I will not shoot at Father! OK?'

Aba Y saw her chance and jumped into it:

'Only on one condition, that I sometimes come with you to keep an eye on you, Mother!'

Her tears had gone, this ten-year-old policewoman.

'Mother is destroying this family,' mMo persisted, sensing the advent of a mad compromise.

Before there was any reaction to mMo, Adu spoke from a different world altogether, 'Mother and Father, I have computerised my early morning fart for the whole family!' One snort from Aba was sufficient for all of them.

'OOOoo, I have a better idea!' mMo shouted with joy. 'I propose that we children start a children's war! Eye buiei! Can you picture me as the commander-in-chief?'

'Yes, yes!' enthused Aba Y and Adu, 'We shall win the war for the adults! After all we can't solve every problem for Mother and Father . . . Besides, they love each other so mech that they should know what they are doing!'

Aba Y beamed when she said the last words. And the children ran out.

There was one silence followed by another. Gentl was going back to his strategies. And Ama was going to the battlefront . . . with her empty gun thrown confidently on her shoulder, and a thrown-back 'Trust me' to her husband. She looked up at the sky, trying to get her long-suffering look back again, and there was the same hawk, still flying the shapes of her face.

It was when Ama was walking and running in bits, and trying to talk to the hawk high to bring her shapes lower that the golden cockroach appeared on the horizon. Its sikadillo smoke crawled on Ama's back without realising it.

'Ama Three!' shouted the cockroach with saliva on its golden tongue. It had a table on the horizon, on which lay roast chicken in alasa sauce, piccadilly biscuits, advanced bond paper for dessert, and the secret kuraba with the leaks of the planet in it. By its side saluting it every few minutes was the silver mosquito, which was getting more and more overwhelmed by the power of the golden cockroach.

'Ama Three, are you faithful to your husband?' asked the roachcock with the hitch on its plate: the mosquito had forgotten the salt again.

Ama heard nothing, and was busy trying out her new battle walk with its greater locomotion of the buttock area. For months now the cockroach had been trying to suppress a growing attraction for Ama with the long legs and the long African neck.

'It is out of respect for the major that I do not want to say that a woman with shoulders like yours needs some insect protection!'

Ama stopped and turned round sharply, thinking she had heard a voice. She listened to what she didn't hear. Kpooh! went the horizon when the cockroach took a bite out of it: the golden crawler was a divine fool – O: when it was hungry it got the mosquito to put tiny bits of gunpowder between sky and earth, so that when it bit the clouds there were small explosions to aid digestion. At last Ama heard the aerial biting and rushed towards the cockroach with the fire in its mouth, this mouth of chicken *à la alasa*. At first she couldn't see the cockroach for the mosquito, and then she couldn't see the mosquito for the cockroach. They all looked at each other for a bit, then Ama gave a curtsy no longer than her nose.

'Give me another bow, you woman of someone else's wife. I have told the major that you have an interesting body, your calves jut irresistibly, but your mind is even better. I think of you by covering your shape with boiled groundnuts! And there's so much length of you, O Allah of the cockroach world!'

There was some golden sweat from this crawling emblem as it ate and talked, ate and talked; and it had the tiniest smile you could ever get on a pin, so that when it laughed its mouth vanished.

'Let us surround her in this deserted savanna,' squeaked the silver mosquito. 'I have never seen anybody naked, man or woman . . .'

'That's what happens when you come from the silver lands,' declared Mr Cockgold with a frown. 'How dare you suggest exactly what I was thinking about the honourable major's wife . . ?'

The cockroach looked over at Ama with a dazzling smile that she couldn't see. It took a bite of cloud as all three stared at each other, after yet another explosion.

The noise of footsteps in the rustling leaves behind them startled them. And there coming towards them with his slow firm steps was the major, holding a bag. Ama knew it was her bag for it swung at the same rate as her hips when she walked.

'You forgot your food for the battle,' Gentl declared with a wave at the golden cockroach, which crawled in a quick circle to welcome him, saying, 'Ah, Major, you just came in time, just as we were beginning to find Ama here attractive! It looks as if she's on her way to the battlefront again. Even her nose is military. But I hope she's soft to you in the house.'

With that it quickly crawled up the trouser leg of Gentl and then crawled back down again, as if to feed the leg with clouds, for coming down Gentl's leg now was some quick steam.

As Ama looked in consternation, the mosquito whispered to her, 'It is the moon dust that is sometimes given to the major to give him more strength when he's climbing up to his rooms in the sky . . .'

28

'And he never tells me about those rooms,' Ama whispered back with a hiss.

Since Gentl and the golden cockroach both saluted each other at the same time, their hands met coming down. Ama laughed at the gratuitous handshake of man and gold, and then shouted, 'My dear husband, your friends here like me too mech! I am late for battle, and thanks for the food, I will shoot you less with my empty gun for your kindness! . . . Please plan the children's war properly.'

There was a wise pause, after which the major said, supplementing his small face with his large hands, 'I wouldn't be surprised if Ama joined the children's war and shot at her own children . . . I know we want a type of closeness that would allow us to neglect each other properly, but this is getting too much, no?'

His snake crawled on to his epaulette as he spoke, moving round the nape of his neck, and finally coming majestically down his chest like a live chain.

'Don't let that snake swallow me whole,' warned the golden cockroach, 'because I'm indigestible.'

'You know the snakes don't devour emblems,' aMofa smiled to his military helper, one small smile obliterating a smaller one.

The major and the cockroach each took out a notebook simultaneously, to discuss and write up the war of survival. The mosquito was the secretary, and would take the fullest notes. Gentl sat in the elephant grass scratching his elbow, as the silver malaria quarrelled with some knowknow flies; and the small neem copses answered to the wind.

'That Torro is trying to get a machine that will make everyone in Achimota City do exactly the same thing at exactly the same time, so that when his troops are doing the very opposite, they would win one time . . . Please give me a double glass of adoka, followed by the biggest calabash you have.'

aMofa stared at the cockroach for a full minute, and then sent the mosquito to his house to meet the request. 'I know that Grandmother Bomb will soon begin working on this, but a new strategy has to be thought up fast . . . and there's a bigger secret: Torro is trying to construct a new type of cockroach, yes construct some huge crawl, made of platinum, a cockroach that will have bigger ideas than I have . . .'

'Who told you?' asked Gentl quickly with this big worry on his brow.

29

Golden cee just laughed, adding, 'Do I really have to reveal all my sources to you! . . . I had a girlfriend in Torro's household . . .'

'Do you mean a human being?' aMofa asked innocently.

Golden cee increased its laugh: 'What is happening to your insight this morning?' it laughed incredulously. 'Of course it was a human being! What on earth would I be doing wasting time with a real cockroach . . . except for a special purpose . . ?'

'What purpose is that?' Gentl asked impatiently.

'Are you the proverbial patient man or are you not?' Mr Goldcrawl asked, 'But anyway, I don't intend to tell you that I know everything. I don't want to fill the head of a man of action with too many things.'

Gentl in turn smiled and crossed the wrong leg, which was already going to sleep. The smiling sweating silver mosquito returned with the calabash, adoka and glass, saying, 'Your children are truly preparing for war, and they are digging shelters, the air at your house is sweet with preparation, I swear.'

aMofa turned round to ask the silver presence, 'Have the children taken the armoured cars?'

The mosquito shook its silver head.

'Why are you holding a torch in your mouth? When you talk I can't hear you properly,' complained Mr Cee, 'and, besides, don't ask me about my girl . . . it's a painful matter . . . On to the strategy then! . . . O I remember Torro laughing in his house that he can't quite understand you, for you should be easy to defeat, you the major that started a bigitive poultry farm but became so personally involved with each bird that you could neither eat nor sell any, eii!'

The mosquito laughed for the cockroach, but both met the glare of aMofa Gentl whose eyes were set against the laughter. A drop of rain landed on his cheek for the tear that he suddenly wanted to give. Gold and silver looked away to give the major the seconds he needed to compose himself.

'Cry free, you fellow African,' declared the cockroach . . . Then they started the strategy in the rain, with some sad writing on paper wet by the sky:

'Major! Are you ready?' sang the golden emblem with an 'h' at the end of it. 'We are having to do far too much knowknow thinking to defeat this alatulala Torro, this man of prestidigitation. Give me a little waakye with the language . . .'

sharper than his pen. And he could still hear the song of Mr Cee in the sky.

Through the stumps of the low plains, aMofa could hear the stamps of marching footsteps. And true, over the nearest hump came a group of Torro's soldiers training in the savannah, hump hump hump hump. And marching up in fine style at the rear was . . . Ama Three . . . with a winsome smile for her husband. She gave him a great big lovely wink, her arms swinging with love for him. The major stared motionless as the marching soldiers laughed in rhythm to their marching. Then keeping the same smile on her face, Ama produced a small placard which read, 'I love you my dear husband'. Before he could recover, aMofa heard further footsteps from the opposite direction: and there marching past was a group of Torro's juvenile army; and marching at the rear with exaggeratedly vigorous movement was . . . Adu, his son. Gentl roared to the sky as Adu ignored him completely. Not even one look. Gentl saluted a passing crow in desperation, for something sane to do. He couldn't go and pull Adu out of formation, for such an action was not complex enough. And he roared again.

ZONE FOUR

The enemy is your friend

Torro was feeling angry, eating one whole roasted cow, with his belly resting on it. His beer was so cold that he didn't dare drink it, not even with his wife massaging his back, boof. By his huge elbow – an elbow with the culture of science, lust, betrayal and invasion round it – lay his rich double-stuffed sikapoo cigars, the tips of which he kept faithfully in salt. He would say, 'Taste the sea every day before you smoke it, no?'

No matter which room he sat in, in his large terrazzo-touched house, the floor sagged to emphasise his authority. His old spaniel had jaws shaped exactly like his favourite Fiat; and this Fiat was the terrible machine that could drive sideways as well . . . In fact the 'Terrible' after his name was named after his car, even though he himself deserved it. And he loved to deserve things so proudly that he stole from the wealth of his own arrogance. Small moths came out of his anus when he was angry, and always went down the right leg of his shorts. What he was angry about was that the major's wife Ama Three would not reveal to him the secret of her husband's snakes. He had asked her three times. She was after all one of his biggest achievements, pulling into his army the wife of his bitterest enemy; and she was so true and satisfied on the battlefront that he was sometimes suspicious. After all, the brain machines had stolen only half of her head-head energy, for the other half was not worth stealing.

Torro's own wife was South American, with the strength of many races in her bones, but the main reason she was so patient with him was that, apart from the wealth, he had promised to reveal to her when and where she was born, so that she could rejoice and enjoy all her past birthdays at once. She was relatively simple under his cunning intelligence, or so he thought. Sometimes when Bianca was doing her husband's back she found the flesh there disgusting; she could see clearly outlined the shapes of her beautiful hands. They had had several children together, who had been in Italy with Torro's mother. The old

34

woman was raising the children under the wrap-round world of spaghetti, and often sent pictures mysteriously brought by pigeons, pictures of the children with spaghetti arranged across their eyebrows. Bianca thought her husband's belly was like the smooth side of a snake, and had finally persuaded herself to have a tiny passion for General Jolloff . . . especially for his moustache, on which she would desperately want to sit. Outside in the tirelessly decorative garden, the pine trees had been taught to try and come into the sitting-room by stretching their branches and their tailor's needles in then out of the windows. The spaniel barked into the orchestral music.

Bianca always objected to the brakes of the Fiat: whenever Torro pressed on them in the Achimota streets the sound of his love-making with another woman appeared through the speakers. 'To suffer all this mucho for my birthdays is too big,' she would say to herself. She had lost half her Italian from worrying over her children, but was now shopping in the best markets of Achimota City for a passable English.

'My darleeng, you are not pressing my back hard enough!' Torro suddenly complained, in the middle of listening to two radios at once. He then switched off one set and said with a glow in his fat cheeks, 'We are brave people, you and me, bravo, no? We live right in the meedle of the enemy city, and we play chess with them with only half a head, ho! My sweet Bianca, do you not admire me pronto!'

Torro usually laughed alone in the company of his wife, for her lungs were busy taking in the inexhaustible air of silence and complaint. She had yesterday decided to try and fall in love with someone else by force as well as General Jolloff, a fine handsome Achimota man if possible; or a passing stranger travelling across the universe and seeing her by chance and miraculously falling in love with her at once.

'Bianca, what are you theenking about!' Torro shouted through the orchestra, for he no longer felt the pressure of her hands on his back. That was when she overincreased the force and sent a stab of pain into his weak shoulder. She ignored his quick scream, with its fat round it.

When there was a knock on the door Bianca gave Torro a knock on his hand without thinking. He turned round to her in an angry surprise, his fist raised to retaliate . . . only to meet the laughing face of Pogo Alonka Forr, for Bianca had taken refuge in the bedroom. Torro leapt up, as much as his weight would allow him, to greet his friendliest enemy.

'I am with mucho oblige!' he said, as Pogo sailed into a chair from the elaborate angle of his silk joromi.

Pogo was trying to separate his laughter from his words: 'So you old Italian fool! You haven't learned not to strike your wife yet . . . if you're not careful, she'll start looking at someone else.'

The laughter hovered around every third word, and could stray into more.

'O, my Bianca is just a little frustrated without her bambinos. The more she strikes me the more she loves me. Mama mia! I have to supplemento her knocks on my delicate head, no!'

Pogo gave his best mocking look to Torro the Terrible, and then went and poured himself out a double adoka with a flavouring slice of lime in it.

'I am nearer the sun than you think,' he said, looking at Torro with an intense but absent-minded curiosity.

'You, Mr Pogo, what is thees you talk about? Everytime you talk about the sun. You and your people are strange doublemento! You can court the sun and have rooms in the moon, but you cannot defeat us at our full might, is that the right word, might? No!'

There was the sound of a door creaking and they looked back to see Bianca trying to sneak back into the sitting-room.

'Woman, go back immediately and hide from me again, in case I remember my anger, I am busy with my authentico millionaire. Out!'

There was a long pause as Pogo Forr gave a wink to the semi-rebellious Bianca, and then announced with regal pride to Torro, 'I want to tell you now now now that I have a silver owl for sale . . .'

'Ditto what you say to me again,' said Torro moving to a different part of the room to vary the sagging on the floor.

'Yes a silver owl that can talk, and the only reason it can talk is that its beak is real flesh. Even the wings are silver . . . it is priceless, and will cost you fifty tanks . . .'

'Nonono, my dear Pogo, you are trying to empty me of my weapons in toto, no? I will not allow you to help me to defeat myself. You have already made mucho money from the supervision of the war! Have mercy on the poor invader with the kind weapons . . .'

'Do you want me to go and sell it to someone else?' Pogo asked abruptly, suddenly looking out of the window to see Amina at the ready as always with her guns. Today, master and female bodyguard came in

36

a pink helicopter, to grace the skies. It was as if Torro was whining in the biggest corner of the room, and the spaniel was whining with him. Bianca looked out through her refuge door, and gave Pogo the happiest smile she could find for her lips: 'Torro, give me more wealth. Buy the strange owl for me as fast as your speedometer moves, pronto!'

When Torro glared, she reflected it back to him adjusting her necklace to match her cocked ears:

'My buono goodo husband, for the sake of my bambinos, buy the owl for me now. Show your love!'

It was when Torro was angry with his wife that he looked deeply at her feet as if to uproot her being. On the other hand, he had never refused an offer from Pogo Forr before; for within his vast war space of the mind, to refuse an offer was almost the same as to accept it. And apart from this he wanted to study further the happy beam on Pogo's face, for a positive spirit could break every contradiction in sight. This was part of Torro's fear, a fear that was met with scorn from his masters abroad: sympathy was spirit and could thus change the whole universe! To make matters worse, he always suspected that Pogo had some secrets up the sleeves of his robes. Thus in a way he secretly feared him even more than he feared the major . . . at least when the major defeated him, he felt he had been beaten by a lesser man, rightly or wrongly; on the other hand, if Pogo were to be a winner over him, he would feel that it was right for Pogo so to be. And this was a dangerous feeling. For since Torro was not at core a complex man, he often yearned for the good old days when he could be, directly, his old ruthless self: robbing banks in Rome, arranging for weapons for Africa South, and selling the latest genetic engineering on international markets. Fighting a war with fractions of one's strength was dangerous paa, even for a heartless cynic; for eventually you saw that the people you were trying to destroy were equal to you, had an immeasurable width of soul and head . . . but didn't have the power. And Torro loved power! Even if he had to pretend that he had only enough to match the environment. Besides, he loved Achimota City with an insane and terrible love.

Pogo looked at Torro, snorting finally into the latter's silence.

'Have some of my fine cow,' Torro said at last, pushing a different mood by force into his face.

Pogo didn't eat much, being a man of genetically exciting vegetables.

So Torro said with resignation, 'All right, I will buy your silver owl, I will be rich in to-whit, no?'

Bianca came and planted a passionate kiss on Torro's chewing lips. 'My darleeng,' she said, 'you are a top-class genius in kindness and in arranging to be born twice, you are my beautiful tulipano!'

'And that is the only way I get kindness from my wife. Scusi, but I must speak the truth,' Torro replied.

Bianca followed her own laughter back to the bedroom, giving the owl a hug bigger than its wings.

'The ball, the ball!' shouted Pogo Forr with joy, 'I have come for our usual game of football . . . and this time, no cheating you Torro of the terrible habits, I will gari you just now with my goals!'

'But is this a war or a game? Sometimes I forget . . .' drawled Torro, suddenly rushing with excitement into the bathroom to change into his football shorts and his fat was his jersey. Pogo changed there and then, with Bianca sneaking a look at him through the crack of the bedroom door barely open. The floors shook more with Torro's haste.

'Bianca! Bring on the silver owl to be the referee, give it my diamond whistle, pronto! And my darleeng wife, do not laugh at me when I look like a bull corpulento, like a clumsy animal chasing its game of ball. When I look too ridiculous, just come and keess meee!' shouted Torro already out prancing in his football boots in this greenest of grasses, and letting the beetles and the grasshoppers scatter.

Pogo, having caught Bianca looking at him changing, left his best wink with her to keep her company. She was always banned from these wild matches between her husband and Pogo, for she insisted that things would be more interesting with a thinner husband . . .

And keeping goal for Torro in extremely woolly boots of the desert was the pet camel of the house; and it had a pipe in its mouth for it was trained to do so, and besides, it wanted to stop Pogo's shots with hard smoke. Pogo's number seven was the police-lizard with a vicious left foot which was most effective in the company of adoring female lizards that preferred half-time to anything else, for they could then feel the magical touch of the resting king lizard. At centre-half for each continent was the same elephant, which was so big that it could play for two opposing teams at once. *Howl, you silver referee! – for the game was about to start – and don't take too long urinating against both goalposts.* And the rest of Torro's team were rats, and the rest of Pogo's were horses, with restless carrots of all shapes as reserves, except round shapes. Ewurade peeep! blew the silver to-whooo, and there was a great roar from the servants, all Italians or of Italian descent; and they all supported: Pogo! For they were afraid of the killings of their master, but not afraid enough to jeer him in permitted contexts. Pogo on the ball! Allah, see his inimitable *leger de pied*, some double-direction waist movement that sent the fat of Torro the wrong way while the camel filled its goal line with its own dung.

'C'mon!' screamed the oval carrots loudest, 'if you can't play well, then call on us the interminably deep roots of the problem . . .'

And the rats had already reduced the size of the ball fractionally by some unauthorised biting of the leather orb that tasted like refined momoni . . .

'Hey fowl,' cried the horses as several chickens crossed the pitch with squawking elegance among the wealth of the compound. Peeeep! screeched the silver owl with its sexy Bukom-bred eyes, as it forgot itself and started to chase the smallest rat which was having a great game on the left wing.

'I will not be devoured by the referee,' said the cheeky young rat with an earring in its left ear.

There was Torro displaying, preparing his massive frame for a run down the left flank, the ball glued to his leftfootedness, with glue provided instantly from the gum of the neem trees. Pogo faced him squarely, with a carrot perched on his shoulder and whispering encouragingly into his ear carrotwise. Torro swerved to the left, Pogo swerved to the complementary right, so that the former had to transfer the ball to his right foot but he couldn't: the glue wouldn't come off. Torro relied on the element of surprise by changing direction but keeping to the same foot. He lobbed the ball menacingly but Pogo, with the help of one of his ordinary horses, somersaulted ingeniously and blocked Torro's space. There was a wild cheer from the makeshift terraces, from the servants who had always wanted to be masters anyway. And then the camel suddenly left its goal, with its dung flying. It burst between Pogo and Torro with a magnificent lunge of fine fur, and collected the ball with a foreleg, heading right towards its own goal. It got over its own hump, then turned round and gave the elephant such a perfect pass that it went clean through its legs and bounced off its tail. . . so that if the police-lizard hadn't made a spectacular save with its head on its way to eating a stray grasshopper Pogo would have found his team down. Then, without provocation, Torro pushed Pogo, the carrot millionaire. Pogo laughed, but retaliated with a dirty slap. They both gave each other a makola suspension at the same time, and when they finally landed on the ground, Torro stood his magic stand: frontal and sideways at the same time; but it didn't work: Pogo raced through the entire defence, and finally sent the camel the wrong way with a brilliant feint for the first goal.

'Goaoaoaoal!' the master servants roared, doffing their hats to the jubilant Pogo, and returning the threatening stares of Torro the Terrible with bold nonchalance; and out of joy, the king lizard wrote its own name with the different droppings of its dung. The elephant cheered for one side, and cried for the other. Torro sat on the ball and burst it, and his rats gathered round him and squeaked in sympathy . . . which the camel didn't share for it knew it would be kicked after the game for letting in that goal, agyeei.

'Bianca, you seelly anca, bring me my asthma machine to clear the air fouled by this goal; and then you can go and get me one of the coffins from the store to bury the camel in,' screamed Torro, looking insanitary in his sweat and mud – some huge, chewed, muddy toffy-lonkwe, ampa.

Bianca brought the chest cleaner . . . sitting on the camel and stroking it to emphasise her protective love for it.

'If the camel goes, I go,' she declared. But was completely ignored by him.

The camel's nose now towered over everything, with its smooth cinematic walk.

The second half of their games always turned into an exercise of strategy for the war, for Pogo loved the peculiar sensation of fraternising with the enemy so closely. He had this feeling of ultimate victory from it. There was an explosion in the distance.

'Ah, there goes the waging of the children's war . . . isn't it lovely to see the bambinos so serious about trying to destroy each other! But the major is a fool: he has arranged weeth the elders of government that for the first few weeks no child should be killed . . . I'm sure that it's because his bambinos are involved. And now I have sent for my own children from Italy to help me win the junior war.'

Pogo was already dribbling the rats, his left foot a mass of tricks. He stopped in the middle of a swerve, and then continued dribbling as he talked, 'You, Torro, it's a carrot you will be buried in when you die! I will arrange for a sexy tomb for you paa, excuse me to say: sepulcunt!'

The words of Pogo came back into the angry face of Torro, whose anger made him move into a wild tackle on Pogo from the back. Peep! whistled the silver owl that had at last, without Torro's knowledge, managed to tear apart the small tricky rat, poor topo, and swallowed it; after which it immediately allowed a substitute on, so that Torro couldn't see the difference. The fine horse with the finely sculptured popylonkwe took the foul, even though it didn't know which hoof to use at first – it eventually turned round and gave a back kick – and the ball sailed on to Torro's foot by mistake. Pogo glared carrots at the horse, as Torro charged at goal, calling to his security helicopter above to come lower so that he could get more breeze for the hot shot coming. Boof, went Torro's foot, but it missed the ball clean, and ended up kicking the king lizard right out of the park, pity.

Torro was panting dangerously, his asthma on fire with his cigarette in spite of the cleaning machine; but he insisted on saying this to Pogo: 'Let me tell you something my good friend, no? The most advanced thing they want to do is to turn thought into a sense, diiirectly!'

Before Pogo could digest this, Torro the bulk went round him with the ball and scored with a wicked flick. Goalll! whistled the silver owl, using its whistling as much as possible to digest the rat. There was dead silence on the park until Torro ordered his servants to cheer, otherwise they would be sent back to Rome in coffins. The forced cheer was in strings of spaghetti. Torro was beside himself with joy.

'I have scored against the millionaire!' he shouted to the dancing camel, and the camel carried the shout freeee with the smile of the desert in its eye, still retaining the suspicion of its master.

As the minutes ticked on Pogo balanced himself on the ball and talked, 'Torro, are you going to sit down and let your bosses invent bypass surgery in the stomach which will take food away from it so that those with that gorge will eat endlessly without getting full? Torro, beware of the mirror that lets you touch your own image behind it, beware of the new car whose fastest gear is reverse gear! I hear from the golden cockroach my precious friend that your least intelligent rulers have decided once again to attempt to retain some of the most primitive parts of the mind; and that is what leads you to want to destroy us. True we want a little more sophistication than this from such clever people!

41

You, Torro, stop pushing me off the ball, or I will call my golden horse, and let my carrots loose on you. I will unfold my fist after it has punched you and rest it on your bruised jaw, I swear! You can keep your advertisements for poisoned wines and dangerous powder . . .'

And just as his voice was trailing off, his feet burst out on to the right, the world was a number seven, and he crossed beautifully for the king lizard to nod the ball home for the second goal.

'Very soon I will attack your Grandmother Bomb . . .' Torro began angrily.

'And she will be ready for you,' Pogo declared with a deadly serious face.

The security helicopter had risen out of sight, and the spectators had vanished, for they had seen real anger on the faces of Torro and Pogo. The former's rats stood poised on hind legs, and would have attacked if it were not for the elephant that stamped with authority and stood between the two men: it wanted to be paid in leaves for playing a double game. Torro laughed over his rats. The camel whispered to the lizard.

And it was only when Bianca came with fresh bananas and sweet apple that the sparkle returned to Pogo's eyes. 'Ah, these games are getting serious!' he laughed.

Torro was back at his roast meat which was still sizzling, but Bianca wouldn't do his back. She was staring at Pogo with eyes bordering on admiration, and wondering whether she should shift her romance on to him or continue to reserve it for General Jolloff.

'It is imperative, yes, that I win when we play, Mr Pogo Alonka Forr,' Torro stated simply, wearing a face of angry pleading, 'I have not built this football park for defeat, you comprehendo, I have built it for victory.'

'But victory and defeat, are they not the same for you koraa?' Pogo replied, staring at the sleeping silver owl, probably now dreaming about its swift rat-dominated refereeing.

Then began Torro's insane laughter, laughter rising into the corners and sagging the floors more, some shoogling of flesh that touched the vast beef on and off. The leaves rumoured to their trees, as Pogo rang for his golden horse with its new garland of oval carrots. Bianca suddenly went and hugged him on an impulse. And Torro stared at his wife, his belly almost catching fire as the match of yet another cigar fell on it. He had reached a point where the contradictions of perception had not yet formed into the paradoxes that could be managed. He had wanted there and then to use his unreal bomb on Pogo, but had just received an instantly transferred psychic message from his bosses to play to the rules: while you were gathering the energy of brains, it was in your best interest to attack this same environment at the level it was at. And what was this level? Torro was becoming confused: how did you deal with a people you could defeat with your full power, but who were stubborn enough to have rooms on the moon, and stubborn enough to aspire to the sun with their golden horses and brilliant gari? Mama mia!

The warring admirers

Nana Mai, the Grandmother Bomb, was drinking lemongrass tea high up in a satellite which had a sexy booster tail to charm the galaxies with. Several oranges had been prompted to the status of fruit planets, and were orbiting the major's rooms to supplement the bananas there, paaa. Nana Mai could be quite gay, with her teeth taking on the polish needed for smiling, in spite of her usual stiff self. She encouraged the wild rumours of romance between her and the golden cockroach, only when she was up among the freedom of the stars near Gentl's rooms. For she would then shed her severity and give in to some uncharacteristic levity. Besides, being so high up she felt she could afford the ridicule of ludicrous facts and situations taken as the truth, precisely on the assumption that the actors of the ridicule would never appear so high to test her normal sense . . . or so she thought.

Lampposts had been installed, suspended in the eternal darkness up there, and things had become so advanced that oxygen had now been spread throughout the entire universe; and there were lanes of gari for rockets, and lanes of macaroni for celestial bicycles, pedalling up to the moon, *I swear*. Nana Mai even hung her single rarely-used headkerchief outside the rocket as she sat in the light of the satellite. After all when ruling a whole district, she couldn't quite afford to be so free at the ruling; so it was obviously easier to rule the universe than to rule a district in Achimota City, Ewurade. Her lips were colder than the beak of her parrot . . . the simple reason being that she had invented an ice cigarette that she ridiculed jot smokers with.

So there she was smoking the steam of her ice jot, beside that parrot pecking at the solar calculator. Little did she know that the golden cockroach was trying to crawl incognito through the aerial gari avenues, so that it could sneak into her satellite to admire her still firm calves of leg. The golden cockroach had always wanted a wife older than it was, a wife that would sit comfortably among the missiles. There were now

44

luscious worm-free guavas in the longlong firmaments, fine chop. And Grandmother Bomb had brought up one of her door professors to attend to the needs of the intellect mainly; but he had been warned not to blow shut at inopportune times. Any time the door prof opened his mouth he was warned to open his whole body, so that he would be faithful to his function.

'I would like a quartic equation quickquick, $x^4 + 7x^3 + 2x + 3 = 0$,' whined the parrot, as it held a joint calabash to drink palm-wine with, beside Nana Mai.

Parrot Koo had tiny missile earrings on, and an outrageous kente bowl into which it plopped its dung, and against which many guests made strong protest since they considered it an abomination. Nana Mai didn't care a hoot whether they hooted or not: in spite of all the science, she considered this the era of the beak, the hoof, the antenna, the crawl. 'One century equals one insect,' she would say with a shake of her elbow. Since the golden Mr Cee had heard her say this before, he thought he had a good chance with her. Where there was a hope there was a cockroach . . . As soon as Nana Mai was born she had power: she was immediately given the choice of bearing her mother back, and she did exactly that, traversing a mighty and wonderful pregnancy to give birth to her own mother in just two hours after herbs had fertilised her.

'I belong to the new breed of bearable babies,' she had said several years later. After a difficult childhood during which she was always accused of being too bookbook – not playing enough ampa according to the gayer girls – she suddenly rose from her books at twenty, and married a flat-headed musician with a neck almost as long as his trumpet. He was an expert in rural Highlife, and he had such volubility in his music that he drove her ears into the lounge when she was in the bedroom, and drove them to the bedroom when she was in the lounge, sharp. After a year she left him, carrying a daughter still hot from a badly heated marriage.

Her second husband was the very opposite: he drove her away with his silences, just at the time when Achimota City had only two million mosquitos to get rid of. What did you do to a man who gave a reply to 'Good morning' six hours later, when the afternoon was already on top of her. He was the mathematician who taught the parrot how to talk, and his habit of breaking off his talk in mid-sentence and continuing the same sentence three days later gave her some inner discipline through

45

the pain of silence. But this was unbearable too . . . and he had one nostril far bigger than the other. So she left him too, even though he gave one hundred silent sobs.

Just as she was getting ready to think up a better strategy for Major Gentl, and then to build up some more scorn for Pogo Forr, Nana Mai heard a knock among the stars at her satellite door. The inner door was the professor, but the outer door was steel. Instead of using the computer, she sent the parrot to check; and the parrot came back stiff with surprise: there following through the human-physics door was her mathematical silent ex-husband, grey now, but with a platinum ring round the entrance of his smaller nostril. Nana Mai too stiffened, momentarily, but she quickly composed herself and waited patiently for him to speak first. He in turn felt that she rather should speak first, since he had made the first venture in coming up the fine rope steps leading from the earth to the rocket. They stood there in silence, each with a grim look on the face, with the parrot alone chattering endlessly the way the mathematician had taught it. During the marriage he had spoken more to the parrot than to his wife. But as the silence deepened, even the poor parrot sensed the embarrassment, and decided to carry this silence from one mouth to the other. Flap, flap, flapped the parrot taking the years of bitterness and apathy from these pingpong hearts now standing so sternly and yet so vulnerably before each other. Then the bird had a sudden idea: it flew straight at Mathematics Professor Kwodwo Dolla, the heartbroken ex-husband, and pecked his neck so hard that out came that scream that had no maths in it.

And then, without hesitation, Nana Mai interjected, 'Thank goodness you spoke first. Akwaaba, my dear husband of the past. Let me get you your favourite drink of Guinness and palm-wine . . .'

She went and got it, and said with deceptive expansiveness, 'Kwodwo, how did you manage to trace me up here? Did you work it out by the square root or something . . ? But let me tell you straight away before you announce your mission: I: do: not: love: you: anymore! I'm sure you have heard that silly odo song that they were singing last year . . .'

Professor Dolla stared straight ahead without a word. The parrot was asleep on his bare toes, putting there some love in compensation, no doubt. Nana Mai's initials were on the reinforced glass by her left shoulder, and the thermometer was passing the new heat of the hearts so

46

fast, up and down, up and down. Dolla put his hand out to touch her shoulder, but she had already moved away to scrutinise the scorn on her face in the supaglass mirror.

As she retained her back to him, Professor Dolla wailed out of desperation, 'I am different now, I now have a car browned by the cigars I smoke, I put the lit sikadillo cigars on my white car, and then over the months the car becomes a distinguished brown, burnished if I may as a mathematician say so. I promise to put much meat paa in your mouth as you eat . . . remember that was one of your favourite things, to have bits of meat put in your mouth as you ate . . .'

'Stop all that, you one-plus-one Kwodwo! I have changed now, and I do not require your meat koraa!' Grandmother Bomb interrupted.

It was her laughter shown sometimes in the silent twinkle of her eyes that worried Desperate Dolla.

'Besides I'm now grey and not easily lovable, so take your silences elsewhere!' Nana Mai added cruelly, but with a cruelty leavened by laughter.

'Give me more of your destructive laughter, I will eat banku with it before I die!' Dolla exclaimed uncharacteristically, extending his desperation and uttering more words ex-classroom, boof, than he had done in the last year.

Nana Mai became stern in one eye, for she had just heard the ominous sound of a trumpet by the physics-door; and was wondering who on earth had opened the steel door to begin with . . . to admit her musical first husband in this connubial memorial among the stars.

'Daaalin, daalin, if I had known that you had changed so little, I would have come earlier to awoof you more! Don't you adore this flat head of mine that has become flatter than ever through missing you and my daalin little daughter not so little now! And who is this stupid stiff gentleman standing lovesick before you? Aah, I heard that you had the effrontery to marry again! Listen to my music . . . How dare you allow someone else to come into you, all this time that I've been imagining you alone and lonely waiting for a day like today when I would burst like a tyre on to the scene and you would stop everything and cook abenkwan for me with great joy, Allah! . . . I am now almost a Muslim. Don't you admire my excuse me to say pentatonic mutability, walai!' shouted Jollo Gyan all in one breath, blowing his trumpet intermittently for effect.

He had yellow silk shorts and a yellow joromi, and his great

47

moustache had risen at the edges to receive his music. Nana Mai, to the astonishment of the two men and the parrot, not forgetting the scientist that had left its door-space out of curiosity, was busy in a corner of the pink machine, working out a problem in ballistics. She had completely forgotten they were there, in spite of the parrot's screech of remember-ance, O you Koo.

So Professor Dolla and Jollo Gyan faced each other. The professor had stuck out his chest as a sign of masterful strength, wanting to bully with the breast. Jollo just blew his trumpet at Dolla's groin, dancing up and down in yellow speed, blowing the trumpet more in well-aimed thrusts at that mathematically stiff man.

'Let's remove our shirts and fight for the love of this great and wonderful woman before us here!' Gyan shouted with joy. Then, pom, his joromi was off. Then he turned away from Grandmother Bomb, removed his shorts, and revealed his yellow pioto to match; then in an act that Dolla would never forget, pulled out his popylonkwe – it had a yellow ribbon tied graciously round it – and then placed it side by side with his trumpet, screaming, 'Yes, I am now measuring it, are you not amazed to see its length? . . . I am so strong that when my mouth gets tired, I use my human twig to blow my trumpet! C'mon fight me now now now . . . you look like some soft booklong abongo man!'

And this was when Dolla decided to use his massive dignity, walking with a restrained swagger to the nearest rocket wall, and filling it instantly with many shoogly mathematical symbols. He declared, 'You see the equation on the right, you see the equation on the left? Join them with another connecting symbol, and you will see, my friend, that I have cancelled you out altogether. You do not exist on the face of this earth kapere ba! And I order you to change into your nonexistence immedi-ately!'

Kwodwo Dolla was standing only on one foot, in anger, his platinum nostril flaring extra. Jollo gave a wicked grin, rushed into the tiny heads-only kitchen, devoured a plate of rice and stew, and then rushed back all in an instant just to give Dolla a dirty slap. With the parrot squawking in consternation and flapping between the two gentlemen, Nana Mai at last looked up in total surprise. She had been eating gari to fully concentrate her thinking. The rocket lurched as she rose to speak, so that her words came out logorligi . . . at the wrong angle to her own tongue:

'Cross the parrot there, Koo, nip both cheeks for me, destroy them out of my life!'

The rocket danced as Jollo blew his trumpet in agony.

Then there was a devastating silence as the two husbands of yore digested the import of what Grandmother Bomb had just said. Then something strange happened: the two of them started to speak at exactly the same time, using exactly the same words – it was Torro's reduction machine no doubt synchronising disparate beings and actions again.

'How dare you woman of the torn heart and the inter-continental weaponry disgrace us in front of the cheeky beaky parrot and the sweaty physics-door like that! Hear our double voice now for stressing effect. We spent years nurturing your labalabalibilibi temperament! When we wanted love, you gave us experiments; when we wanted to give you some sly night embraces, we ended up embracing bombs instead, O Allah of the fez that is so high that it can reach an aeroplane's underbelly! We implore you to bring some divine justice into the medium-range heart of this woman! Besides, she likes koobi too mech . . .'

'I disagree with the Allah bit,' declared Professor Dolla, getting his voice and his individuality back single again. 'You may have some leanings towards muslimry, but err . . .'

'Stop chattering about butter now you nonally of the midget popy-lonkwe. Give me my single voice anytime. I demand that you and me, we have some serious fight, some boogie ntokwa, to see which one of us will win the heart of this lady that doesn't want us . . .', Jollo Gyan said, smiling disdainfully at Dolla.

But all Dolla replied was this: 'What weak logic you have . . .' And he took out his pipe and smoked it fresh-fresh.

It was when everybody was quiet that the golden cockroach made its entilahatic entry. It wore a pink hat above its especially decorated entrails . . . some ludicrous modern inner colouring, *I swear*. It said, 'I am a hypnotic animal, be careful with me, I mean just look at me. Am I not a sight for the magnificent? How do you gentlemen of the husbandry expect a lady of genius like this to waste her time attended by men who may be gifted, yes, but who cannot measure up to her singularly sankofa gifts! Look at my hats, my ribbons, my ghana-flag shoes, my eternity-dark glasses, look at my sexy standing hey!'

49

Even Jollo and the parrot were incredibly silent. There seemed to be a margarine tin of awe before the corporeality of an emblem.

'Give me an embrace, Madame Bomb, before the very eyes of those men!' ordered the golden cee.

Nana Mai had already rushed to get a tin of Raid insect spray, with a sardonic look on her face, to spray the golden C pronto . . . She was fed up with admirers, especially likeable ones.

'Wait!' exclaimed Mr Cee, 'Wait, and do not spray me, for gold does not die.'

The golden cockroach stood in mock astonishment, knowing very well that Nana Mai was too intelligent to forget that it was a golden presence that would not die. A chasm of the heart separated Nana Mai from her ex-husbands muttering together in the background.

'She has betrayed us,' wailed Jollo Gyan, ignoring the cockroach altogether, 'and she will cause a scandal by rejecting us for an insect.'

Professor Dolla had decided to give up talking again, and was busy scribbling mathematical symbols on the palm of his hand, stroking Koo the parrot at the same time in the feathers of a psitteciformes science.

O in came the silver mosquito carrying an electric sword.

'This golden cockroach is using me too mech, what if this sword electrocutes me? . . . I am here to drive all unwanted visitors away . . . and if this golden Mr Cee thinks it has really won the heart of Madam Bomb, me I know her better than that! She wants to use him . . .'

The golden cee was quite unperturbed, and was busy staring at Nana Mai who in turn had gone back to her ballistics. The love of others flowed around her closed heart. And the husbands waved and waved on their way out and she didn't even look up; but they had been reassured by what the silver mosquito said about her heart.

Professor Dolla suddenly burst in and cried to her, 'If you don't come back to me, I'll be forced to fight on the side of that mad Italian Torro! I have certain secrets of war that you may find useful . . .'

Out of respect for the professor, the golden cockroach lengthened the laughing space between one grin and another; and it was only after Dolla left that there was no space left at all, for one laughter touched another and another. Koo sulked in the distance when its master went, but went to make the lemon tea. The physicist was shut again; and the golden cee had a smirk on its face. The morning coloured the rocket as the tea was brought with a touch of ginger it it. Ginger morning here.

'Shape me, shape me!' screamed the cockroach with desire. 'I am talking about love between you and this emblem that I am . . .'

It turned round to present its best feeler towards Nana Mai for a feel or for good effect, but she wasn't even looking. She was navigating a new course, and wanted to land in the graveyard in the Achimota plains where the recorded voices of the dead, played through tiny speakers, reached out to the rocket in massive discord: there were those with their last words, there were those in moments of love, those who were brokenhearted, those emitting their first sounds as babies, and those wailing at the funerals of others.

The golden cee was bewildered, not knowing why Grandmother Bomb chose such a spot. What was he going to do with his romance here at all? And he was getting suspicious about the impossibility of the old lady loving him: you didn't send fresh love to the graveyard one time lalat.

Nana Mai had a bigitive gleam in her eye among the graves, as they descended from the satellite. Even the parrot had to fit in the pervading silence.

'Pogo Forr almost found out that it's the dead that I love and sell things near. Everything else is secondary . . .' Nana Mai said almost laughing. Her face glowed when the dusk came quickly.

'I am the originator of rooms in the moon,' declared the golden cockroach, 'so it will take more than graves and darkness to put me off . . . I believe you may take off your clothes soon . . .'

Nana Mai glared at it with such intensity that its golden wings unfolded involuntarily; the parrot landed on her wrist, Kooooo. Her left eye seemed to protrude that little bit more. She said threateningly, 'How dare you think I love you! Lesser men have tried and failed, and the greater will fail more. Don't you have any sense of dignity, chasing me in a graveyard?'

There was a silence as the golden cee adjusted its hat to a less debonair level, to some abinkyi angle; and the parrot reflected the yellow moon in such concentrated form that you would think it was blood coming from its beak. Mr Cee was getting desperate for romance. Old Koo threatened to assault the graves with its peck and screech to balance its sanity, for it had seen something it didn't like at all: while Nana Mai was preoccupied with a soothing dead voice, the golden Mr Cee tried to crawl between her legs. Koo dashed to swallow it, gold and

51

all, but Nana Mai had already shaken her long cloth in anger and consternation.

'I only tolerate your madness because of the war . . .', she declared, finding the golden crawl repulsive, shieeee.

'How do we defeat Torro the infinitely Terrible through the major?' the golden cockroach asked, sensing a change of mood, and speaking loudly above the dead voices. 'As you know, we can't fight him directly, and yet he must be beaten. The major is the first direct hope. Pogo is almost as indirect and deflected as we are . . . different wings of the army fight differently. But I wish I was the direct type . . . I have the power of the skies, yet I can only use this power through the beloved major . . .'

Out of a corrective impulse, Nana Mai took the cockroach up in her arms and gave it the marvellous embrace it wanted. There was the joy of gold, but the golden cee was clever enough to know this: the obsession of Grandmother Bomb to defeat Torro so wanted to be direct that it was prepared to enter into embraces and other pacts to achieve its end. So the hug was a miltary manoeuvre. And she in turn agreed that the indirect war raced through the direct; and yet this didn't stop her from wishing to be closer to those condemned to the indirect method. She admired the patience of Major Gentl, but she admired the sounds of the dead even more . . .

The golden cockroach was deeply quiet as the silver mosquito came with the helicopter to take it away to simpler plains.

'I do have human girlfriends,' stated the golden cockroach, its soso mouth almost disappearing with sadness.

Nana Mai snorted, then said, 'Then why do you need me?'

Golden cee hesitated wryly for a second, and then replied, 'Isn't it lonely being an emblem that wants to be more and more physical everyday . . . and you and me, we share the same type of brains, brains that need the touch of fruit or gunpowder, the dead or parrots, or at least a jump at the moon as if we were children . . .'

While the golden cockroach talked, Nana Mai fed Koo a dose of nivaquine, for it swore that the silver mosquito had given it a bite among the dead, oooo.

As Nana Mai went back to her district among the welcoming neems, she shivered at the nonsense that she sometimes took her life to. She stared with contempt at the physics-door; for she knew that if she didn't retain her sternness all the time even among the stars, they would not see her status, nor her invention: she kept her mind open by closing her temperament, and no one except the golden cockroach truly understood her passion to scatter the bosses of Torro very much in addition to Torro himself. She found Pogo too expansive and too wealthy, and Gentl the major not aggressive enough, as if he was prepared to push for victory without taking on the trappings of the victorious at all . . . You ma-know. The great Koo with the scientific beak went to sneak some adoka to add to the nivaquine, and was now chattering with theorems at great speed, boofboof. The flowers on Nana Mai's roof were in full bloom, the cornmill sang above the dead. Joy to the woman of victory for she kept the wisdom of her age in any situation!

ZONE SIX

War within war

The major knew that the children's war was becoming popular paa. There were telephone pennies and pesewas there for ringing different commanders soon after Torro's children joined the war; there were security flies with guns across their wings so small that any deaths from such firing would be smaller than the triggers. First of all everybody from both sides – Gentl's side, Torro's side – laid down their guns and decided to sell hard toffee. The market women complained bitterly, but the security flies drove them away. mMo sold toffee to Carlo, and it was commanders' toffee; Editta sold toffee to Aba Y, and it was deputy commanders' toffee; Adu sold toffee to Mensah, guncarriers' toffee, Kwesi sold to Giovanna, Giovanni sold to Abebrese, Edoardo sold to Mansa, and then Ugo sold to Agi; Oti sold to Ottone, Baba sold to Barbara, and Beniamino sold to Bediako, sharp. The sun was hidden with hundreds of toffees thrown in jubilation. There was cat toffee, dog toffee, gorilla toffee, mafia toffee, puberty toffee, existence toffee, and beeny toffee. But best of all tufu toffee, tafa toffee, tifi toffee, tofo toffee, tafo toffee, twifu toffee, and then tafla tse: toffee tougher for all, toughest for the sweetest war of all.

'But what is happeneeing here?' Torro would say in disgust. 'Isn't anybody dead yet? I warn you, Major, not to let any of my cheeldren die first!' Gentl standing there with his sergeant shadow, still being beaten by Atinga the bodyguard, would say nothing. He would just shift his snakes, just as Torro shifted his rats. Snaking and ratting under the toffee sky was good–O, *I tell you.*

It was in the mid-year 2020, when the bush-coloured bullet pushed off his cap, that General Jolloff decided in a brilliant manoeuvre away from the presence of rice to add the supervision of the abofra war to the adults' war. His decision was made in good grains of thought. He created a deputy immediately and warned him that any obsession he wanted to have would have to involve fufu, and not rice.

'You are not allowed to have the same odododiodo as your boss, myself. No rice is allowed in your thinking. Besides, supervising the children's war may be more difficult than a supervisitation of the adultery . . . I mean a supervisor of the adult war. I order you not to assume that I have looked at any other woman apart from my late wife, just because I have made a slip of the tongue! And my moustache is one of the sights of the battlefields, it is better than aMofa Gentl's I swear. And I want to give you another order: do not look at the lady soldiers when they are bending down; as soon as their hips come into view as signs of temptation to you, just shout, "Hip hip hooray!" And the temptation will go away. I am talking to you as an extremely married man. I have never looked at another woman . . . unless I'm absolutely forced to, and even then I put on my goggles and use only my military eye. I will never reveal the secret about which is my military eye, and which is my civilian eye. Now go and supervise the big war now now now before it starts to cool.'

Captain Owusu never failed to shake, nor to feel confused, in the general's presence. He hated fufu, but was now being forced to start an obsession with it. He loved women, but he was being asked not to look at their bendability. Then in a moment of bold rebellion, he proposed to several women working under him, only to stand crushed under the weight of what each told him: he was neither attractive nor independent-minded enough. Ewurade, better divide his eyes solider-fashion just like the general's. But in a desperate attempt to walk like General Jolloff, and to acquire darkglasses so dark that he couldn't see and was always tripping, he was finally laughed out of love altogether.

General Jolloff found it absolutely true that supervising the children's war was more difficult than the adults' war. He woke up after a small afternoon siesta to find his great moustache trimmed without authority, and neither of the juvenile opposing commanders would admit to ownership of the smooth Kokompe scissors he found near his chin. Which woman of Torro would love him now?, he thought. He called the commanders from both sides immediately, and screamed, 'Don't you know who I am, you undertrained choochoo mosquitoes? Your little brains are made of the material of the keteke. Now you have made my moustache smaller than Major Gentl's, how dare you . . ? I have been cultivating this hair spiritually for more years than you have been born. Now look! Junior Commander Carlo of the ears of pizza, what do you have to say with your tongue like one macaroni after another? Shame to you, doing this to a general of general importance . . .'

The junior military band suddenly came by, drowning out the words of General Jolloff, who instinctively rose and marched for a full thirty seconds before realising what he was doing. There was a deafening silence. Jolloff refused to walk back from his reflexive march, for he knew they would mock him now and tell their parents later.

'Dignity before the wildness of children,' was what he snarled out before taking a series of ludicrous hops to his waiting bubra, Achimota brewery in Achimota City, by the settee now brought out for supervisory purposes . . . but which was now tightly holding the dignitarial doona of a whole general. And the breeze came in various shades of mango, banana, tangerine, and guave, Chop.

'Now, young soliders,' began Commander mMo to the gathering of junior soldiers, 'are we going to accept such bullying from a distinguished gentleman of the uniform, lalat?'

'Noooooo!' came the reply.

'We no eat pizza for the general at all!' ventured Commander Carlo, promoting his English to one stripe of language.

'Nooooo!' came the second reply.

'We are all brothers even though we are enemies!' shouted Commander mMo with the confidence that came from stealing one of his father's snakes for his epaulettes . . . and unfortunately he had stolen the snake that was notorious for its stubbornness: as soon as the mutually exclusive Torro–Gentl children's army blew an extraordinary number of balloons in celebration of the first battle, which nobody won, the reptile with the nkonkonsa wriggle burst every balloon with a wonderful show of speed and agility; a supercrawl so appreciated that they all decided to promote the crawl and leave the snake as silly as ever: why should it show such talent in such a burst of energy, asemni? Also, this same snake ate Torro's third-favourite rat, secretly brought on to the battlefield by his son Carlo. This caused a reptilic furore, since the amiable and soft-furred rat had become everyone's pet.

'We have secrets that can be useful for the adult war,' Aba Y declared in the midst of the junior army deciding what to do with the silly snake.

Adu was all for cutting the snake open to see whether the rat was still alive; but mMo was appalled by this, since he continued to see the disloyalty of his mother and his brother as treason. He shouted out, 'This snake will not be cut, no way!'

And that was when General Jolloff interrupted the proceedings, declaring that the war was getting too agromentous, and that the shooting should resume: the enemy, born, bred and citied of Torro, was to shoot to the west; while the home guns with the ritual lavender on the butts were to commandeer the east. Shots on any part of the anatomy were to be forbidden at this stage except with the express permission of the elders of government of Achimota City, O you toffee war.

The two rival commanders were just preparing for a full-scale attack when Aba Y repeated irritably her assertion, 'I said we have secrets that can be useful in the adult war.'

'Then promote her to the adult war immediately now now, this girl is too proud,' someone shouted from the back.

And next to that someone was the youngest member of the junior army, Sama, the one-year-old tyrant, who decided on the use of battle spaces for Commander mMo. He was an infant strategist who would brook no nonesense by any stream in the bush: he loved the use of water space, and would let both armies stand for hours shooting at their own reflections in the water, wet bullets. And as soon as General Jolloff tried to put his bootfoot down on the need for a drier children's war, Sama assessed his rights with a pee by the crowded banks, so that everybody would see the increased wetness of both the stream and his authority over wet space.

'I was talking about the adult war,' persisted Aba Y.

The infant strategist looked at her with scorn, even though she was the commander's sister.

Aba Y continued, 'If my father the major's men could come down to the water here, he could double the strength of his army by making use of reflections in the stream, so that . . .'

'But you started to mention your secret idea before we came to the water . . .' began Sama doubtfully.

'Do you think that you are the only one who has ideas about water?' Aba Y asked with impatience. 'Besides, I was going to suggest shadows at first, but I know that reflections are better, especially wet ones . . . and the Grandmother Bomb has almost finished inventing something for the military use of shadows and reflections.'

57

'How do you know?' demanded Sama, who had just rushed home secretly to partake of his mother's breast milk, and come to the water.

He was feeling extra defiant, this infant, simply because he knew that Aba Y and one or two others knew that he was still on the breast. The reason he secretly admired Aba Y was that even though he didn't treat her too well, she had never teased him about it. He should not push his luck though, he thought.

'I want a dry space now, so everybody including Commander Carlo's menkids should go up nearer General Jolloff standing on dry land smoking his pipe over the mad and untidy war . . . Don't forget, we have some dying to do . . .' ordered Commander mMo.

'But, errr, no one is dyieeng yet,' protested Commander Carlo, echoing the words of his father, Torro.

The armies marched wet out of the stream, and entered strongly into the smell of fried onions. There was Major Gentl cooking squirrels' entrails with Torro the Terrible. The armies stood there stunned among the onions.

'Ah, you beauuutiful leetle cheeldren, fight on fight on!' began Torro. 'We have just come to get a few heeents from you, no!'

Gentl gave some onion to the snake so rapt wrapped round his weaker ankle. Some pythonic amulet, bangle in the ankle, agyeei. The entire double army watched the frying as Torro fanned the fire.

'Why don't you go and fight your wars and leave us alone to fight ours?' asked Adu, staring with resentment at his father the major, and continuing, 'Besides, how can you win wars when all you do is to fry onions in the bush . . ?'

'Papa, weee dooo nottt want vigilare-vigilare, leeeve us alone, our guerra is good without you,' Beniamino said to his father Torro in his spaghetti English while looking at Bediako.

The trouble with Beniamino was that since he arrived in Achimota City, the only person he could speak to in the afternoons was Bediako. All his questions, all his answers were directed through the latter, even his greetings to others . . . all done with a slow sad voice that was just about to break into puberty. But when it came to toffee and other distinguished things of the belly, he ate them direct without passing through Bediako's mouth; and he insisted to himself on one thing: all his memories of Italy had to pass through Achimota first, momoni

Achimota, fruit-tree Achimota, anthill Achimota City, everything a second memory.

Torro was livid with anger and surprise, his belly heaving higher, then lower, so that if he were not careful it would end up pancaking his chin.

'Is thees what all my bambinos from Italia want to do to me! Me I fan my humble fire with my best nemico, my major enemy, then youuou want to spoil our onion show, no? Spank–O sculacciare! Dio!'

Gentl thought: Torro was having one of his inexplicable angers again, he would have to learn how to be kobolo from passion. Torro's rats suddenly appeared at his shoulder, as they sensed that their master was going to use them for the kill.

'You cannot keeel me, your own son, your figlio favourite. I am not a servant, Papa. Weee weel say what weee want on our own battlefield!' Commander Carlo commanded, his defiant stance looking immensely like his father's. Besides, his mother Bianca, so ecstatic to have her children with her again, even if for a war, had told him to be himself in this beautiful land . . . irrespective of any devious plans his father might have for him.

Gentl allowed himself a smile of exasperation as he looked at the look in Torro's eye; and the look said that he was really prepared to turn the rats on his own children.

The major prepared his snakes. The armies moved back silently from the two men now staring at each other, as of old.

'Let me deal with my own bambinos, Major!' Torro hissed, hardly opening his mouth.

The snakes writhed round their master's waist in anticipation. There was the silence of hundreds of children. Then, as snake and rat remained in sprung stillness, Sama rushed between the two men after consulting General Jolloff, and shouted, with a smell of breastmilk on his eyelids, 'We will not allow you to come here and fight! And we will not allow you to fry your onions here! What's all this! We children are protected by law . . .'

'What does thees leetle baby know about law? Major, you are letting your bambinos get too advanced,' Torro said sardonically, taking the silver owl out of his bag to feel superior with.

General Jolloff didn't want to come into the restrained fray himself, since he admired Major Gentl too much. And he didn't quite understand why he felt a near uncontrollable need to fart in Torro's presence. He continually smoothed his reduced moustache as he watched Sama exert an authority that was related to babymilk, koko and other weaning food. And the stolen snake that mMo used for his epaulette slid back to the major who showed no sign whatsoever of having seen it.

The major suddenly turned his back, crowded with snakes, and walked away from Torro, leaving the onions to burn. Torro too turned round, decorated with stiff rats, and walked off in the opposite direction. General Jolloff suddenly saw his freedom.

'Now you children, you are free from the warring giants! I want you all to march to the sound of rice falling! Isn't it a beautiful beat! C'mon, more rice to your souls, rice, rice! left right, left right, rice rice rice rice rice left rice right!'

The general started to beat the drums himself, but no child moved. They looked at him with contempt, as Gentl and Torro disappeared over the different horizons. But General Jolloff Rice didn't care: he knew he had a gigantic dignity below all the fooling he was doing now, and that a distinguished man had to enjoy himself sometimes. He marched and beat his drum to the terrible silence. And the fish drank the stream to his marching. Commanders mMo and Carlo had now decided this: even in the middle of fighting, they would try hard together to become more powerful than the adults.

The power

The elders of government were eternally careful to hold their big starched beards at specific angles but, not necessarily, always at the same one. One of the Elders was short, one was tall, and one was medium and fat. If it were not for the existence of the golden emblem cockroach, they could easily have used these beards as the regalia of office. Each had a missile in his toilet, but being men of peace, all they did was to personally polish and repolish the missiles until they were absolute shine papaapa. Bees, fruit and honey were popular in the cabinet rooms; but the honey was carried in small cans on the backs of extremely haughty rabbits moving from table to table. *You had to show some deference to each rabbit before you could take a tiny calabashful of honey. You political pets.*

In order to increase his sense of humility, Elder One would every morning use a ladder to climb his own height and then dismiss himself every ten inches, so that each inch would enjoy a humility that had been thoroughly mocked by himself to prevent false pride. He was the originator of the honey rabbits in Government House, for apart from what he considered the ecological morality of interacting with rabbits, there was also another good reason for this extraordinary interest: he had ears exactly like a rabbit's; and when he was feeling very governmental, he walked like one.

Elder One had boldly decided that it was not necessary for him to have a name, since he preferred defining actions to defining things. He could therefore be named when he was doing something, but nameless when he was not. But the populace thought it good to name him Kofi Kot, a name that they did not dare say koraa in his presence: add a particular vowel, and you would end up in the territory of the genital dangle, some cool kote. Every month he had a special wedding ceremony with the same wife. Mrs Wife – this was exactly what she was called – had become so outraged with the frequency of this ritual that sometimes she would disappear, feigning sickness. This would not perturb Kofi Kot at all, for he went through the ceremony alone, grinning at the abusuapanyin and dexterously slipping the ring on to his own finger shipsharp. Otherwise he was so simple that his only other ceremony was his beard. This beard was undoubtedly the property of the government, just as it was for the other two beards of the ruling troika of hair: whenever the golden cockroach misbehaved by shedding its emblem, the law immediately allowed the beards at certain angles to be used as semi-symbols of authority, ebei. Kofi Kot was paid chin allowance for his beard, but in a moment of extreme independence, he demanded from the populace, without consulting the other two elders – he was in fact insulting them instead – that he was prepared to have his beard shaved off in the interest of the state, and that his chin was his own property entirely.

There was a small national debate over the beard. Eventually the matter was solved when the official Government Goat, such a post being necessary to keep the bush down, took a wild and illegal bite out of Kot's beard; and that was when he decided to keep his hair on his chin – for a third of it was missing. And as he slept, his wife, *you Mrs*, held it in a passionate embrace before giving it a very gentle trim that returned it to its original angle . . . the approved governmental angle.

Elder One was often Kot boasting that he had many times sat on a pin because of careless typists, but that he had never emitted a scream in the middle of important meetings, the only sign of pain being that his ears flapped gently like . . . a rabbit's.

Elder Two was patapaa. He bobbed up and down with his fat, and then would increase it by chomping enormous amounts of food during cabinet meetings. He would argue in one place, and then release his fat in another place to bolster the bluster of his arguments. He never stayed too long on one subject for he was afraid that the fat in his head would congeal, boof.

He one day caused an inferno in his girlfriend – his wife had left him long ago claiming he was impotent – by failing to finish a sentence, 'I love you,' as she had asked him. After 'I love' he had failed to insert that most important last word, 'you', simply because he had moved on to another subject: himself, Jojo Digi. He caused an outrage in the ruling council by catching a rabbit and eating it right there in Government

House. The succulent smell led to a one-hour adjournment of the cabinet meeting, and a small reprimand from his other two comrades, especially Kofi Kot the originator of the rabbits in the first place.

'Fruit is our subject, not meat,' Kofi Kot had snarled. And that was the only snarl Kot was allowed to give that day: each Elder was allowed by law only one large snarl a day, and Jojo Digi had looked around in triumph, for he knew that for once he had not used his quota of snarling first. He would thus soon growl back in revenge, without reply.

Digi was the only one of the troika that seriously considered the use of the missiles in the War of Existence. He was impatient with the roundabout way that Major Gentl and Pogo Forr were going about trying to win the war; he wanted heavier more direct fighting, but since he had been outvoted each of the thousand times that he had brought up the subject, he decided to keep mute if possible.

Elder Three suffered from a surfeit of love, bigitive love was his asem. He neither scrambled after eggs nor poached his enemies. He rarely boiled. Neither did he guard gari not watch waakye. Frogs, lizards, crows and hens sometimes slept on him, he was so kind. He often had to carry his wife to cabinet meetings for he had overwhelmed her with love and she was thus immobile. If the three elders hadn't sworn in law to suffer each other's idiosyncracies, there would have been riots at such occasions. Elder Three was called Amos Kittoe, though his maleria was a safe series of bites. His hard head for facts was his strong point, so as soon as anyone thought he had outmanoeuvred him, he would bring out a contradiction or an obscure fact, and thus cut the ground gently from under the logic. He was especially fond of Major Gentl even though sometimes when they met they couldn't communicate for their gentleness koraa. Even good mornings could be too agressive. Kittoe was the spirit behind all the fruit in Achimota City; and he was also the official architect for anthills, the adviser for ants and termites. You should see Amos relaxing in his banana garden listening to African symphonies.

Thus Elder One's wife was called Mrs Wife, Elder Three's wife – she stuttered in love – MMMrs WWWife, and Elder Two's girl Miss Wife. They shared the Ms while the three elders had made themselves experts in many things. In spite of temperamental differences, they had a vast store of wisdom and courage. Everybody had confidence in them, yet everybody laughed at their idiosyncrasies, creating an easy complexity between the rulers and the ruled that did not have a history before them.

Kot was talking to Digi was talking to Kittoe was talking to Kot. They were discussing the war when a loud snore from Kittoe's sleeping wife interrupted them. Amos carried his beautiful wife out of the cabinet rooms while she still slept. They looked at her askance but Amos ignored them. Digi gave an impatient scowl. And the confidential secretary was seen writing fast, even though nothing was being said: she always insisted that she knew what each elder was going to say in advance and that each meeting was different combinations of the same-same points from the same-same people . . .

But the elders didn't mind her at all, for she was so ugly that she was attractive, and the only person she told state secrets to was her handsome husband, who was too busy eating twenty-four hours a day to divulge any of them. The chairmanship alternated, and so did the wind, blowing on to the three different beards with varying intensity among the termite mansions.

Kot, the current chair, began, 'We may have to call in Major Gentl, Torro, Pogo Forr and others to this meeting to review the war, but now we go on with business. There's the problem with the Ministry of Fish. The fish are still getting rebellious in the sea, and are refusing to be caught no matter what nets are used, for the smaller ones slip the smallest nets, and the biggest ones slip through the biggest nets. The minister covered herself in fish, including a brassiere of tilapia, and then boldly approached the sea to see whether any fish would rise and meet her fairly and squarely in the political arena of the tossing waves. Sometimes she got fish that were interested in the pol but not the itics. She braced herself, waiting to see Mammy water herself mermaiding in the deeps, but all that happened was a huge shark gave her a threatening grin, and after summoning up all her ministerial courage, she swam away fast for further instructions. It was after everything was lost in the personal approach that she used the sonic equipment with the fishy music, adowa in the water. The fish are now being caught in adequate quantities, but I am seeking authority for the fish themselves to be represented on the new Council for Fish . . .'

'Brother no-name Kot,' shouted Elder Jojo Digi patapaa, 'I know we have built tolerance and the new into the fabric of the termites and the fruit, but you are overdoing it . . . At which point in the brew of ideas do you consider that we are tearing the ordinary apart? . . .'

'Ahh, there you go again, going on to some differdiffer subject before you finish what you were saying!' smiled Amos Kittoe with his bronze-brown lower lip carrying the smile, 'and I can give you several dates on which you did the same thing . . .'

'Gentlemen I declare koraa that this meeting has a chair . . .' began Kofi Kot.

'And I table the motion . . .' said Digi with a laugh in his brighter eye.

Kofi Kot suddenly called for the ladder to attain his height of humility yet again but then changed his mind, for he had to assert his authority immediately: the others were eating fruit nosily, and were now oblivious to his frantic attempts to restore order. He continued regardless. 'And I understand that the fish have already passed several intelligent motions insisting that they have the privilege to devour any small fried human being in revenge before agreeing to show the scale of their involvement in the Fish Council.'

There was some silence, the rabbits stood sullenly with their honey. *You would take dung rather to the elders if you could, you sweet fur.*

'What do we do about the Fish Council, then?' asked Amosssss, trapped in his own sibilant sound.

'Fry it!' cried Digi with the oil on his brain, 'And to go back to the ordinary world of pona and cocoyam, I believe we must be careful with our philosophy of variousness, otherwise . . .'

'Other fools will take it over,' Kot declared, assuming his chairman-ship with speed again; and stubbornly holding a live fish to show the other elders how serious he was about that council that was based in the sea, that wet committee.

Jojo Digi exploded, 'How dare you assume that we want to see a real fish? I have always told you that the thingness of Africa is the headness of somewhere else, and what . . .'

'. . . will save us is not a present attachment to the concrete but an ultimate one,' declared the confidential secretary.

'But how did you know that I was going to say exactly what you have just said?' Digi asked with surprised anger.

'Sir, you said the same thing three days ago,' the lady with confidence said.

'Yes, and you said it at exactly 3.55,' concluded Kittoe, the man with the exact amos and the gentle smile. And the telephone rang and answered itself long before the confidential alombo ambled over to pick it up. The message was that her husband had rung for food even though he had just returned from a succulent chop-bar, and that he was insisting that she choose between him and her work for the elders of government, for whenever he needed her she was not there to listen to the sound of his chewing. Mama the secretary left one tear on the telephone, for even though she was strong, she never failed to feel exasperated by her husband, this exasperation showing in one advance tear and in her pen moving so much faster.

Before the elders could drink lemongrass tea at the same time – this Tea Law allowed for uniformity in trivial things and divergence in important things, according to the wisdom in the threedom – Amos said with genial force, 'Jojo should not carry around in his head still this artificial difference between the concrete and the abstract, for we all know that we accepted the whole long ago, and we now know quite well how the elements change within it . . .'

'The only whole I know is the hole that the rabbits came out of. I will never agree on fundamental things except when a decision has to be made, and immediately after . . . Could the chairman indicate whether it will be necessary to postpone science for another week, so that we don't remain slaves to it . . ?'

'There you go again, you did not finish your first point, please go back to it,' Kot declared.

'But I thought we were still discussing the Fish Council,' Digi protested.

Kot saw his chance in spite of his humility, 'Ah, I'm sure you are suffering yet another headhead disconnection, suffering your usual abrupt about-turns. It's because of the unauthorised rabbit you ate. But let me remind you that we have not only fried the Fish Council under a general motion, but we have also eaten it, in spite of the several points of order raised by the existence of throat-pricking bones . . .'

Digi used his snarl at last, just when he was not ready to, snarling taller than his own jaws.

But the termites didn't mind what the elders were doing at all, for they just continued to change the architecture of Government House when they wanted, with their inspired saliva plus earthen engineering. And wasn't it the cheapest way of building strong mansions, using termites intelligently? And the way the biting combined the different forms of red, grey, and brown was beautiful to behold. And would you be so kind as to hold your page while one elder went to the toilet, thought the troublesome rabbit as it tried to steal some of its own honey, kayakaya sweet.

Agoooo, came the stylish knock of the golden cockroach as it walked unannounced into the cabinet room, preceded by the silver mosquito in a ludicrous procession of two stiff insects. As the walking emblem of Achimota City, it was the duty of the golden cockroach to walk round the tables twice in perfect silence, and then eat its mango necklace immediately.

'What secrets have you come with today, our dear emblem?' Kot began. 'Akwaaba, you gold and silver beings.'

The silver mosquito loved Amos Kittoe for they shared a desire not to quit life. The golden cee was still silent, for it had not yet finished chewing its necklace with its golden grin koraa. At last Mr Cee spoke, after rescuing an incipient laugh from a burp of mango.

'Greetings to you, you elders of the political deep! You must know that the War of Existence will be getting more serious now, since Torro feels under greater threat than ever from his masters. Torro has come to the conclusion that the reason he is fighting an unserious war to the death is that his masters abroad are themselves leading extremely trivial lives, obsessed with mere processes, and trying to create yet more power and wealth for spirits that died long ago. Now, don't get me wrong, Torro is not going to run right now to our side: he is not necessarily interested in power in relation to his bosses but power in relation to US! Ha! He has become very possessive about this city! and he may even be prepared to be replaced by the synthetic leader if it means he will still have some sort of relationship and control over diminishing aspects of our lives . . . Can I have some honey please, into which I will dip my khebab of soft goatskin . . ? Besides, Torro has done something which has put his bosses on edge: he has trained the brainthief machines on his own head for a very good reason: how will his masters continue to want him if his already limited but usefully wild faculties have been reduced by their own inventions? I am telling you gentlemen of the beards, things are getting more complex than you can see behind your waakye! And things have been made worse by the fact that Torro is suspecting more and more that his wife Bianca is moving more openly towards General Jolloff. This has increased his urgency, but this urgency hasn't gone into the jealousy that he would be expected to feel: it has gone into a frantic desire to survive in Achimota City, for he loves also his reputation of evil put together with generosity. Here he is not mocked in that thin status-conscious way he was in Rome, where his bank-robbing exploits were ultimately used to reduce his fullness as a human being. Not that he wasn't admired, but that they felt he was too human to be a hero, even if a hero of the left hand. Can the rabbits please stand up while I'm talking? Good, I feel far better that way . . . And he has used his special synthetic bombs several times on himself, for he's now trying hard to give his masters the impression that he is DEAD! Dead in a war where no one is supposed to die very much! Torro is not very intelligent, but at this stage, and for the first time in his life, it is to his advantage not to have too much of a bookbook head . . .'

'But is this emblem telling us anything new?' asked Jojo Digi irritably.

'Of course!' replied Chairman Kot, still remembering the poor devoured rabbit. 'Just because we have a commanding view of every-thing doesn't mean we should listen to nothing. As you know we have two advanced sources, the golden emblem, and the major's binoculars; and sometimes for a short while they may know more than we do . . .'

'But the golden cockroach sometimes assumes airs, errr. But. What I want to say is that we all helped to work its gold, and there's no need for it to lecture us.' Digi's irritation was now arranged across the curve of his lower lip, but nobody passed the curve. So Mr Cee returned to its breathless words with their mango fragrance . . .

'And in a strange way Torro's first military problem is neither victory nor defeat, but victory BY THE RIGHT PERSON! He wants Pogo Forr to defeat him, but he's worried that Pogo is going to do this in such a sly way that there will be little difference between Pogo winning and Gentl winning . . . Isn't my crawl sexy O you Elders with the avooo rabbits . . ! He is afraid of being defeated by a contrived mutation of Pogo's carrots. And to tell you the truth, so are his bosses! For they have nothing to fight carrots with, just as they have nothing to fight sympathy with. Allah! I am sometimes a Muslim cockroach, I tell you. But that doesn't end things for Torro at all: for as soon as his bosses start fearing exactly what he fears, then he becomes worried; which means that he's now trying to force himself to be afraid of Major Gentl, so that he will be FREE! Free from one source of worry but imprisoned in another . . . and the arrival of his children has increased his love enormously for Achimota City. But deep down and out of honour he wants one of his children to die in the children's war, a ludicrous wish that usually ends up with a tiny amount of guilt mixed with underdone roasted chicken and copious red wine into which he would drop a drop of Achimota evertime lavender plus six tears for the future. The man is mad!'

And then slowly without warning, the rabbits surrounded Mr Cee and mated sullenly, and then they returned to their honey. Amos Kittoe was still quietly conferring with the silver mosquito, they must not quit talking.

'And where does Gentl's life turn these days?' Digi asked scornfully, looking at the insect that confidentially ministered unto ministers and elders.

'Ah,' said the brightening Mr Cee, 'Major Gentl still remains the best bet! He's making good use of the rooms I gave him on the moon. He's doing some lunar spying; and in addition he has the magic binoculars . . .'

'. . . which unfortunately we have discovered to be a two-way spy machine: when you are using it to see abroad, abroad sees you,' Kot interrupted with regret.

The cockroach stood there bristling, its mouth open over the bristle, 'So that's why I've been getting a third feedback from my supercables . . . anyway I took some precautionary action. I inverted the superfluous feedback, so that the double viewing was cut off by the new triple view. You see, in life I AM AFTER THE TRIPLE VIEW! samia. I carry this principle in the war: take a third decision immediately you suspect that someone has taken a second one against you secretly. And that's why I am confident that the major's wife will soon sort out the problems over her fighting for the enemy . . . Who IS the enemy anyway? Ama Three does everything thrice; and I believe that one day she may make inroads into the soft core of the enemy. Even though I love Grandmother Bomb, I can't keep back my attraction for the major's wife koraa. I have to control myself when I am in her company . . . and I have a strange vision, which I told the major, of her left breast constantly changing places with her right breast. Nothing makes the major angry except anger itself, I swear! And I don't believe the rumour that sometimes when he's asleep the snakes slither over his popylonkwe. But Pogo's wife still dreams of the major, and Ama is still not beyond taking second looks at Pogo. She finds his millionairing attractive . . .'

'This is a serious meeting of government,' complained Digi. 'We will not tolerate rumours here at all . . .'

Digi was potent against rumours, for his ex-wife did start the one that he was impotent. And there was an uproar in the cabinet rooms the night he had to walk on to the television screens with an erection to prove his potentability, as he put it; and he would boast at meetings that this was the first time in any government anywhere that a popylonkwe had been used directly as official evidence, albeit ensconced in pioto and kente jeans.

'Order, order!' ordered Kofi Kot, waving a hand to signify that it was time, as required by law, to hold all three legislative beards at the same angle for five minutes. Talking was allowed while the heads were tilted, and so was the chewing of carrots that Pogo Forr had just sent to the elders in a fruit and vegetable helicopter.

The resizing cockroach that could enlarge and shrink its own shape was now silent before the emblematic beards. And it found something problematic: they seemed to be making more rituals for beards than for cockroaches. Amos Kittoe put in sharp words.

'Yes I know why the golden cockroach is silent! I remember the exact date when it started moving about from one corner of the national flag to another, and this caused a great commotion: the city's emblem had metamorphosed into a physical being, had regressed from sunsum to mogya. But at that time it refused koraa to leave the flag, and what it said was that it was giving everybody a warning about the problems of existing in the late 1990s when, in spite of our ttttremendous efforts to survive, we were still required to prove our right to exist; and to prove this to the forgotten capitals of some other worlds where wealth and advancement have been foolishly extended to manifest a so-called entire and universal superiority. And our golden emblem asked what, after all, was so intelligent about going so fast on the journey, the journey of life, that you couldn't even see the scenery? Even if we call them and insult them that they are the people of pure speed, physically fast but spiritually snails, we will not be saying the whole truth: it is a tiny beeny proportion of these speedsters that drags the rest of its countrymen along! And so the only hope is for this slower rest to insist on putting a stop to this cosmic nonesense. After all, Mr Cockroach had continued, no people with such vast wastelands of spirit and heart could possibly have any right to produce art; and besides, the greedy quantities of this art produced – probably book mountains, canvas mountains, and sound mountains of utter profligation – don't hide the fact that there is a spiritual and human narrowness that is a tragedy to behold!'

Digi's cheeks were sometimes so round that they were like buttocks. He was looking with a frown at the unusual passion of Amos, and then he asked with his extra bot in the face, 'So in what way does the great and golden cockroach think we are better? Yes I agree we are broader, and emotionally and spiritually deeper, but we have nothing to boast about if all we do is to fight for our physical existence. Nkwasiasem! If we don't wake up, we'll find ourselves on the high road to extinction, kicking and screaming that even though we are being physically liquidated, we are yet spiritually superior . . .'

Chairman Kot rose to his full height with his ladder on his soul and declared, 'We in Achimota City are fighting this strange war with great resources. We are not static! We have won one war already, and I have the confidence that we may win the next one now.'

There was another silence, but Jojo Digi snorted into it: 'If we have been so great, why is it that we are only a city? Yes I know it is the great secret that we should not say out loud, but WHERE IS THE REST OF THE COUNTRY? Why haven't we regained it yet?'

There was a stunned silence. Kofi Kot then said with more sadness than anger, 'Elder Two is always giving us trouble . . . All the people of this city have agreed that we must win the Second War of Existence before we can start looking for what we have lost. It's like history: you forget the great absence, the great hole behind you, until you make your immediate earth firm enough to start the great search . . .'

'Too much searching!' Digi persisted. 'Let's do everything at once.'

The cockroach coughed golden into the talk. And then asked, 'Am I going to continue to be your emblem or am I not? Are you going to use your beards on the national flag, or are you sticking to the golden me? You should remember that without me, you'll never win the war! It is only because of Nana Mai that I have so far failed to crawl back into the flag . . . for it is tiring going around looking for truth . . .'

'Well I'm happy you found love first and truth second,' Kofi Kot observed wryly, and then added after an imperceptible pause, 'The beards are second to you . . . You are our hero.'

The elders then looked sternly and in unison at Mr Cee the golden, and Mr Cee stared back with its legs dancing a suggestive and philosophical agbadza. The silver mosquito, to the consternation of

71

Amos Q, was crying quietly in the background, and dancing simultaneously: so full of love for this city of trained termites that were yet free; of skyscrapers that were yet smaller than their own juts of sky, of the spectacle of Pogo's golden horse, and Bianca's silver owl.

The meeting was dispersing because of the unspoken truth spoken by Jojo Digi: 'Let us find our missing country while the city still grows!'

The rabbits stood in line as the closing drums were played. How many fronts do you fight a war on? Shadows from the fluorescent light reflected in the honey.

Just beyond the happy honey with its sullen rabbits stood Chairman Kot. Some people had eyes like their toenails, hard sharp and transparent; and Kot's were like that now, quite unlike their usual soft sponginess, sapo eyes. He usually met a nagging doubt with large amounts of humility. Now he had left the cabinet room and gone up to the tower, from where he stared down at the city coming to dusk.

Three men smoked their cancerless sikadillo cigars between six cars and nine double-brown houses. Sometimes the architectural bamboo stilts wore severe wooden sandals, so that you would think they were going to walk away with the houses. Beyond the vast banana groves, squeezed in at intervals between the bright avenues, the cola continued to be sold; pineapples planted on extremely high mounds pricked the sky, and the planned bites of the termites continued to be creative. And spiders too laced beautifully the celestial routes of all flying machines. Behind the pond of dancing fish, by the transitional missiles that you could buy but couldn't use, Kofi Kot saw the gliding shadow of Major Gentl.

The promoted shadow was moving about the city quite freely, bullying other shadows, and avoiding Atinga the bodyguard as much as possible. Atinga had finally sent a strong petition to the elders of government over what he thought was the unfair promotion of the shadow, at his expense. Shadows just followed substances, but bodyguards actually guarded, no matter how advanced certain shadows were. The streets were sometimes so clean that you could see a sneeze coming to rest on the pavement.

In spite of the troublesome and usually uncoordinated Jojo Digi, Kot knew that the elders would continue with the original plan: chess with the enemy, oware with the enemy through trusted players like Gentl, Forr, and Grandmother Bomb, with magnificent intermediaries like the

72

golden cee and the children, not forgetting the armies that continued to obey the most ludicrous of orders: for the holders of guns that shot up and guns that shot down knew that one person's ludicrum could be another one's victory. Unless the enemy changed drastically, Achimota City would continue to fight the odd oddder oddddest war with an eternally flexible fixity. The city would continue to fraternise with the enemy, even sometimes love him, but in all the moves and in all the planning, victory would live.

ZONE EIGHT

The system

It was after Chairman Kofi Kot came down from the tower covered in electronically spun cobwebs from advanced spiders that he perceived that things must change, for circumstances had changed, and he was very sensitive to tactical nuances usually at noon, and often by ants. He had been drinking coffee at the time. Kofi coffee. And had to convince the other elders plus the rulers of the districts and areas, as well as the populace. The pineapple populace agreed with the tangerine elders, and they all sat round mushrooms to work out the new strategy. Guava came later, touching alasa in fine fruity nudges, sweetsoursweet together. Jojo Digi had been digging his garden by the yellow chandelier flowers, but thought that the garden suddenly looked strange, and it was: he had been digging Kofi Kot's garden by mistake; and so as a matter of national semi-priority, he was rescued from the wrong dig immediately. But he still kept his Digi. A bee flew between the heads of two elders of government, by the strategic durbars; and the shell of bees gave the children earrings. The children had been against any change in strategy, including Torro's children of the opposite army; but had later agreed to reconsider their decision in a month's time after being given an unlimited number of motor-bikes. Sama, the baby tyrant, rode very fast to his mother's breast.

And all the districts were demarcated again, so that Gentl, Torro, Pogo, and Nana Mai all gave up their areas, and had to form one government. One of the most amazing things done by the elders was to appoint Torro the Terrible as the Minister of Defence.

'But how can our biggest enemy be our Minister of Defence?' asked Abomu Kwame with his lips on fire from injudicious tots of akpeteshie. 'For me, I see that these changes you are making are nyamanyama madmad changes!' *You could speak your mind koraa in Achimota City, and even talk to the government while sitting on the toilet.*

Gentl smiled at the changes, Nana Mai poured scorn on them, Pogo

74

made money out of them immediately, in a way that was morally defensible in the mornings, and morally indefensible in the afternoons; and Torro just ate more beef to make his neck thicker, keeping his words in reserve for once, keeping his options in defence of his new ministry, so that if he had to betray anyone he would do so without committing himself now.

But the next most amazing thing the elders did was to appoint Commander Zero as the deputy minister of defence. At first Commander Zero was not even a human being: he was a convergence of shadows from various parts of the city. But he was so adept at collecting himself from shadow to shadow that, first, there was a general shortage of shadows, with even the most intimate of people accusing themselves of stealing each other's shadows; and second he burst into a human being out of the profusion of his insubstantiality. When he thus became a real man, there was a problem: his nose wouldn't fit, for it had been taken from the commanding shape of Major Gentl's nose; and Gentl only got the shadow of his nose back after General Jolloff ordered a general inspection of available noses, and then punished Commander Zero for nasal thievery.

Immediately after he became a human being – arranging to be born simultaneously with the copulation of his parents – he marched into a bag of charcoal and thus dirtied his uniform and became a beautiful black blacker blackest man. But what worried the commander most after this was that the whites of his eyes became black, and the black of his eyes white. He could thus look at everything reversed, and wondered, sometimes even with a whimper, Ewurade, whether his snivelling attraction for wonderful women would reverse, turn on him, and devour him altogether. At one point he even developed several degrees of love for Nana Mai. He had also proposed a passionate embrace for Bianca, in spite of the terror of Torro, but she had pushed him away, all six foot six of him, warning him that if he was not afraid of Torro the minister, then he would have to be careful about General Jolloff, who would sometimes try to occupy the spacious rooms of her heart. Bianca to Jolloff to Bianca, hmmm.

For the commander to enjoy the fruits of his new humanity was not always easy: he sometimes forgot he was no longer a shadow, and would try and walk through trees with his most confident swagger; but would end up with reversed bruises on his left eye. *Commander! come under a better fate!* And no one should ever blow a whistle when he was around, for he would follow the sound wherever it went: into occupied toilets, logologo bedrooms, strategic meetings, silly salutes, and the arms of long-lipped women who usually found his lower half attractive, but rejected his upper half.

In spite of these difficulties Commander Zero, with the fatherly prodding of Major Gentl, was beginning to coordinate the war quite well. And Torro was uncomfortable with him: how dare the elders send him such a ludicrous yet effective man for a deputy! Give him a straight rascal and a fellow rich man like Pogo any day. And since Torro's whole position with his bosses and his enemies was so uncertain, he felt that this Zero just added to the confusion.

One of the first things Commander Zero did was nothing. And then after that he did the following: nought. And then something else: he sent all the soldiers on leave, and replaced them with thousands of rabbits with reduced honey on their backs; rabbits were to fight the enemy for a week or two, and were to fertilise the battlefields with their dung, so that Pogo Forr could grow carrots nearer the heart of the fighting, thus saving transport and effort: after an exchange of fire, a soldier could just rush into the carrot fields and serve himself. Pogo was overjoyed, for since the soldiers were all rabbits, with the exception of the children's war, you could not get a faster turnover of the carrot rate. The elders had agreed, for this meant Pogo buying more weapons from Nana Mai, who in turn ploughed most of her profit back into the war. Torro felt his back to be against the wall, and had to make twists and turns in his very small inner life to try and contain the new complexity that Zero the nought of difficulty had brought. He resented the fact that Chairman Kot had connived with Major Gentl enough to produce such an advantage in the war. He would shake Commander Zero's hand several times in a day out of sheer hate koraa. Gentl was more cunning than Torro thought.

'Major!' Torro shouted on the battlefield of rabbits. 'Why you send me such a seeelly deputy!'

The major took a drop of honey to sweeten his smile, but said nothing. Today his cap was a snake.

Commander Zero hadn't yet touched the children's war out of fear of the moustache farmer General Jolloff. But the children loved him, driving their motor-bikes all over his height, and boasting that they too had commanders. The commander sometimes had to hold his popylonkwe away from the marauding bikes; and that was precisely when General Jolloff would make an appearance, and bellow out, 'Commander! You are not allowed to hold your genitals in the war!' And the commander would try and hide a stubborn tear by appearing unperturbed in his opposite-coloured eyes. Thus minister and deputy both stood in defence of each other, trying to deal with a wariness that neither could control.

'Why you are so funnie funnie man?' growled Torro in the office one morning.

'Good morning,' replied Zero.

'Why your head hold your cap in so seelly seelly way?' went on Torro.

'Good morning,' Zero replied again, his hands occupying quite uselessly the space in his extra large pockets.

Torro rose with a little anger, his neck thickening with his raised voice. 'Why you change tacteecs all the time without telling me, sciocco! You do not trembare in my presence?'

'Good morning,' Zero persisted, rolling the words from a different part of his mouth. Then he went on and said another one hundred good mornings, while Torro stood up fuming and holding his neck intermittently. Sometimes the whole ministry would stop work and everybody would come and watch their bosses for minutes and minutes. The laughter would go into the missiles: 'O boss, your balls are anti-ballistic–O.' And Commander Zero's good mornings were meant to be the salt of defence in the Torro's wounds.

Torro stood there in a moment of utter transmogrification, with gari running out of his pockets, from a sudden impulse in the market to buy some for his children. Commander Zero got the gari gathered, and gave a series of silent smiles as his boss shook and reshook his hand out of anger. This was a green office and a blue office, this was a red office with a mirror that made your reflection move independently of you; this was an office of subordinate rats that nibbled fearfully at their master's feet, not knowing which one was going to be crushed next out of which mood.

Long live the ministers' toilet, for that was where sometimes minister and deputy met to continue to shake hands. Torro would be consumed with further anger right in the middle of his excuse me to say ni, and would send for Zero for nothing except to wash his own hand in the toilet immediately and shake Zero's slowly. And sometimes arguments about strategy would start immediately after the flushing.

'My dear Minister Torro, I know you are my bossi, but you do something too mech. Pardon me but how dare you send for me to shake your hand while you're still in the toilet! I am a six-foot six deputy minister, properly appointed after a snap elastic decision, during which I quaffed one hundred tangerines to the jealousy of the legislative bananas. I have set a record for the fastest materialisation in the city from some lonely and thin collection of shadows to a substantial political and military being! I deserve something more than always ministering unto my minister's anger. Is this ebufu politics or what . . ?'

The usual office audience had already started gathering, this time at the door of the toilet; and two of Torro's rats had appeared on his shoulder ready to strike in a dutiful and masterful manner if so required. Sayoooo, the bosses could obliterate each other!

Torro snarled, 'All of you, give me silenzioso! I weesh to announce that my deputy and myself are the best of friends, get away from here pronto, and go and draw the war on the notice-boards, no! This is serio!'

But is was only after Torro grimaced terribly while stroking his sprung rats that the groups scattered to do their work.

Zero began, glowing with the sheen of his commandership, 'Minister, we must learn to manage the rabbits better. Some of them haven't mastered how to carry the missiles, but it's only because they have been carrying honey and mating too mech. And some of them have demanded to be put in command positions. Fish and rabbits have ambitions. But I advised those with the greatest ambition to eat as many carrots as possible in order to feel less frustrated. I told them that if I can become nothing but something out of nothing, then they have every hope to be everything out of anything. And I believe that we must send the armies to the eastern side of the battlefield more often . . .'

'And whyeee?' asked Torro, absent-mindedly eating tolo beef.

'Because we are in a difficult position: we belong to opposite sides, yet we are planning from the same side, we have to plan together against each other. Our strategies are twofold: we must plan better against ourselves so that it will be much easier to plan for ourselves; and then whatever we plan, we have to reveal secrets to each other straight away, what I do is what you haven't done, and what I haven't done is what you do. But I have some supertobolo hope for victory . . .'

'Victory for whooo?' asked Torro with the beef mouth.

'I will tell you after you have been defeated,' Commander Zero

78

declared, raising himself to his full height majestically and then bumping his head on the ceiling.

Torro rushed to get a chair and patted the culprit ceiling, 'Heet him more, heet him more, break his head!' he shouted.

And the next day the armies were sent to the eastern side, with the massive complaints of Torro on the western side. Commander Zero boasted that when he was a shadow he could float on air and that he was so daring that, as a human being, he could still float, but that the floating this time was done on ministers, alleluya.

Part of the army was still rabbits, part was human beings; and for some time anybody was fighting on any side, the enemy in magnificent formation with the home forces, and everybody singing war songs, some obscene, against each other. The home army's march was the easiest of dancing; the enemy was stiff, with its hundreds of mercenaries crowded against each other without Rome to move, and they sang above the rhythm of Achimota City.

One rabbit was accidentally shot while it was both devouring a carrot, and regretting the honey finished on its back. It was buried immediately with full military honours, in an architecturally daring coffin full of . . . honey: and the bugle scattered the honey bees.

> Shoot your guns up
> Shoot your guns down
> for we shall remain
> fully alive in this war
> and give the elders the best reason
> for continuing with the present strategies
> Hurray to Gentl
> Hurray to Pogo Forr and to Grandmother Bomb
> for her missiles are so considerate
> that you can carry them carrying themselves
> no complaint sir
> for if you want
> to see us magnanimous in victory
> you shall see us
> if you want
> to see us dignified and arrogant in defeat
> you shall see us

we march among the carrots
And who dare not keep
a big hurray for Commander Zero
and for Torro the Terrible too
to share half each!
Sang the armies.

And in the distance the children's war returned the sound of fire. The two wars seemed to be synchronised in alluring syncopation, high bullets, low bullets, artificial bombs that returned to their missile-cases immediately after firing, and the music was ballistic, joining with the roar of hundreds of motor-bikes.

Fight on, you stalwarts of the fruit city, for whichever direction the subtleties will lead you towards victory, you must take it!

Some very old rabbits had epaulettes on their fur, and insisted on marching immediately behind some alombotic female rabbits, some diddling shoogly does, ampa.

Chairman Kot the nameless had arrived in person on the battlefields, accompanied by Nana Mai and her parrot. He was happy with the confusion, knowing how many times what appeared to be a historical confusion was really and truly a masterly strategy. Nana Mai tucked at his joromi, and said, 'Chairman, aren't you ashamed to witness such disorder! And it's so necessary!'

'Nana Mai, Nana Mai,' said the modest chairman, 'you speak the truth with your eyes, but your mouth is mocking! In spite of your sarcasm this city is privileged to have you as a daughter, hmmm . . .'

The two pauses met as the bullets flew into the useless sky. The firing and missiling had stopped, and every soldier, rabbit and human being was saluting Chairman Kot and Grandmother Bomb. Nana Mai retained her ironic smile as Chairman Kot saluted back a hundred times. As soon as the passing bird with nowhere to land laid its egg in mid-air, it was caught by Chairman Kofi, to the roars of the soldiers.

'Catch the government too!' someone shouted. 'Uncle Kofi, you have the wisdom paa to lead us, no palaver, we want you now now now to lead the government for the next twenty years, du by du . . .'

It was when Kot held up his hands in playful exasperation that the brass band burst into music, with Amos Kittoe and Jojo Digi leading the music with stately steps to the battlefields.

'What's going on?' Nana Mai asked with a twinkle in her eyes. Kot looked at her suspiciously, for what was she doing with her sudden insouciance? In moments like this, Kot never failed to desire the eternal ladder for the height of his soul. But this wasn't possible now, for the other two elders had already approached a hastily constructed dais with banana decorations. Kot had taken on a massive stiffness as his perplexity grew. Digi gave him a wink which he didn't return. Mrs Wife had also appeared and in a whisper had offered, to Kot's great surprise, to go through yet another wedding ceremony immediately. He refused in his stiffness as she wiped his brow regardless. Jojo Digi was suddenly annoyed because the brass band had played a single note too many after he demanded silence. You could only hear the sound of the military rabbits chewing Pogo's carrots. Digi wedged his talking into the chewing.

'We have met here now to change the system of government again. We spoke to every person over ten years old, except that Baby Sama had a special dispensation to be consulted in spite of being an infant. We didn't tell Chairman Kot, because he would refuse. He initiated the changes from the tower, but there are certain changes the people want. Some are major, some are minor: the first one we are putting before you Chairman Kot is that we want a fish to be appointed as Minister of Fisheries . . .'

There was a silence, as if Kot wasn't even listening, for he had pulled his hat lower and lower.

Digi continued, '. . . for we have found the fish themselves highly intelligent on the Fish Council, and these fish have graciously agreed to be eaten by us in reasonable quantities, provided that one of them gets the Fish portfolio, and of course neither the Minister of Fish nor his administration can be eaten. It's the scale of the matter we are interested in, sir.

'The second one is that the people no longer want to have turns each at governing, for some of us are fools and some of us are wise; and what do we do when it becomes the turn of the fool to rule? And that is why Pogo Forr refused to pass on power in his area. On the other hand, we have just discovered two good candidates for executive duties in government: a wise frog among the carrots that restricts the number of insects it devours on an hourly basis, and which is extremely philosophical between its leaps; and one of Torro's children who hates his father,

81

but who is prepared to drop this hate provided he comes over entirely to our side, while remaining utterly anonymous to his father . . .'

Chairman Kot was just walking away when a severe embrace from Mrs Wife detained him. And there were several magnificent salutes.

'. . . And then the next thing we want is that you, the present chairman, should continue to be the chair for the elders for the next two years or more . . . We have got the necessary majority for this so no matter what objections you raise, we will not agree. And I want to put in the next point fast before Mrs Wife is forced to give you yet another largelarge embrace, some bigitive hug: we think it's about time we appointed another person on to the Council of Elders . . .'

There was a huge roar as Baby Sama walked majestically on to the dais, peeing in his pants.

Digi shouted, 'No nono no, take this arrogant infant off, we cannot appoint him yet! And we think there are enough beards of government. So we have decided irrevocably that Nana Mai the Grandmother Bomb will be appointed on to the Council of Elders, for she has shown she has the originality, the strength and the wisdom . . .'

It was the turn of Kofi Kot to give Nana Mai an ironic smile, as she stood there with an open mouth that she closed instantly with a look of angry scorn. Neither Kot the nameless, nor Grandmother Bomb said a word. Her mathematical parrot sang a whole page of theorems, and ended up releasing a plop of victory on the motorway of Atinga the bodyguard, who immediately seized the opportunity to ask the august gathering of the eighth month, 'What about my promotion?' and then delivered himself of an aerial slap to the impertinent parrot. Chairman Kot went and gave Atinga a hug as Mrs Wife waited for hers; and while this hug was purely to calm Atinga down, the crowd roared and roared as if he Kot was showing joy at the points raised by Jojo Digi.

Kot suddenly shouted to the increasing crowd, his hat thrown to the ground, 'What wisdom do I have to give you? What wisdom do I have to give you! I agree fully with all your points, except the one concerning myself. We should continue to rotate the chairmanship . . .' The roars had drowned him out, and as he turned round to congratulate Nana Mai, all he heard was her helicopter taking off with her on board, and with her shouting down imperiously, 'But how can I do my inventions if you want me to come to Government House and talk and talk and talk!'

They all waved and waved at the disappearing helicopter, knowing

82

that it would only be Nana Mai that would have the impatience to fly off like that just when she was being honoured. Digi had already become preoccupied with other matters, and as Chairman Kot got ready to leave, 'to think about things', Digi rushed into the brass band, seized a trombone to everybody's surprise, and played a beautiful rhythm which took over the battlefield. There was a percussion shot from the distance, for the children had refused to stop the war for a few minutes since they had already agreed to the changes proposed now.

The golden cockroach glided mysteriously over the battlefields, alone now, for the silver mosquito had deserted it and joined the household of Amos the elder. But not far behind it in the sky, and certainly without its golden knowledge, flew the silver owl, now happiest when refereeing football games involving mice, so that it could eat any of the players when it was hungry. The silver owl had been pulled by some force beyond itself to follow the golden cockroach; for it had been decreed, perhaps even beyond the firmament, that there always had to be silver following the golden emblem. And this golden emblem was angry at the elevation of Nana Mai, for it made it more difficult for his foolish love to have results. Heaven only knew what it would do when it discovered it was being followed by the silver owl . . . The voracious sounds of the brass band took over the battlefield more as the war resumed and the soldiers shot with joy.

This ambition

The camel sat on the major, then the major sat on the camel. Torro's camel had deserted its master, after serving dessert to him on its hump as usual. Bianca's kindness didn't save the camel from the numerous kicks from Torro, especially after it had made mistakes in the interminable football games it was forced to play. Its powerful farts couldn't save goals either, soccer kwee. So it ran away to aMofa Gentl's house, and then had impertinently phoned its master to ask him to be bold enough to come to the major's house to get it. The camel boasted that Torro would again be defeated by gentleness, and this time the gentleness would have strong camel stubborness behind it, as well as the secrets of Torro's existence gathered and hidden in its hump. Torro gave an angry laugh through the telephone, and the camel laughed back; big hump faced bull-neck, the phones couldn't take the intensity of hate. And whenever the major tried to take the camel back, the camel complained to the government. In the end Torro didn't want it, even though he had sworn to kill it sooner or later. How the camel laughed! Thus the major sometimes used it to move around when he became tired of helicopters. The camel had even visited the lunar rooms, its dung bouncing behind it scientifically, veeeeee.

So it was that Major aMofa Gentl rode slowly on camel back to the glass and bamboo house of Pogo Alonka Forr. The glass framed the major in such a curious way that you would think it was riding the major again rather than the opposite . . . which in fact it was, this difficult tricky rider-ridden leele camel . . . aMofa threw it off his back, and mounted it with authority again.

Gentl always felt somewhat wary in Alonka Forr's presence, for it was as if the latter was keeping something back from him: carrots. And because of the secret looks that he felt Forr's wife gave him, he knew there was one phallic symbol that Pogo would never give him towards the thrust of war: carrots.

Gentl arrived just before the second-last dream of Pogo's wife Delali, for she had materialised him in her afternoon siesta, and was just about to test some fikifiki with his polished logologo when the last dream came: Gentl himself, looking quite handsome by the contrast of the camel's face even though they shared the same semi-desert of the nose. Kokoooko, knocked the camel for the major through the highhigh bell of the glass door. Its reflection knocked back as the major dismounted, right into a tub of: experimental carrots. And when he looked round for a donkey to balance the pervasive carrots, what he saw was the golden horse with its intermittently golden dung dropped by the throne of the king vegetables of the house: king carrots of the golden nature. But the oval carrots didn't mind at all not being king, for it was only a matter of time before the oval would become gold too, and everything powerful would be oval, including Delali's breasts which she was now standing boldly showing to Gentl, who kept perfectly still and dignified himself, but whose snakes had risen in reptilian lust in unison with the camel. *Major, Major, don't salute like when you were a baby, for if you do your neat hand will be taken under present circumstances for a rising popylonkwe!* And when Pogo Forr came in an angry strut to meet the scene, all Delali said was, 'Breasts for victory, my darling Pogo. I'm trying to help us to win the war.'

'My wife likes to keep abreast of the situation,' said Alonka Forr the carrot millionaire, wearing his usual white robes and ludicrously crawling about the floor looking for 'revelation, my deardear major, revelation'.

Pogo's eyes were not twinkling this morning; they had on the contrary taken on a massive defence: he felt insecure too mech when Delali showed affection for anybody else, including their new six-month bounciest lactogen baby whom Pogo had brought into the house one fine dusk, saying,

'Some woman said she was willingly and willy nilly penetrated by me some time back when I was not dedicated to gold and carrots, and that this finefine child with my eyes is mine.'

Delali had not said a word. She just went with her lithest walk, and produced a birth certificate plus a photograph of this same baby, which both proved that he was borne by Pogo and herself. Pogo had stood in irredeemable confusion, his robes blowing about him uselessly. It had turned out that Delali had indeed given birth to this son Poco, but that she had kept the whole pregnancy a secret, since whenever she had her wild bouts of jealousy about Pogo's awaygaming embraces, she took wild decisions. Alonka, who knew so much about everybody else, didn't even know when his own son was born, for Delali had gone to her mother's, and had always insisted on meeting him while she was sitting down, so that he wouldn't see her belly. She had explained that she needed a rest from all that money he had, especially the smell of it. Delali had arranged this whole surprise so well that Pogo had immediately given her one third of his fortune to look after, sharp. She knew though that all he was doing now was to plan his women more carefully in between extreme insights on carrots; so she retained a resentment that she sometimes showed on days like the visit of Gentl today.

The more Delali saw of the major the less she saw what she saw in him, and the more her infatuation grew. And as soon as she had finally perceived that the major's wife was showing more than a little interest in Pogo her husband, she had taken on an enormous happiness, her tiny guilt dropping off immediately. She sought out and sought in Ama Three until they became friends, spending hours in opposite talk about opposite husbands.

Pogo Forr with the thick thighs had risen from his crawling – usually done on Mondays to keep him in touch with the lower levels of reality – and gone to wash his hands before shaking Gentl's. They sat down to tangerine juice and palm-wine. The major kept staring at a picture on the ornate wall that kept changing colour, shape and size. And he stared at a stylish post-Adinkra goldfish bowl, which contained guppies and tilapia mixed together, as well. It was separated by a thin pressurised wall of orange-coloured water; and the bowl refused to give its shape to the water, and thus water and bowl had entirely different shapes, much like host and guest now sitting silent and facing each other. It was extraordinary for Alonka Forr to remain so quiet for so long. He had gathered his robes around him, and kept looking at the major's small head with its thick side-hair, some side-burns with three grey hairs each, which Ama Three kept counting when she returned from the battlefield – she would thankfully sigh that her exploits were not giving him any more such hairs. aMofa's tiny smile remained fixed. He and Pogo scrutinised each other's eyes.

Then without warning, Pogo Forr shot up and gave the major a hug, saying, 'Now I understand better the use of your gentleness! What sort of calm do you have that can stand the agitations of me, Pogo Forr the carrot million man? You can go and have a look at my wife's breasts again if you like, for I know that I can trust you, you the man of victory that doesn't want to celebrate that victory!'

Then, with no warning at all, Pogo lapsed back into his unusual silence, staring far away into the distance, and meeting the scowl of the camel who thought its new master was taking too long. It stamped among the bananas.

'They all say you are a man that can listen to confessions,' Pogo said to aMofa, and before the latter could say anything, he continued, 'Well, I'm getting more worried than gari about my lifestyle. I have six coffins in my bank accounts, yes I'm talking about coffins. Death and money . . .' He looked carefully to see whether Gentl had changed his expression or not, but saw no difference, and went on, 'Every now and again, I withdraw one coffin, sometimes made of sapele, sometimes of gold or gold plating. And then, in the secret of my room, I practise death. This is why I got so annoyed with having to bury the old woman on Nana Mai's road, for it wasn't yet time for me to be reminded of death. You can't die in the middle of a war, can you? before you know the result . . . the banks have ledgers for my coffins, but I'm only allowed to make an overdraft when I'm about to die, since I decreed that I should be buried, several times, to get my revenge on those of you who arranged to be born more than once! . . . and do you know that Torro is copying my coffin revelations? He's a fool–O!'

Pogo moved his laughter between his points, and watched the major shift his left leg without really seeing. He didn't see the faint smile on Gentl's face either, a smile the same colour as water.

'And another thing I want to tell you is that I want to win the war . . .' Pogo paused again, giving the major's face another careful scrutiny, and still finding nothing new. 'I want to win this second war. You won the first war. I now want to win the glory of the Second War of Existence!'

Major Gentl scowled, and watched all the glass around him mirroring the world. Outside, the tiny blackberries kept their berries cool under the shadow of the camel; and the frangipani had settled their subtle smells behind the proud golden horse where the big atua tree grew. It was when his mother died that Gentl wondered whether his hopes would really remain beyond the mere interim, with or without the moon, with or without the now compromised binoculars . . . How dare they look back at him while he was looking purely to survive! Then he turned his attention back to Pogo Forr before him, this vain man who might be truly sincere about the survival of Achimota City, and the finding of the rest of the country; but, the major thought, it was conditional sincerity, it was a desire that looked to glory. On the other hand the correspondence between a new oval carrot and the shape of the sun was something that could give a gigantic surprise, and unsettle Torro and the bosses. Pogo was useful, but since Gentl was not one for glory, he suddenly got up to leave.

'Sit down Major, sit down, it's far too early to leave. And you haven't answered my request yet! After my golden horse, my carrots, my suns, and my coffins, all I want is glory and recognition. Help me!'

After looking across at the sky through the big glass windows, aMofa said, with his smile gone, 'At the best of times we can't even tell who our enemies and friends are. We all won the first war, not only me . . .'

'Put your gentleness at my disposal, Major! I know we are already an alliance, but I want us to have a double alliance, under the protection of the golden cockroach. The cockroach prefers you to me, and so does Nana Mai. We all need you, but I need you most! I will remove your wife from that disgraceful strategy that forces her to fight with the enemy. How many convolutions must we go through before we are victorious, my brother! Listen to me and we'll have a shorter bush path to victory . . . We will begin by killing that insane croo Torro . . .'

'But you know his body has now been programmed to die within our geography,' Gentl reminded Pogo Forr.

'Yes, but that's where I have to tell you a secret: my oval carrots are close to breaking that code that keeps Torro protected and alive . . . and look at him, he's now a minister on top of everything else!' replied Pogo with animation.

'But why don't you tell the elders and all the rest who make the strategy?' the major asked, and then felt himself naive for asking it – after all wasn't it Pogo Forr that at one point refused to hand over power to the next in line in his area? His reason, Abomu Kwame, was no doubt legitimate, but why choose that particular way of retaining power? *See the glory of Pogo's story.*

aMofa Gentl got up again to leave, but then remembered the oval carrots, and persisted with Pogo.

'You should have told the elders of any new developments, so that the plans would have been better based in fact . . . I insist that you inform them of all your weapons against Torro,' Gentl said, still standing, 'and I don't want any alliance different from what we have already . . . So you want power and glory for yourself, eh? And you are prepared to use some of your own weapons in secret until you reach where you want to reach. I am beginning to think that this is a filifili case of bad ambition . . .'

'Stop your nkwasiasem!' bellowed Pogo in exasperation, 'I am not offering defeat to my city! All I'm saying is that I want to lead the victory. Surely with your knowknow modesty, you should know that winning by itself is more important than who does the winning; and you have been the hero once, now I think it's my turn. Me, I vex!'

'But surely it's the elders who lead,' said the major, 'and they have been leading since before I was born.'

'So what?' interjected Pogo Forr, his eyes meeting the threatening gaze of the camel as he looked out in frustration: the man who aspired to rooms in the sun for his hotel was not being listened to by the lunar major. 'If you don't listen to me, I'll start calling you "minor" instead of "major!" How dare you be so greedy as to want to lead the second victory too! I'll ask you one more time: let all your helpers back me directly so that I come out the hero, and I'll receive all the cheers on my golden horse,' Pogo Forr shouted.

Major aMofa Gentl gave him a curious look, as if to search for some areas of sanity in his face. His patriotism of a good millionaire kind was not to be doubted, but why go to all the trouble he was going to now to secure a power and a glory that they would all share anyway; why choose a different path to reach the same destination?

'What will you do with the glory when you get it?' Gentl asked sarcastically.

'I will of course spread it back among the rest of you, especially the elders . . .' Pogo replied.

'Then why want it alone in the first place?' Gentl interrupted.

Both men were sweating. The camel had raised its front legs on to the glass, and was scratching irritably at it.

'Tell me what you really want,' Major Gentl said, raising himself to his full height, and taking a snake out of his pocket so that he could have access to the handkerchief there, Pogo jumped small, even though he knew that the major was a man of reptiles.

'He wants nothing less than the sun, and if he has power he will use this power ruthlessly to get this sun that he wants . . . him and me we share nuts,' said Pogo's pet chimpanzee.

The two men turned round with surprise. There was the masterful chimp standing with a silk adinkra cloth on, and smoking a sikadillo cigar.

'I have trained my pets to say the opposite of what I really am,' Pogo declared suddenly. 'Is that not true, chimp?'

The chimp thought for a long time, and then agreed. 'Yes that is so. Now can I go into the garden to chop my one hundred bananas?'

As Major Gentl moved away from the chimp truth, shaking his head, Pogo rushed back into the house on a wild impulse, and gave the major a ten-gun salute, each explosion having a small subsidiary one attached, big sound small sound; and after the last shot aMofa heard Pogo's voice far away, losing sound and authority at the same time:

'Major, let us share the glory, but give me a little more!'

It was a banana echo. And the major suddenly stopped. He dismounted from the camel, took four snakes from his pockets, arranged them carefully on the ground by the tall savanna grasses, placed the camel on them, this tired camel, mounted it again, and then blinked as the snakes carried along gently man and beast in a kayakaya crawl, some roller snakes. To avoid the pricking of pineapple stalks, the snakes had to move carefully, touching the bananas instead, but sometimes forgetting that they were carrying their master and the cheeky camel, for they would suddenly rush after rats and frogs, leaving their master sprawling under the camel. And whenever the snakes apologised in a series of supplicatory wriggles, the major saluted below the camel. Boof, came the salute, shining in the savanna through the reflective gloves that the major wore now. Neems, pines, flamboyants, and frangipani bordered the vast outskirt borders of bananas, pineapples, oranges, and other fruit, crisscrossing the separate areas for carrots.

It was when the camel, now rested, finally jumped off the snakes that the major saw his wife Ama Three. At first she seemed bigger than the horizon, higher than the sky of his vision, and firmer than his feet on the earth. He in turn jumped off the camel as the snakes tensed themselves as usual in the company of Ama: there she was: carrying Torro the Terrible on her back, Ewurade Nyankopon. Gentl put some ice in his own eyes to defend his heart, but the heat still came, pushing his frown higher and his lips tighter. But Torro looked very odd, his eyes closed and his tongue hanging out; and beside Ama Three was their son Adu, frowning as usual, and carrying on his back one of the larger rats of Torro. And the rat duplicated the oddness of its master. Father Gentl looked at Wife Three and Son Adu, and said not a word. The anger was in the major's eyes, and had not yet reached his mouth. As he started to move slowly forward to push Torro off Ama's back, she stretched her hand out through the shower of sweat, and beckoned him away. Adu did exactly the same thing with the rat, which was not moving at all. And then, down from the pines, with a neem berry stuck in its wing, flew the crow; round and round Torro's head it flew, and as it finally landed just above the bull neck, Torro's . . . head . . . fell . . . off.

Nobody screamed, the major just moved back one step. The rat's head fell off simultaneously with Torro's. Adu rushed into the neems to vomit, and the snakes lay absolutely still. To the left, the camel, which had rolled Torro's head with a short and secret kick, was retreating surreptitiously to celebrate the joy of Torro's rolling headless death. More crows had already come, and would have started to peck the dead eyes out if Gentl hadn't chased them off with a confused salute. He went and collected his son from the shivering neem trees.

'Aren't you going to jump with joy? Your biggest enemy is dead . . . and not a single drop of his blood went on me koraa,' said Ama Three, looking at the peculiar expression on her husband's face.

All Gentl said was, 'And you carried him all the way on your back!' Ama protested, 'But I did the carrying for you! I wanted to bring him to you personally, to let you see that fighting on his side didn't mean that I didn't hate him.'

Gentl looked with longing at Ama, in her profound defiance. He put his head on her shoulder and it looked strange in the crawling snake-dominated dusk, as their two heads held themselves against each other; and immediately below them, with its eyelids pulled back by the scattering crows and the new vultures, Torro's head stared at them banefully, with a useless grin suspended somewhere on the lips between life and death. In the distance stood Commander Carlo, Torro's son. He stood there with a child's massive self-control, coming forward to drive the flies from his father's head.

'I have come to bury my father, I am hees oldest son, no?' That fresh tear that fell from his eyes was not followed by another. 'I have to have reeevenge for my father, but I do not know who to keeel, because you are all my friends, all my enemeees are my friends,' Carlo said with a firmer voice, standing there holding hands with Adu, some close defensive comradeship.

There were two helicopters descending, one for Nana Mai the Grandmother Bomb, and one for Chairman Kofi Kot. There was an urgency in the skies. They almost landed on the Italian flag that Carlo had spread on his father. Was it the Italian flag or the flag of South Africa?

Chairman Kot was shouting, 'Whose handiwork is this? Who was in such a hurry with the wrong type of victory that he has killed the enemy at the wrong time? The more this Torro dies in the wrong way, the stronger he becomes with his one life left . . . Major Gentl, who did this? Of course it was Pogo Forr! His ambition has overtaken his own millions . . .'

Nana Mai, after having Torro's torso and head gathered, went abruptly back into her helicopter with only a nod to Gentl, who said more to himself than to anyone else, 'The oval carrot has worked sooner than I thought.'

The helicopters had just taken off when Pogo Alonka Forr rode by with great speed on his golden horse, carrying a victory banner, and shouting with his disappearing sound, 'Major, I told you so! I am riding through the town to celebrate! When I told you to join me, you didn't listen . . .'

aMofa Gentl knew that the Grandmother Bomb was going to sew Torro's head back on: if he was left to come back to life himself, he would be far stronger. There was a great rush in the skies to bring Torro back to life. Nana Mai, Nana Mai, if you really want Torro to breathe again, trim his neck, trim his neck! A Minister of Defence, even if he is an enemy, should not have such a huge neck! When would the elders make this an ordinary war, so that people could die in an ordinary way and enjoy some wonderful shooting directly at each other, even if fighting for their very existence? Carlo, Adu, and the camel had already gone; the camel was in ecstasy, wanting to join Pogo to celebrate all the joy they could share.

Gentl stood there in the evening savanna, with Ama beside him. They started to walk through the pineapples. Winning a war was more difficult than killing the enemy. Pogo was a danger, even if his oval carrots were an advance, an advance that should have been used in a wider strategy. He was celebrating for nothing, Gentl thought, he was just adding to the expense of bringing Torro back to life quickly enough for the safety of Achimota City.

'Whose side are you going to fight on now?' asked Gentl of his wife. He restrained that urge which he had to hug her.

'Can I go and fight with Pogo Forr? For him and we are on the same side,' Ama asked, 'and Bianca wants to join General Jolloff to supervise the children's war.'

Gentl was repelled by Ama's intrigues. He said, 'If you leave my side again, don't come back.' Each carried the other's silence, but they were holding hands so hard, so hard . . .

ZONE TEN

Song of the pig

With the lampposts now low in light and the bamboo rustling to be cut, there was Commander Zero in the deserted savanna, right at the outskirts of the city. The small light was shining through him, for it was as if he was almost a shadow again. He was waiting for Major Gentl, and he was in agitation; which didn't stop him from playing his dirty saxophone by some high-rock light-torn saxifragaceous plants with moss at the tips. And the giant windmill struggled with the wind. His face was dirtier than his handkerchief, this fair-brown visage that gathered dust when it was worried, as if it were a duty to do so. The Highlife music that came mournfully out of the instrument sometimes went right back in by force; and the saxophone would get so hot receiving the same sound it was giving that you would think it would burst. *You saxophone*: it could then play on its own when put down, with its double-charged excess music, Allah. The rain wet his epaulettes.

Rain indeed, for there was Major Gentl, with Ama, coming towards the sound, after some bitter sweet romance by the blossoming oranges – where immediately after a wildly restrained hug, there was a scratch of man and woman by the thorns. Besides, he had forgotten how soft her left thigh was with its permanent smell of frugally picked frangipani. Zero looked at their coming, and blew his saxophone at them. He knew he couldn't fit into the love between them, no way. He replied to Major Gentl's greeting with a blow of the sax. And when he was asked how he was, he blew again to reply, short notes for worry, long notes for joy. This was deputy minister music paaa, thought Ama, squeezing aMofa's hard shoulder once more; she walked for him and he walked for her. Commander Zero went into some short-note frantic playing, blasting the Highlife with his agitations.

'Why can't he talk instead of playing his language?' Ama asked with a yawn of love.

94

What Gentl said to himself was, 'If we can talk through love, then he can talk through his saxophone.'

Ama heard the moaning of his silence. Never lose a mood of love ust to listen to someone else's pain, Ama Three thought, gazing with intense absentmindedness into the major's eyes . . . which were just then looking elsewhere, right into Zero's troubled look to see what this pain was. Trouble could easily drive a fine minister to music at the mouth in the savannas, Gentl mused, his snakes suddenly appearing on the rocks, as if to harden them. The reply of music to language continued, with Zero losing flesh intermittently to his shadowhood, once even ceasing to be a human being altogether. So there was the commander more of a deputy human being than a deputy minister. At last the saxophone was put down as they all sat in the grass in between the music-laden pineapples. Ama saw that mango that touched the tangerine, and sighed.

It was after the commander searched for his flesh and found it that he spoke. 'Major, Major, you know you are my hero. I love how your shadow was promoted, and I marvel at the controlled way that you calmed down Atinga your bodyguard afterwards. I base myself on you even when I am a shadow ampa. Shadow sergeant shadow commander. But I am soso surprised that you are still close to this woman standing up now and sitting down and then standing up again . . . I mean I was witness to the times when she would have shot you but for the quick alanta dives you made just in time . . . and you may not know, but once, having turned into a shadow without any warning, I had to rematerialise pronto and stand in front of you to stop this woman's bullet from commoting you koraa. You see, I live for your hero soul!'

Ama Three was sitting down now with utter disdain. She said to Zero, 'You, whether you are some awam minister or not, I want to warn you that my husband has been offered a seat on the Elders' Council before, and he refused. I want to warn you that you do not understand the nature of love.'

Ama Three took Commander Zero's staring so easily, putting some in the scornful swivel of her hips, putting some in the fire of her eyes. Who was this see-through man that wanted to spoil the spell of love that had come to balm her heart small?

'Besides,' Zero went on, 'there are rumours that she loves the carrot millionaire . . .'

The major stopped the proceedings now, saying with a deep smile, 'The only million in her life is the million times she sometimes loves me.'

Commander Zero stared incredulously at the major, and then shrugged. *Don't get burnt with the heat in his epaulettes, ei.* The silence was in different grades. Then the shadow commander spoke through his corporeal deputyship, 'Your love is your business, Major, I swear, but what is making me cry out in my kakalika anguish is something else. It is to do with aspects of my job . . .' Commander Zero suddenly wailed into the savanna, and then pricked himself on seven pineapples in the rush to trap his own wailing. Then he composed himself in song.

'Stop singing, you man of nothing!' growled Ama Three with a flower on her head for effect.

But the commander continued to sing his points of sorrow, hoping that the minor keys would win more sympathy from the major. 'I am the one that teamed up with Pogo Alonka Forr to kill Torro the Terrible, I beheaded him before he was finally put on your wife's back at her own insistence . . .'

Major Gentl demanded silence through the writhing of his third snake, for things were moving too fast for him. 'You will be tried for destroying our strategy without authority!' he said with a force that surprised himself. Then he retracted what he had said, adding, 'Don't some of you know that there are ways of winning wars, and there are ways of losing them? How dare you take it upon yourselves, you and Pogo Forr, to alter things without letting the rest of us know? I am telling you now that you have not got the width of perception to work out a strategy of survival! Your friend Alonka Forr may have the width, but it is always narrowed by ambition. I reject this ambition that wants to lead us short and take us to destruction! Did Pogo offer you something, did he offer you money or dreams?'

It was the commander's turn to look pained, for he hated being accused of anything to do with money. His voice shook as he said, 'Major! This is not how heroes behave! You should acknowledge that I saved your life once! I only killed him because he was our greatest enemy. I was in the best position as his deputy, so none of his technology could save him from the new poisons of the oval carrots . . . and in his wish to stay here forever, he had reduced his brains so much that he had completely forgotten how to switch on his protection machine . . . it was so difficult cutting off such a thick neck . . . finally Pogo himself had to send one of his supervising soldiers to help me do it.'

There was a terrible silence as Gentl stared into the nothingness before him. The commander had changed out of fear into a shadow again.

'Nana Mai the Grandmother Bomb will sew Torro's head on again, so that we can really win the war . . .', the major said, with his mind elsewhere. The ministerial shadow fainted, but turned into flesh again before it hit the ground.

'But how can I continue to be his deputy when he returns and accuses me of cutting off his thick head?' Commander Zero had finished singing long ago, and had now picked up his saxophone again.

Ama redoubled her scorn as Zero cried through his music. 'My dear husband, let's go now', she said.

'Let's be patient with this man who has saved my life once,' Gentl replied, with that reduced tenderness that came from a preoccupation of the mind. He felt some presence-bi behind him, a new wind had come and pushed his snake to the other shoulder; the saxophone blew on its own again.

And there rising out of the guinea grass with pineapples in each hand, and bigger rats on his shoulders, was Torro the Terrible. His neck was stiffer than usual, and he was two inches taller for he had insisted on and got an operation to lengthen his ankle bones, in his great desire to be nearer the height of Commander Zero. Revenge height. The rats saluted in unison as Torro rubbed his neck threateningly, throwing with a playful snarl the two pineapples he held, one at Gentl, one at the staring Zero.

'Genteelmen, genteelmen, how nice to see you after my death, no! Do you like my new height, no? For the first time I have found out that when I truly die, mama mia, I weel go to hell rather than heaven . . . death ees hotter than the African sun! I come in peace and in revenge . . .' Torro gave Commander Zero a long look, and continued, 'Ah, my deputyeee, I did not see you in office this morning, why? You must teach me how to cut off people's heads . . . I prefer to shoot of course, but it weel be useful to know . . .'

'You were not at the office, dear minister, because you were dead!' declared Zero, raising himself to his full height, and hitting his head on a neem branch. His head jangled to the tune of his automatic saxophone.

Ama Three wasn't even looking at Torro; she had become bored with her months of military service to him. She adjusted her chewing gum yet again, and it was the colour of Torro's nostrils.

Torro laughed at Zero's logic, and said, 'Why should we keel each other when first we belong to the same ministry and second we are in a cool peaceful war, eh, sciochezaa!' When Torro rubbed his neck, so did the rats. He glowered at Zero, and said, 'You see, Commander, I am very special. When I die, I rise again, and I will get you back in a very friendly and dangerous way, no!' And then he turned to Gentl, saying, 'You, Major, you are always cleverer than I theenk. But now I am changing this war. How can I have so much power and not use it, no! Me, Torro, I will make events happen before they do, I will erase the memoryee of your own actions, I will fight thees war with soldiers from any century, you cannot challenge me anywhere, neither in thees city nor on the moon. As for the sun, eet is my brother now!'

The rats had circled his neck twice as he spoke. Out of the darkness to their master's ankles came two of Gentl's snakes. In the distance you could hear General Jolloff supervise the night session of the children's war. And over-ambitious mosquitoes fell into the sea, as if from Torro's mouth.

Major Gentl was going to walk away with his wife and his snakes when Torro barred his way, shouting, 'Major! You must show me your first or second sign of manhood today! I want you to get angry with me. C'mon, push me out of your way. Let us have a fight, no!'

Ama was just about to lunge at Torro when Gentl held her back, and walked round Torro.

'I am your Minister of Defence,' screamed Torro, 'show me more respect, rispectto! I couldn't care less whether it was your Grandmother Bomb who put my head back on. I weeel never lose my head again!'

Torro had moved back into the path of the major. He wanted to block him again. From his constant training with his snakes, Major Gentl had developed massive wrists, which he used now to twist Torro's arm, pushing him with a steady gentle heave out of the way.

'Ah, I was just testing you, Major,' Torro said with scorn, picking himself up from the grass, 'I weel not fight with rabbits and children, I weel not fight with wrists. Everything I do now weel be in memoryee of my neck! We are going to fight the true war!'

aMofa Gentl was already regretting the force he used. He helped Torro to get up, as the latter tried to push him off, and then told Zero, 'Commander, go back to your office with your minister. You are both to plan a new strategy for the War of Existence . . .'

'But Major, the whole plan is confusing me! Do I plan with him or against him? Does he get to know everything and then use the information against us? Major, help me!'

Gentl had already walked on, but turned round with a faraway look in his small face, and said, 'Commander, here we don't solve paradoxes, we just win wars . . .'

Zero looked at his disappearing back for a second, and then turned round to tell Torro, his minister, that it was time to do some late work on strategy in the office. But Torro had disappeared, and all that Zero could hear was the squeak of rats in the distance. He saw a golden glow in the sky, very low, towards which Major Gentl and Ama Three went. Commander Zero didn't rush there for nothing: there on a mound newly cut with a langalanga stood the major and Ama talking up to the golden cockroach in the sky. It was surrounded by fireflies, and followed by a silver sheen that Zero wanted desperately to talk to, for he wanted to solve the whole world.

Commander Zero called 'sssssss' to the silver owl which still had Torro's diamond whistle, for it used it to whistle filial love at the golden cockroach. The silver owl which enjoyed being the train to the golden cockroach was momentarily flattered as the commander asked it in a whisper, 'What is the secret of the existence of the golden cockroach, my dear sister owl? I'm happy you left Torro's household. Can you tell me how it gives the secrets of war to Major Gentl for him to win wars? Is it the moon, or is it the ancestors that are the secret of his gentleness, or does his gentleness hide a supertobolo ferocity? Tell me my dear sister owl, take me out of my misery, for I am a deputy minister, as you may know, and I must learn how to help this city to win its wars!'

'Follow the strategy, follow the strategy!' said the silver owl with a merry laugh.

'But what is this strategy?' Whenever I think it's the opposite, then it's not, and when I think it is not, then it is . . .'

The commander had said this so loudly that the golden cockroach heard it, and edged sideways from Major Gentl towards the milkbush where Zero was crouched.

'Major, come and see your protégé the deputy minister, whose shadow may come in useful in the future, as you were aware when we discussed his appointment with the elders . . . Ah, you talltall commander, was it Pogo who led you into this killing misadventure? We will still keep you as deputy minister, because we liked your rabbit strategy, and we have to make mistakes at times, otherwise the enemy will consider us stronger than we are and attack us harder. They want to take our brains and our energy, for this will help them to leave the galaxy! Since they have more power, the greatest subtlety is needed. But we are not too far behind them, even if they believe they can overpower us in five minutes . . . We too have our power! Don't allow yourself to be misled by Pogo Forr, eh! His problem is not existence but glory!'

The golden Mr Cee was now laughing uncontrollably. But the commander refused to be overawed. He asked, 'If the strategy is so deep, why don't some of you make it simpler for some of us?'

Mr Cee glared hard at the silver owl, for it had still not got used to its silver following. Major Gentl was nodding in the distance at the words of the cockroach.

'Take the strategy on a weekly basis until the elders tell you that the world is a month instead of a week, or that the world is a year instead of a term, you hear! . . . Look at the doubt in the face of the gatherer of shadows.'

The golden cockroach returned both to its laugh and to its serious stare at the silver owl; but the owl didn't care, it just continued to adore Mr Cee through its diamond whistle. Peep, went the whistler of the skies, with the smell of gari and raw mouse in its hooked beak. It didn't know that Mr Cee was planning some revenge on the silver mosquito, for after all this owl was too devoted, except when it came to mice.

The sea was quite far from Achimota City, even though it sometimes threw small fish into the sky for all to see; and the light of the sun could catch the fish suspended in the sky for a few seconds. The moon was worse with herring. Commander Zero had left for his doubtful office, and Ama had gone to check on the sleeping children, and had found all Torro's children sleeping in the house too. What was a trick, and what wasn't a trick? Major Gentl had ordered his snakes to slide over the garden to keep the grass short. The mangoes rode the wind, and the disturbed crow jumped beyond the ginger growing at the edges of the garden where he had spent the night, for there was too much love inside from Ama, too much love for poor Gentl to digest in one night. Besides, she had talked about joining General Jolloff to supervise the children's war, and he had removed his hand from hers; for she seemed to be growing away from him again. She wasn't: the more love she felt, the more independent she became.

So Gentl set out for the sea to talk to it, to tell it to stop throwing its fish high, for the talking would not only raise memories of childhood days by the shore but would also improve his strategy, or. As befitted a man with accommodation on the moon, he wanted to pull the waves this way, and then pull the waves that way, all with some lunar look in his tiny face that didn't fill all eyes. Twice he thought he saw Torro trailing him among the termite architecture, among the fruity columns, but he dismissed the vision.

The camel walked behind stubbornly, in spite of being ordered to stay at home; and behind the camel was Atinga who had also rebelled against his master's constant orders not to bodyguard him too mech. Atinga was often annoyed with the world, for he was displeased at the way his promotion was dealt with: one shoulder was promoted by Commander Zero, while the other was asked to wait for greater assessment. He therefore walked about disdainfully, with one shoulder higher than the other, and swearing that very soon they would promote too his upper lip and leave his lower lip. Now at least half of him was the same rank as the hated sergeant shadow . . . which also frequently deserted the major, possibly for shadows of a female nature, for awam indeed was the love that had no substance, *ebei you zero love*.

The major moved on with his slow deliberate walk, passing and repassing the rising markets in his procession of three, and seeing a fat frog suspended in philosophical sankofa: was there too much future in the city, and if it jumped too high, would it hit its head on a fish?

Further on, nearer the sea, there was Nana Mai high up in a helicopter, with a huge needle and thread, sewing up a part of the sky that had been deliberately torn that night by a wicked missile released by Torro to prove his terrible nature, and to give a warning of his new ruthlessness. Grandmother Bomb shouted down to Gentl with a frown. 'It takes a lot of humility to sew the sky at my age, but when that mad Torro starts to change his tactics while remaining the Minister of Defence, then we have to change our way of doing things too. Certainly I can't find any love up here can I, Major!' And then she laughed and

laughed, for in truth she had been profoundly shaken by her appointment into the Council of Elders. To protect herself Nana Mai had
written two restrained letters of rejection to her two ex-husbands,
warning them to stay away from her, especially in her new and more
vulnerable position . . . which she still didn't fail to pour scorn on,
even at meetings. Her laughter improved the rhythm of the camel's walk.

Gentl had passed through Labadi, and had ended up at a fine part of
the beach where fresh morning horses threw the sand right and left.
Under a high coconut tree with erosion at its roots stood an extremely
serious pig trotting on the spot, with bacon shining in its eyes. It
approached Gentl and said, still trotting, 'Please, Major, I am the
president of the New Pig Experience, an association formed for pigs,
through pigs and by pigs. We salute you as the orginator of the
heightened appraisal of animals in Achimota City. Through you snakes
have become important, fish have become ministers, rabbits have
fought wars, and pigs have been put in charge of their own African
bacon. We salute you! There are even pigs driving satellites in the city
skies. But unfortunately we have been approached by Torro the white
South African Italian, and present Minister of Defence, to kill you. At
first we were outraged. How dare this thick-necked beast suggest your
death to us! But then as time went on, we saw merit in his argument:
first of all he, Torro, looked very much like a pig himself, including the
new scars on his resurrected neck; second, since we pigs loved you so
much, we thought we could turn you into an ancestor since you are so
good. We now want you to become a piglet saint. And thirdly, we
believe that all the strategies are so subtle in this great city that we could
gain something good by killing you the good person, and leaving the bad
living. I believe you don't solve paradoxes here. The association has
therefore sent me to demand of you an answer to the merits and demerits
of your own death, as proposed by Torro. If you agree to die, then as the
president, I am authorised koraa to kill you on the spot, with or without
your snakes. If you don't agree, then I have the same authority to kill
you immediately, since we have already decided in advance that you
could be more useful to the city dead than alive. Please tell me your
views now now now, so that I won't have the tension of waiting, for a pig
with hypertension is a sorry sight. I have also been empowered to shoot
you before you give your view if I have the premonition that these views
will be contrary to what every pig stands for . . .'

Major Gentl stared in disbelief as Atinga raised his eyes to the sky with exasperation: here was yet another occasion to save his master, without the immediate possibility of having his other shoulder promoted, Allah. As the pig was talking, the camel was climbing the coconut tree immediately behind. There was thus a small soft race between the camel and Atinga to save the major.

'I want to save the major today!' screamed the camel without thinking, and half-way up the tree at that. And, when the President of Pigs turned round to see what was happening, Atinga pounced on it, giving it a dirty great slap, and disengaging the pistol from its pocket.

'You are not a pig, and therefore you have no authority to stop me koraa from carrying out my legitimate duties. I demand you return my gun, otherwise I will report you to the Minister of Defence!' shouted the smooth-faced pig.

Atinga stared at it with utter contempt and without a word. When the major hugged him, he passed the hug on to the descending camel.

Then, quite slowly, out of the corner of his eye, Gentl caught a glimpse of Torro standing in the sea with an octopus on his back. He turned round quickly and true his eye confirmed its own corner. Torro stood there glistening, magnifying his limbs with the octopus. He said, 'Thees octopus will help meee to defeat you, because there are more hands for grabbing you, no! I have your success locked up in an octopus, Major, beleeve me. And behind me is the ship of truth. You and me will go on to this ship one day, now eef you like, and only one of us weel come out alive, for there are strange things there. Sharks and giant crabs . . .'

Torro pointed out behind him, a hundred metres away, an old wreck with its brown tripled with rust; a slippery rock guarded it, and miraculously its horn still worked.

'The shark blows the horn!' Torro added.

Gentl watched him with a complete lack of surprise. Torro walked quietly with his bulk and his raw neck, and gave the pig a slap; and another and another, until the camel faced him, its former master, and dared him to slap its hump next. Torro laughed mysteriously at it, and then turned to Atinga.

'Atinga, come and bodyguard me, I am better than your master. I weel give you plenty meat, and I weel give you instant promotion too, eh! You suffer too mech, no!'

Atinga stared at Torro and cocked his gun, his legs wide apart, and

103

his eyes full of fury. 'You, you Torro bombole, you go die for second time, sharp!'

Torro ignored that too; he was almost merry. He pointed once again to the ship of truth, rusty truth, and repeated, 'Major, come with me to deescuss your death and my death too on the ship of truth where all battles are won. I do not like this land fighting, it's too weak, and too seelly for me!' He had a huge smile which impossibly reflected itself in his own odd-angled eyes.

Gentl didn't return the smile, but said quietly, 'I gave your son Carlo some chloroquine last night. He was feverish, and muttering against his food and his army. We have been feeding him and his brother and sister for the last ten days. I can take them on to the ship of truth for you. Sometimes they ask for you, and their mother rings every day to thank my wife for looking after them, and helping them to settle in this country with its single city. I believe you should make your love for them a little clearer . . .'

Torro stood there with his mouth open. He was thinking: 'This Major is a fool paa, me I talk of truth and the sea and death and war, and he wants to bring in his silly kindness, seelly, and then make me feel guilty sosososo.' Without another word, Torro threw the octopus after the squealing pig president.

'Trotter off, trotter off!' he screamed after it. He then stood looking at the sea for a long time; and then he walked off, shouting back at the major, 'Your sympathy, so what, your sympathy, so what, galantuomo for nothing, trying to reduce me by bringing in my bambinos, how seelly, kindness is for women, no!'

The camel measured the sea with its strides, as Gentl walked on between the mist and the waves. Atinga was asleep with the tides just leaving his legs; he had fallen asleep immediately Torro went. And, after her aerial tailoring, Nana Mai was no longer visible in the sky. aMofa went on to a hump, camel, and another hump, mound, from where he stared deeply inland. GRACIOUSNESS OF THE EARTH! There, miles off beyond Achimota City, a rectangular piece of land slowly crawled through the void, and joined the land of the city! Major Gentl was crying, with the camel looking in puzzlement at him. He hugged the camel, and then rushed to hug the sleeping Atinga, who jumped out of fright, his gun at the ready.

'Atinga, this is not the time for shooting! Don't you see the land of the rest of the country coming back in bits? We are at last getting our first crumbs of success, the strategy is not so silly after all! Who is saying we should not leave the contradictions alone. MERCY! Let me phone the elders through the sand, and through the water that if a small tract of land the size of a football pitch has come back to us, then we are doing some things correctly in the war!'

The telephone kept behind the camel's hump was already ringing, and when he went to answer it, all he heard was 'graciousness of the earth', spoken by Chairman Kot too. They had rung each other's ringing, and the sun came out and ignored the ship of truth, which, after all, had missed entirely the biggest small truth of the newly settling land. *Here comes the long-missing country in bits, Ewurade!*

The city is finding its country at last! And Gentl's helicopter took himself, Atinga and the camel to Government House, where the elders, minus Nana Mai who had just finished polishing the missiles, went with Gentl and landed fast on the new bit of land.

On the land, sitting forlornly, was a short fat man, his head in his hands. He wouldn't say good morning, but raised his head, and howled, 'Why have they brought me back here? I was quite happy as a captured labourer in the cold lands, and there are thousands and thousands of us there; and they are sending us all back WITH OUR LAND because we have not ceased to be human! And I don't even remember the name of the city I was in, where the blacks had one life, and the whites had another. I can't understand why everyone here is so happy! Let us go back and eat long long plums alone! And how torn are the roots of being there! And yet they do not want us to heal them!'

There was a pause, an astounded silence, for neither Kot nor Gentl knew whether this was a Ghanaian speaking, or an Azanian.

The man continued, 'And the belief is that they destroyed all the black people there in what was called a legitimate genocide by the western and eastern nations – I can't even remember the name of one country – and then blacks from other places were imported, yes imported like goods, to replace the lost indigenous people, so that there would be such rootlessness and economic gratefulness that the old system would go on without rubbish being talked about voting and majority and humanity. And then the cycle of genocide would be repeated. Who am I and where am I? I ask you even if this place seems familiar . . .' *The new land had bananas, that's all, the new land had fruit.*

Chairman Kot recognised the man as the brother of Abomu Kwame. He had left years and years ago, before all the barriers and metal walls the rich countries had put up. But Gentl was shattered: did you rejoice over the return of the land? Or did you grieve over the paucity and ravage of the few people that came with it? Did you just limit yourself to the city alone, or did you broaden your strategy in such a way that you hoped for the return and eventual success of those who left your shores long ago? Or did you just pray for the land, and hope the people would never return?

All that the powers abroad of any persuasion were doing was to listen to their computers which were telling them that Africa, apart from its resources, was expendable, and that the vast lands were to be ultimately acquired – with most of the people dead – for space, for sun, and for materials; and for sanctuary in case of nuclear war. This was all in their plans and computers, in their secret files and in their top-level talks. Ewurade help us to overcome this evil, Gentl thought.

'The broad strategy continues!' shouted Chairman Kot as hard as possible to convince himself that more than the city needed to be saved. The entire missing country had to be saved! But the doubt persisted: shouldn't they save this city alone and damn the rest of the country?

ZONE ELEVEN

Punishment and after

Jojo Digi, the second elder, had the job of disciplining both Pogo Alonka Forr and Torro the Terrible: Alonka for arranging the killing of Torro without authority, but Torro? Torro for dying without authority. It was felt that Torro, with his vast reserves of power, could have stopped himself from being killed, but that he wanted, first, greater power from his death, and second, a small victory against Pogo whom he still stubbornly considered his most dangerous enemy. Some thought that Torro continued to want Pogo to be his enemy either because he had reduced his own intelligence too much, or because he secretly knew that Pogo would be easier to defeat; or conversely, it would be easier to accept the humiliation of a defeat from the considerable tricking of Pogo Forr. Whatever the reasons, the two men, both with their massive thighs, had to be punished for straying from agreed strategies. Digi the Jo had some little difficulty at first in disciplining one man who had a supervising army, a golden horse, oval carrots, millions of cedis, innumerable helicopters, and aspirations towards the sun; and another man with a vast store of technological power, rats, interminable beef, more rats, and a frontal and sideways stand both simultaneous.

'How dare youou come to deescipline my thick and sore neck!' demanded Torro doing his double-direction stand, one hand on his advanced belly.

'I will put a carrot between you and your discipline!' snarled Pogo in chorus.

Digijo kept surprisingly cool, smiling on top of a calabash of palm-wine just before it reached his lips; but he didn't smile with his eyes, his forehead was thunder complete. And the crow that usually drank akpeteshie vc-10 kiss-me-quick with Abomu Kwame was pecking at the windows of Government House, hoping to chop a stray termite even though it was unlawful. The crow seemed to carry with stubbornness the crossing thoughts of all three men beyond the glass.

Elder Digi had suddenly risen from his cane chair, and had demanded and got a frying pan and stove to fry an egg, in order to retain his unusually even temper. It was difficult, but his anger went into his egg highspeed. As he fried right in the middle of the conference room with rabbits bringing and taking their untaken honey, Pogo Forr and The Torro, as Elder Jo called him, ignored each other. The Torro had an ostentatious red ribbon round his roundabout neck and his khaki shorts-so-fat seemed to contain two people; while Pogo Alonka was wearing joromi robes so silken that you could be excused for thinking it was glass. This Pogo was getting impatient, for the egg was taking too long: Jojo Digi had forgotten to switch the power on, so that Torro had gone with a curse to do so, warning his new favourite rat not to fall into the pan and be fried by the government. Jojo gave a reluctant grunt for thank you, and slapped the rat with irritation. The Torro stiffened, but took his stiff to his seat, pressing his popylonkwe down with ceremony. A snort came from the Government Frier, Elder Cook Digi, for he was thinking how disreputable these important men of means were. As for himself, he knew that his temper was always his alibi, but this ostentation put him on edge. The crow put its back to the glass and slept.

'Who is going to dare punish Pogo Alonka Forr?' The Torro said suddenly to the smell of the fried egg, his new height simmering. Elder Jojo didn't even turn round.

'And who is going to discipline Torro the Terrible?' Pogo asked with a corresponding growl.

'I can see one speaks for the other, eh?' Jojo observed, trying desperately to suppress his anger, and then using it to help the egg fry again.

'And does eet take as long to fry an egg as to make a law?' Torro asked.

Elder Jo turned round at last, and banged the frying pan on the conference table, with the egg scattering on the cabinet papers. He started to shout, but controlled himself yet again, and said, 'If you Torro have changed your strategy for the war, we are ready for you! We are ready to sack you as Minister of Defence if this means fighting the war direct and mortally.'

There was a pause, during which the crow, wakened by the smash of the frying pan, cackled against the glass, insulting the government termites with impunity.

'I have a heart too, I have a heart too!' screamed the crow. 'Let me in,

108

let me in at least to finish off the eggs!' And the rabbits took the egg to the crow. Boof, chopped the crow, laughing and hoping to graduate to rabbits later.

Torro looked pained, and now put on an almost pleading voice.

'But Elder, you know I love this place, and I know you have the authority to do anything to me, but do not threaten me with a direct war, otherwise . . .'

'. . . otherwise, your bosses will replace you!' Pogo shouted with triumph, hating being lumped with Torro for punishment, but wanting by temperament to assert himself anyway; and he suddenly thought: power exercised by sad sly oldish men could be acceptable, even though he passionately believed that it was time to introduce glamour into power again in Achimota City, forgetting that one of the most difficult and one of the wisest things the city had achieved was to extract glamour, wealth and prestige from power. This was how it got its wisdom and stability, and sometimes even its creativity, even though politics even of the Achimota kind could never be for long the source of creativity, koraa.

'Pogo Forr,' roared Jojo Digi, keeping his thoughts linear for once, 'you have been banished to fight in the children's war for a period! You will have to discuss openly the new properties of your oval carrots; and you will also have to confirm or deny the rumours that you have reached an accommodation with the sun in connection with hotels and weapons. And the golden horse is to be ridden by the poorest man in the city as a penance . . .'

'Your last point is impossible, so let me say it now now now! No one rides the golden horse except myself! Besides it is unmountable. I am insurmountable and my horse of gold is unmountable. I would rather pay a fine, or offer a free missile . . .'

'You, Pogo Forr, you will not choose what punishment you will get!' boomed Elder Two. 'But as you know, if you want to appeal, then you can appeal. We will call you before the other elders, and before the golden cockroach . . .'

'But the cockroach doesn't like me!' protested Pogo.

Digi glared at Pogo, glared at Digi, and then Pogo stormed out, his robes in suspension . . . only to find the last door shut. When he stormed up to the cabinet rooms, he found them empty, except for the rascally crow which had somehow managed to come in and was sitting trying to persuade the outraged rabbits guarding there to allow it to eat one of their number. And the crow told Pogo, 'Mr Carrot Millionaire, your South African Azanian Torro has been ordered to go and fight among a platoon of rabbits every Monday as a punishment, but he is to remain as Minister of Defence, working directly up to the Grandmother Bomb. A real punishment, I lie! I tell you, The Torro wept, and he didn't even try to hide his big boozy tears from me a mere crow! And another thing: they are considering putting half your wealth in a trust to keep you in line for a year . . .'

Without any warning whatsoever Pogo took the crow up and danced with it. Yieee, the old crow can dance O, with its dirty wings fluffed out, as the rabbits invaded the dancing and threw it out, sharp.

Pogo took honey twice and left. He hoped the crow was lying about his wealth in a trust. The crow was a liar, for he knew they would not dare interfere with the wealth that more or less financed the war. He carried an oval carrot on his head as he reached his horse under the neem trees. He put the carrot on the brown horse that wore darkglasses – it preferred darker galloping – and ordered it to canter home, having put a golden ring round the oval carrot, which made it impossible to steal; and the other order was that a helicopter should be sent for him driven by Delali herself.

Into the palm-wine and fruit juice bar he went. There was a perceptible silence for a second or two as he entered the cocoa- and flower-dominated room, with some of its barpeople smoking Nana Mai's ice jots.

'Pogo the hero, akwaaba! We admire you paa for letting Commander O cut off the head of Torro the Terrible,' came a deep voice with a laugh at its top, from the west of the bar, 'but you have to be as sophisticated as your carrots as far as strategy is concerned: you should have killed within our agreed strategy! Allah knows you are good to all of us, you buy ceramic-made alokoto for our children, and you give perfume of guava to our wives, so nicely that some of them fall in love with you straight away. Pogo we love your horses, especially the golden one! Now have you solved the mystery about whether it gives off golden dung or not? I beg you, Pogo, SPEAK! You seem quiet kakra. Have they been punishing you about your headhead cut of Torro's neck? Just forget their wisdom for a while and sit down and admire your millions! Very soon we understand you will have very cool hotels in the sun. Why? We have enough land here, why don't you build some superalombo hotels right here? Eii, only your ambition-O!'

Pogo moved his robes away from his arms as he smiled his silence. Pogo silent? The deep voice was the friend of a friend. And the second voice came in at a different octave.

'Pogo give me your alonka for my gari! I love the way you have been handling your golden horse when it jumps, you do it with such soso style, and I'm in love with your woman bodyguard. Does she guard you from other women or what, ha! I believe your glass house mirrors everything, the first glass even mirrors the second glass. O what do you do when there's some fikifiki on the compound? Do you all lie and watch each other doing it, Allah! I beg you, please have some of my adoka-diluted river-drink, some freshwater fermentation in my calabash. The world is sometimes the kindness of a rich man with laughter in his robes. We all sometimes wonder why you have not yet been appointed to the Council of Elders. Perhaps you are too young, too frisky, and would your big thighs fit under the conference tables, O Pogo! One, two, three, everybody say P-o-g-oooo!'

Pogo brightened considerably, he couldn't resist the mood he had met. He took hold of six elbows and pushed them into dancing. Ke-ke-ke-ke-ke!

'Now I will talk, my friends and brothers. You have brought me out of my dark mood! Hail to Achimota City, where to love is to know the root of everything. I sleep on gold! . . .' There was a roar of approval. '. . . I sleep on gold, but that doesn't stop me from giving my life over to the War of Existence . . .', Pogo continued.

Then there was a high dissenting voice that cut across Pogo's new mood: 'Yewura Pogo, but some of us are existing more than others. No don't get me wrong, I believe in the value of the carrot, for everybody sees better with it, and I agree with the strategy, but why is it that you are making money throughout the war? Is it right? I beg you, don't vex, for I believe that you have the patience to explain everything to those of us who need the explaining . . .'

'Shut up, my brother! You are going to spoil Pogo's mood again!' a voice interrupted. But the voice of dissension continued.

'I too will brother you big to shut up! Here is a free city, I can say what I like, and nobody can stop me. As you all know, there's no security schedule in government, no arrests . . . Now Pogo, tell me, are you not making too much money in a time that we are fighting for our very existence? Answer me my dear Pogo!'

There was utter silence as people saw the look of thunder on Alonka's face. Then the same Forr face burst into laughter, and carried its body along to hug the dissenting voice, saying, 'My brother, with the different voice! My money goes into the war, and the war goes into my money and as you know I look after hundreds of people free . . .' The spreading laughter reached outside the bar. And Pogo continued, 'You know that a small slice of new land has come to us, though we are all so disappointed in the man that came with it. He just sits and complains and refuses to leave the new land. No one knows why he does this, apart from his own silly reasons about going back to the Exile Lands as a captured labourer. But me Pogo the Alonka I know: I know that he will only become integrated with us AFTER WE WIN THE WAR! So we have no TIME koraa! I have told the elders and Major Gentl that we must make our strategy faster. Why O Why is the major actually spending time tending to the children of Torro? Why is Torro the Minister of Defence? Are we not getting too subtle? Are we not practising that type of goodness . . .'

'. . . that led us to victory in the First War of Existence?' came the chorus led by the dissenting voice.

'Ah!' shouted Pogo with triumph, 'Then since I had my part to play in this first victory with my money and my ideas, why should you criticise my role now, eh!'

There were roars of approval, for there were many who didn't want the image of Pogo destroyed, for they loved him. They loved him more under the palm tree, because Gentl and the elders did not want to be heroes, and everybody found that quite wonderful, but a wild hero every now and again shouldn't be turned down . . . but shouldn't have power either, in a just system, thought the dissenting voice: this voice was Kojo Tolo who shut all avenues of sarcasm up, but could never quite deal with Pogo Forr, nor his own sarcastic remarks either.

'More fruit and adoka for everybody, more palm-wine!' shouted Pogo just as his helicopter arrived, with Delali piloting it.

'Hail to Pogo's lady, the woman who never looks too deeply into her husband's life!' Kojo Tolo shouted, turning round, looking for applause. He got none, for they had had enough of sarcasm, and wanted to roar Pogo on in front of his wife.

'Pogo for the Council of Elders!' someone shouted. But he wasn't

112

cheered either, for after all the city had been through, the people were very careful about giving anybody their blind adulation. Adulation was not even for children, for they too had been taught about the disgust of adulating power. But all the same they were happy with Pogo, they loved him, and even knew his limits; and at the same time they were prepared to ˹recognise that he could make a great contribution to the war.

So there they were shouting, 'Pogo, Delali, Pogo, Delali,' to see the helicopter off, but they didn't want Pogo to lead them. They felt safer with the quiet persistence of Major Gentl, or with the long reign of the elders. They had fought and fought with the elders for their freedoms of all kinds, especially the freedom to tell their rulers, in a rude way if necessary, that they did not like this policy or that policy, that they were prepared to throw them out when they went wrong.

ZONE TWELVE

The duel

By the authority of his limpingly sore neck, Torro declared a duel on Pogo. His neck had been very useful before it was cut off, for it used to help him walk better, he was so fat, with some bull in the eyes, the same eyes that had allowed a tiny bit of sorrow to come at the edges; for everybody except his rats seemed to be growing away from him, even Bianca hmmmm who spent long periods sitting beside and yet not talking to General Jolloff, some awam silences among the romantic yearning. Torro couldn't bring himself to kill Bianca, for her conscious-ness couldn't care less whether her varied life was ultimately ended by that same man who sometimes terrorised her; and besides, she had seen Torro kill too many people, in Rome or in South Africa. He always ate a fine tangerine before he killed a servant or two, and then wept bitterly afterwards, showering the family of the deceased with post-memorial gifts. It wasn't difficult arranging to be born in South Azania, being born for the second time, after a shortish life of robbery and lechery in Rome, where one of the best things he did was to roam looking for money and excruciatingly fresh beef. The drip of beef blood reminded him of the blood of his victims, this bonsam with a bounce. The small sorrow was eked out between both eyes, for even the present seemed to be finishing, let alone the past. He was proud of his terrible past, but was terrified that no one would accept or praise it, not even the jolloff-sick Bianca who seemed to be caught between each grain of rice that General Jolloff admired. It was thus with his whole past, including his recent decapitation, that The Torro challenged Pogo to a duel. He had wanted to challenge Major Gentl, but eventually considered that it would be too quiet and cunning a contest; for with Pogo there would be roaring, pogofoolery, and basabasa. The victory or the defeat would be wild and immature, just what he and Pogo would like paaa. So there was Torro both defiant and sorrowful, silly and vigorous. And he did an impetuous thing: he resigned both out of levity and strategy as Minister of Defence, but continued to exercise his functions, out of spite for Commander Zero; for no one had told him to vacate his office, nor had anyone written to him that his resignation had been accepted.

Eventually after some careful thinking in the northern cabinet room, the elders of government had agreed to the duel, provided that it was to the wound but not to the death; and provided also that Major Gentl supervised it closely, in a strategy within a strategy. Nana Mai the Grandmother Bomb had refused to contribute anything significant, insisting that there were more important things to do than to make executive decisions on duels between the most cantankerous characters in Achimota City, charactankerous. So what she did during the debate was to make a hole in the sky long-distance, for the loser of the duel to be thrown into, for reasons of strategy and security, which she had failed to state; Major Gentl was still constructing a fine light road to the moon to make his rooms there available to all, and Nana Mai was planning to throw the loser of this ludicrous duel on to this road through this hole in the sky. This would teach him cloud sense, especially Torro whose letter of resignation the elders ignored.

So, in the morning, Pogo was at first only so-so. He had risen early enough to push the moon out of the sky to make way for the great sun, his wonderful friend. He was a son of the sun, and when he looked into the morning mirror to shave, the sun brightened it. As soon as Pogo said 'hotel in the sky' the sun got cooler. He deliberately bathed in the garden among the cola trees, coolest.

Delali was watching all this with foreboding, for she was completely against the duel; she hated the sight of wounds, and was getting worried about this grotesquely burgeoning ambition of her husband's. He had forbidden her to go and watch the proceedings, but she had sworn to go there anyway, even though she would have to suppress any secret desire to see Major Gentl. It wouldn't be fair to have eyes for another man while your husband was fighting a duel, deeebi. But it was Pogo himself who encouraged a feeling of festivity – she could perhaps look at the major with one eye – by announcing that to make the morning generous and victorious, his right pocket had given a loan of celebration to his left pocket, deep in his robes.

There he was, eating the tasty locomotion of his horse-and-helicopter breakfast on his golden horse, right in the dining-room. And he had put on his golden robes after a quick lie down on Delali, who laughed as he

115

gave her a huge hug fit for the fikifiki if only there was time. Pogo chopped early-morning fufu by his golden robes, golden reins, golden horse, golden koko, and golden handkerchief. And the sun changed to the colour of his horse, so that even the sky was ready to make gold for him. For some seconds he couldn't move for the sparkling.

As for Torro, he began the morning with a snarl because the dawn wouldn't wait small for him to rise; and he continued it with beef, plus an extraordinary amount of sheabutter on his neck, quick quick. If you were to hear his breakfast you would think he ate curses, the way he threw them around the table. He had recently become so suspicious that he used a computer to map the route of food from his fork or his hands to his mouth: he couldn't trust what could happen in that tiny interval of oral travel. Bianca was around to calm him, but he exploded her calm by cursing her for not arranging for his children to come to the house to give him support. He wanted innocent support, not the rehearsed support of his soldiers. But his children were busy eating breakfast in the house of Major Gentl and Ama Three; and thus in a compensatory fashion, he suddenly missed his runaway camel, and his silver owl. His bosses seemed to be communicating with him less and less, though this didn't mean they didn't know what was going on; indeed, they were probably disgusted with the use of the brain machine on his own head, just because of a desire to stay longer in Achimota City. And his threat of being master over time was yet to be seen.

In order not to let the occasion stand still, Major Gentl had arranged for three old steam trains with one carriage each to move all over the battlefield, whistling, steaming, and rolling among the people. They were the type of trains that automatically laid out their own tracks as they moved, and then picked them up from behind to reuse in the front again. Train, train, train the duellists, for the engines gave an atmosphere of past and present that brightened the future immeasurably. Birds were on the trains, and so were rabbits; and arrogant at the controls of the second engine was the old crow, now appointed Government Crow, flapping about with black-and-white impunity and throwing insults and felicitations at everybody. The brass bands, headed by the indomitably drunk Abomu Kwame, played to the rhythm of the trains.

'Aluta continua!' shouted Government Crow, 'This aluta too, it continua paaa, provided you chop enough aboloo! All of you protect

116

your popylonkwes in case my ship-shape can-you-dig-it train bumps you in the most unnnnseemly places, true African private matter, I tell you! Hey, Abomu Kwame, owner of all the spiritual bottles in the universe, make way! Agooo!'

When they cursed Government Crow, they put their laughter in the curse. *Forge the joy out of the war!* And the crow left its train, flew up high, and returned to drive again. Government Crow flew very close to an irate Commander Zero standing there looking strangely preoccupied, blowing his famous sexagesima saxophone given to him by a priest who called the gods through horns without a shadow of doubt. His eyes looked even more reversed, whitening when they should be blackening, and blackening when they should be whitening. And he had a number of riderless horses beside him galloping interminably with his music that could hardly be heard above the brass bands. Zero minus brass bands equalled peace, true. Except for the chattering and the roaring, for the people wanted to know who be who between The Terrible and The Forr. And commotion equalled grapes: the former expanded among the crowds so much that the latter grew quite involuntarily over the highest walls, grape cement; they talked and ate, they talked and ate, the grapes grew in the duel. Look at the people, look at the people! They were so closely packed together that when they were jockeying for better positions, you found that one Kofi was miraculously wearing the joromi of one Yaw, and one Yaw hadn't even noticed; and worse, Abomu Kwame tried to exchange fresh piotos through the crush with one beautiful lady with odolontous backkeepers.

'I will now now now make a report to the police about your sly attempt to exchange pants with me while I'm still wearing mine! You play me! I will show you pepper just now!' came the cry from the lady of the odolont.

Abomu pretended he had heard nothing, and concentrated on his akpeteshie and his proverbial stew. Hoot, hoot! roared the trains, keeping track of the way the crowds were moving. And there was a woman standing there with a fractured heart because she had fallen in love with both Pogo and Torro, and she couldn't bear to see one of them wounded.

'We are the most intelligent electorate in the world!' someone shouted with no provocation whatsoever, 'because when they give us play, we play; but if they try to fool us, we are there fighting the government in

117

spite of the war being fought! I love these trains moving in and out of the thousands of souls watching here! As for Gentl he's gigantic . . .'

Seven thousand starlings came to watch the proceedings immediately, changing the colour of hats with their aerial droppings; the sharp metamorphosis of hats from aerial dung increased the number of raised arms, raised in festive agitation, and it increased too the number of souls rising for a change that was at present absolutely unnecessary. Ebei, the wind was asleep, or it would have blown the horns of the trains away koraa. Hoot, hoot! If the trains were now going backwards, you could trust the joy to shoot on!

'Major, Major, minor, major, if you don't want a spectacle, then you lie bad!' someone shouted to poor Gentl – standing among the carrots next to the pineapples, thinking – 'and surely for once you are going to stop your serious adwendwen thinking, and act like a hero referee for this duel of high hu! We congratulate you for having your wife back on your side of the war, for even though she may have been carrying out a strategy, she was overdoing it. Ewurade, how dare she take so many pot shots at you, she almost killed you! But we of course realise that in between the bullets, she loved you dearly-ooooo! besiai-ei!'

The major gave the talker a short wave that needn't have risen at all. He had appropriated the diamond whistle from the silver owl; and the golden cockroach was soon very high up in the sky, talking to satellites, with its tiny nose shaped exactly for smoking the sikadillo. It snorted profitably in the sky! Fifty metres from the major, Commander Zero had laid down his sexsax, which was still playing. He was walking thoughtfully up to the hills of neem and pine and almond. Gentl wondered what this deputy minister was up to, but soon forgot about him, for you couldn't plan all the time with everybody. A ripe guava fell on his cap.

People would say that Pogo Forr's genitals were younger than the rest of him, philandering sometimes from dawn to dusk without being caught. A proper sexual manager, with some ayoungi popylonkwe pogolaaaaaa! And just as they were talking about and laughing at him, there appeared on the horizon towards his glass house a magnificent sparkle that could be seen for miles. It was the shimmer of the winner! They roared. Pogo Alonka Forr was coming on to the battlefield for the duel. He could hardly move for gold. And ten golden starlings flew everywhere around him, even in and out of his thick hair, with traditional music mixed with Highlife stretched and shaped to symphonic level playing around him. All music stopped as Pogo approached so slowly; even the trains had stopped, puffing with impatience to start disturbing again. Puff puff puff, utter silence.

Pogo wore his kente-coloured beatific smile, his golden spear arranged under the golden horse, so that when its popylonkwe rose it would raise the spear too. Someone had wanted to bow down and worship this approaching vision, but was dragged up from his knees, and reminded that this war was the middle of the year 2020, when idols were friends not deities. Pogo slowly rose and stood on the saddle of the moving horse. Up came the huge roar from the crowd, which wanted to mob him, but was kept back by the gold, and a child asked its mother, 'Mama, can I borrow the golden horse to go and buy some toffee with its gold?'

When Pogo waved, you couldn't count the hands that waved back, and if they were getting a feast for their eyes, then they wanted an extension of it into the mouth: they ate and ate more grapes, they devoured pineapples out of excitement. Chop chop and chop.

'Halt all proceedings!' came a sudden authoritative child's voice over the loudspeakers. It was Commander mMo, with Commander Carlo standing beside him on an improvised platform. 'We the children of the war are still using this battlefield for the war right now. We cannot interrupt our war of survival for some small fight between two rich men . . . and Pogo Forr hasn't even come to supervise the children's war yet.'

Then the child soldiers surrounded the huge crowd and started firing up into the sky. The rabbits joined them out of reflex. And there was confusion. Pogo however retained his golden dignity absolutely, still standing up on his horse. Gentl ambled across towards the junior commanders, and then stopped half-way. He wrote a quick note, gave it to one of his snakes, and the snake slithered towards mMo and Carlo. They read,

You may pay your first visit to my rooms in the moon, even with your armies. Rocket has been arranged. The war can continue there for a day. It is an important part of the strategy, please.

The two rival commanders were so close that they usually forgot which side they were leading. They ate kelewele together very often on the

119

battlefield, while their troops shot up, and their troops shot down. They conferred over the note. And then they gave a secret sign which stopped the firing immediately.

'To the moon, my young troops!' they shouted simultaneously.

The crowd roared as its exasperation disappeared. Still, no one saw Commander Zero go higher and higher up in the hills, with his empty horses. No one saw the magnificent new missile he had hidden in his pioto.

'Isn't it time now for Torro the Terrible to appear, or is he afraid or what?' a voice shouted.

'Yes, where's he hiding at all?' came another voice.

But Torro didn't come, yet: he sent ahead six sexy arrogant rats – all with uncontrollable erections – with a note that if that seelly Pogo didn't want to be given a mortal wound, then he better leave the battlefield immediately; and that he Torro was insisting on a dangerous municipal football match between him and Pogo, and that his favourite rat should be either a linesman or the referee; the match should be combined with the duel, play should be war, and war should be play. When Pogo read the note, it turned to gold, and he pocketed it amidst shouting and cheering and oseee yeee. The rats then defecated one after the other in utter provocation, and then rushed off in a tiny helicopter when the crowd tried to attack them. The helicopter had the flight power of rodent erections!

Major Gentl said nothing as Pogo shouted after the disappearing rats, 'Tell him I accept his terms! Everything is ready, including my golden boots, for I knew that fat scoundrel would want to have a football game! He is aaaaafraid, Allah!'

The starlings attacked the ratty helicopter, but let it go after a shout from Gentl. When Pogo's advanced music got finished, the brass bands took again to the convolutions of subtle rhythm, beauty started with rhythm and not symmetry. The crowds danced under the trains, as Government Crow decided that the engines should do some celebratory flying, up you go and don't touch the chins of the gods. Torro brazenly sent another rat, but it was killed immediately in anger, without the message being heard even; and the starlings sent the dismembered bits of rat back to the irate Torro, who fried it to preserve it for revenge, sharp.

Now now Torro the Terrible was coming, flanked by a small

computer, six large scorpions, and innumerable rats, and he had dragged the ship of truth from the sea, and had fitted it with oval rollers the same shape as Pogo's carrots. The old wreck rolled slowly but threateningly down the valleys, covered in the slime and rust of the metamorphosing sea. Torro stood on deck, carrying a big cutlass exactly the same length as the one used to behead him. He spat every few metres. The hooting and the booing had a stratum of awe, for with his new height and his thickened neck, Torro looked more of a killer than ever.

A sudden shout of frustration from the sky told that General Jolloff had been carried to the moon forcibly, through aMofa Gentl's lunar road, to proceed with the supervision of the children's war, this general who wanted to watch the proceedings right here on earth. And the faded moon was still visible, opening its smallest craters to let the children in . . . but not before Baby Sama had crawled up to Torro's large leg and urinated against it, with his mother fearing for his safety. Torro didn't even feel it – pee pee peeee on an ogre, and he may not even feel it at all!

Gentl watched the proceedings impassively, stroking his snakes without a word, adjusting his small face against all the bigger faces around, his nose standing out as the best brown in the world.

Torro raised both hands high in triumphant acceptance of the jeering, and shouted out over one of his own microphones, which was one of the six scorpions, 'How can you jeeeer at your own Meenister of Defence! I laaave you all very mech . . .'

'Me I think he's talking about the laaavatory . . .' someone interrupted.

'. . . I laaave you, now I want to become a ceetizen!' Torro stopped for effect, rubbing rust off his knees from the ship of truth.

Pogo Forr was now off his horse, and was already busy supervising the erection of the goal posts on the battlefield as well as any other type of middle-thigh erection. He paused to shout at the crowd, 'This is the most leisurely genocide I have ever seen or heard of. Ask Torro to ask his masters questions about the quiet killing of whole peoples . . .'

There was one type of silence for Pogo's truth, and there was another type for Torro's. Torro ignored Pogo and continued, 'I have the power to keel you all, yet because of my laavlaav I do not do eeet. And I have no bosses,' he added disingenuouly, taking out a kente stole and putting it round his neck with ostentation, 'and as Meenister of Defence, I have improved supplies, I have made deescipline better, I have toldtold the secrets of the enemy which ees myself. Don't you want such a useful and friendly enemy to fight weeth, no! And your elders are not fools to appoint me as the boss for your armed forces . . .'

'So that they can watch you better,' a voice interjected.

'. . . for they know that as soon as they start fighting me directlee, they will lose the war.'

Pogo shouted into Torro's ear, 'Torro my enemy brother, are you here to lecture or to make a duel?' Then he took out the golden ball and placed it in the centre of the field. He sat on it.

'Peeeep, peep!' whistled the fat rat with darkglasses on. It said, 'It is a foul against Mr Pogo . . .'

'But the game hasn't started yet!' roared the crowd.

'Ah, precisely!' squeaked the rat. 'It is a pre-foul. How dare Mr Pogo sit on his own ball just because it's golden!'

'If this is how you are going to referee the match, we shall blast you!' shouted the people.

'Try it!' replied the defiant rat. 'I am in charge of the duel match . . .'

'No you are not, the major is. You are only the referee,' another voice shouted. The golden horse and the ship of truth had now been moved to the touchline. The trains were quiet and cooling in each other's steam.

A great roar went up as Pogo Forr removed his robes to reveal a silken outfit of red, gold, and green with a small carrot necklace. Everybody could tell that General Jolloff was eating in the sky, for rice fell out of the invisible moon. Pogo ran round the park, newly marked out, showing his massive thighs to trotting effect. The proverbial butterflies were coming out of Torro's anus, but this time they were hidden, and sent near flowers for natural effect. When the referee stood next to the ball, it couldn't be seen not even in its darkglasses, so it was given a motor-bike with which to control the match. The camel was the only linesman. 'Peeep!' whistled the motor-biking referee, after Torro had taken that pre-foul.

'The ball is too heavy!' screamed Torro; and the referee whistled in agreement, while the camel threw up its hump in exasperation.

Pogo said not a word, retrieved the ball, and peeled layers of gold from it.

'Is that light enough?' he asked.

Before Pogo could move Torro had already rushed past him, with his equally massive thighs, and put the ball in the net for the first goal. There was an enormous silence.

'This referee wants us to destroy him even while the game is so young . . .', someone said with suppressed anger.

'Cheer for your meenister!' shouted the triumphant Torro, rubbing his scorpion necklace. The camel jumped over its own hump irate. Then they all saw General Jolloff come hurtling out of the moon, for he had finally escaped from the children to come and watch these important proceedings. He had rice in his eyes, as he looked at Bianca looking at him. Bianca was sitting in a neutral corner, with her children ignoring her, but was prepared, out of duty, to go and massage her husband's back if necessary.

Delali had just arrived, and was chatting with Ama Three. Pogo placed the ball at the centre, and wiped his face. Then the ball disappeared before everybody's eyes. The muttering was moving into consternation when the golden orb suddenly appeared; right in Torro's net. There was a small silence before the great roar of jubilation. Pogo had scored, using the new magic of his oval carrot necklace! The referee rode in bewildered circles but, after seeing the grave look on Major Gentl's face, pointed to the centre spot, as Torro spat at it, some intimidating spittle koraa.

Ama and Delali chattered about their husbands' noses intimately; and then wondered how tortuous the next strategy was going to be.

The new man that came on the new land had refused to come and watch the duel; and so far it had proved physically impossible to move him on to the land of the city. He always ate with his hand propping up his chin kuse-kuse. A tiny house had been made for him, and they almost built it on his back because he had refused to move from the appropriate spot for it. His favourite occupation was refusing. Major Gentl knew that this man said 'I refuse' one thousand times a day, but he was waiting to see whether a second bit of land would come, and with a better man or woman on it.

Gentl strolled between Ama and Delali, and felt some love paa boxed in between them, but his mind was elsewhere, his mind in fact was round: right on the golden ball which Torro now tapped from the centre and lunged to the left with; the universe was a feint. Torro was moving with such surprising speed that they had to look at his feet again: he was wearing computer-controlled roller skates which kept the ball almost glued to his foot. Up rose a roar of anger from the spectators of war. Torro went one way, the ball went another . . . then the ball followed him to the wing, it followed him to the inside left, it followed him when he wiggled to the left, it never left him. Then there he was moving full speed 440 towards Pogo's goal. Pogo was desperate. He suddenly whirled away from Torro, and signalled to the golden horse; the horse raised its forelegs . . . and the ball rose and landed on Torro's head.

'Head it, you beef man!' taunted Pogo, 'Head it sharp.'

Pogo then gave a huge jump, turned horizontal in this millionaires' game of history, and then headed the ball with his carrot-hard head poised for the goal.

'GOAOAOAL!' roared the crowd as the ball shot into the net, with the referee driving away from Torro in terror. And the golden horse put its front legs down for the ball to descend.

'If you produce a move I will market it into your own goal,' screamed the jubilant Pogo forr nothing, Forr or rrof it's all the same. *If the life had to be backwards before you won it, then so be it, so be the language.*

Then there was a crisis: Torro had swallowed the ball, and run into Pogo's goal and had lain down, with his hands saying it was an indeesputable goal. The crowd had spilled on to the pitch, but the camel galloped everyone off with its humpish arrogance, shouting, 'One man's indisputability is another man's cheating!'

Torro regurgitated the ball, and trotted contemptuously into his half. The frightened referee whistled for a goal as the motor-bike spluttered with the disbelief in its fuel: it knew that the petrol and the oil were lying about this goal.

'This is not a goal, this is a laog, l-a-o-g! Ataamme!' came the cross shout among the crowd's cross chattering, criss.

The crises on the pitch continued: Torro wanted to make a substitute, knowing well that there were only two players, one on each side.

'But do not forget, I am an original Italiano whitebred in some South African city, and always loafing about in a jam. What I want to do ees to substitute myself with myself . . .'

'Why not subsitute yourself with one of your rats, no difference,' Pogo said with his eye still on the ball.

'I inseest I must substitute myself with myself, immediato!' Torro persisted, ordering a rat to fetch his special camera from the ship of truth.

Then out came the camera. He called Bianca to take a picture of him without delay, for she looked reluctant, and as usual ready to show gross signs of independence in public. But she took the photograph all the same. And then lo! what came out was not a picture but a full-size clone of Torro. There were two big Torros on the park! THERE WAS TOO MUCH OF TORRO FOR TORRO HIMSELF TO MANAGE. When he spat, his double spat. Both of Torro approached Bianca. She screamed, releasing a large complaint that her husband never told her anything about his silly technology; he hadn't even told her where and when she was born yet.

The hooting started as sympathy for Bianca, but ended up as hate for the two Torros. Pogo saw his chance, dribbling both Torro and his visionary clone; and then he gave a perfect shot towards his adversary's goal . . . but then found to his horror that a steam train had crossed Torro's goal inadvertently, and stopped the ball. Government Crow pushed the guilty train out of the pitch, but couldn't stop both Torros advancing towards Bianca for a sudden half-time embrace, which they both needed badly because of the hostility they were encountering. How dare they hate the enemy so much, even when they had made him a minister! Just as the two players were walking towards the improvised pavilion, Torro's clone died, and then disappeared altogether.

'Hee has a life of only fifteen minutes, but thees is enough for mee to defeat you all by using only myself! My army will only farm spaghetti for all my different selves, no! Haaa ha!'

Nobody was laughing with Torro except his rats, and the referee. And his belly. *Look at the late afternoon pushing the moon forward, with the children invisible in their noisy wars still without General Jolloff.*

When the second-half started it was seen that Torro had decided to be violent. He rushed at Pogo with two knives, with the ball nowhere in sight. Pogo's shields were carrots. Gentl had risen ready to stop the match because of this violence, but Pogo sent a wink of disagreement, and then he locked thighs with Torro. The gigantic thighs struggled and squeezed, the sound of muscle, flesh, and skin multiplying in the microphone. Somehow they locked left thighs as well, with cramp attacking both of them, and throwing them to the ground, writhing. Then hup-up rose Pogo in agony but with the ball still at his feet. He rushed with his limping muscles, and scored his third goal. The crowd went wild with delight – two troubles one god for Torro – and the referee disappeared out of fright, leaving his motor-bike to do his job.

'No more tricks!' ordered the bike, snarling its engine at both players. 'If you think you can bamboozle me easyeasy like my rat ratter rattest master, then you lie finish! We shall have a straight dirty game, with trips allowed, I swear, but no gadgets, no animals, no magic, no nothing except Commander Zero . . .'

Gentl remembered the commander again. Where was Zero going? Just as he asked himself this there was a huge explosion from the direction of Torro's house. Bianca screamed for the second time, and she could feel her children stiffen in the moon. Torro called for the telephone on the pitch, and just before he started to speak, he released a powerful shot, even with his painful thighs, and the ball raced into the net. The cycle blew through its throttle for the goal.

In the silence that followed, the telephone told Torro that the computer which stored all the important information on Torro's main adversaries had been blown up by Commander Zero now now now. And Pogo had won the duel three-two.

ZONE THIRTEEN

The serious conventional war

After the duel all strategies changed, for Torro had announced that he was now going to fight a serious conventional war, as far as possible; and he had also insisted that he was perfectly sure about his resignation as Minister of Defence. He announced that he was going to mount a campaign to win his children back, and that his dual position as both enemy and minister was getting in the way of this campaign.

Before the elders of government had given any answer, Torro had rushed to the office of his deputy Commander Zero and declared, 'Now you will be made meenister, and I will then have the chance of cutting off your head too. Now I am deputy everytheeng: I am deputy rat, I am deputy Bianca, I am mama mia deputy toilet, and I am the deputy ship of truth. I say thees because after my defeat I will defect to the second of everytheeng until I win the war and become numero uno! My rat was telling mee I should become deputy to my own peenis, but that animal is mad! If it's not careful, I will keel it for the other rats to eat, mangiare! As for Gentl and Pogo and Grandmother Boooomb, I will destroy them, rapido.'

Zero had said nothing, he just gave his popylonkwe a wild scratch . . . and then hopped straight on to Torro's desk, in case he was telling the truth about the elevation to minister. Another very good reason that Zero didn't like Torro very much was that Torro had an extremely long umbrella, so long that it went beyond the clouds giving the rain in the first place; and this made Torro superiorly wet, for who dared not admire a whole minister who was not afraid of rain, and was in fact on the contrary positively attracting it. Torro would love headlines like 'Minister gets wet out of love and patriotism for the city, for his umbrella is too high!' And 'The minister is our biggest enemy.' Torro now loved to run round red roses, and stand behind the biggest petals to eat beef.

When the elders were talking about money to finance the new strategies, Jogo Digi blew his nose very loudly, nostril finance, and insisted that there was too much linear thinking. After which the compromise was that the golden cockroach and Government Crow should strike up an alliance, the object of which was to loosen things up a bit, and to treat all established relationships as unsacred, some disestablishmentarianistic cockroach and crow. The crow loved it, but the golden cee was rather haughty, wondering how an emblem was being suddenly linked with some feathered physicality. An owl, even if silver, was bad enough. Now a crow too, Ewurade! So Government Crow went and bought a kilo of tomatoes and dumped it right in front of Mr Cee the golden.

Mr Cee took a whole hour to chop one tomato, casting looks of scorn at Crow, and not saying a word. Crow almost burst under the silence, flapping its wings noiselessly to let the pressure of the silence escape. Government Crow opened and closed its beak with several silent words. Golden cee enjoyed its discomfort enormously, the up and down of its jaws duplicating the flapping of crow's wings; flip flop flip flop, went the crow's wings, like some walking chalewate of the sky; strong winds would come and blow the language back down the throat of the beaky crow, kwankwaa.

Then old crow couldn't bear it any longer, and shouted to golden cockroach, 'I know you are an important cockroach whose genitals are gold, but respect me, respect me, for we have been given an alatulala task to be as foolish as possible, so that wisdom may come out of the foolishness. Let me tell you also that as Government Crow I have had air-conditioning installed in my belly! Everything about me is cool except my beak, so I respect you, you respect me. True or no true?'

The golden cockroach had crawled inside the tomato most dedeeede, so that it could eat it faster, but it jumped out in spillings of red juice, and then translated the jump into wisdom: 'Let us be wise, old crow. If you hadn't brought me your sudden tomatoes, I would never have spoken to you. I value my own gold. Now, what we are going to do is to get rid of this mad silver owl, silly silver, by feeding it with toffee from the children's war, and if it eats too much, its beak will get stuck and it will not be able to blow its diamond whistle, which Torro the Gorro has sworn he would get back. Now, what sort of ideas have you got for us to make our short rule together memorable?'

Government Crow laughed, and then made the first disconnection. 'Don't broach the subject while I'm wearing my first brooch. Isn't it beautiful? It was given to me by Mrs Wife for the distinction of supporting positively other people's wisdom with my madness, I swear! She told me that apart from the constant marriage ceremonies that her husband Chairman Kot troubled her with, she otherwise felt she was leading too perfect a life . . . I am offering my crowbrooch as the first contrast to bamboozle the antidisestablishmentarians, if there are any: beautiful pendant, ugly neck, eh!'

The cockroach had a tiny laugh like a jug that it used to pour scorn on others. It had acquired some extra scorn from Nana Mai free; which of course hurt it, for Nana Mai was so serious about laughing its love away, boof. Imagine rejecting golden love, hmmm.

The first place the team went to was Pogo Alonka Forr's house. First of all they ordered the foundations of the house to cease being foundations for things were now different; but the order had to be rescinded for Pogo was livid that his glass house was shaking, and had indeed thrown a frozen oval carrot around the duo to freeze their actions. The golden cockroach had absolutely no problem with this level of technology, since for the last few months it had been practising against a possible invasion from the barbarian hordes overseas. So it jumped through the force of the carrot, but the crow was stuck with its wings aflap, until it too was pushed through the force by Mr Cee. Pogo stood there thick-thighed and immensely popular from his victory in the duel.

'O, I didn't know it was the emblem itself that I was trying my carrots on! Sorry, your worship. Forgive me, exercise your forgivability on me! Now what did you disturb my foundations for? Please come in and let me offer you something before I ask your mission which I know already of course. Come in, and be careful with the glass, for some of it is so clear that you may be tempted to try and walk through it . . . akwaaaba! Isn't my wife beautiful and understanding even though she's always accusing me of being girl orientated and she's never seen me doing it? Allah be kind to my robes.'

After drinking water followed by orange juice, the golden cee went straight to the point.

'Do your carrots fit into the general strategies as elements of defence or attack? Do you think it's necessary to have such high ambition in a city like Achimota City? . . .'

'What about you, Mr Golden Cockroach, do you think it's proper to be chasing one of the elders of government when it is quite clear that she is beyond love? . . .' Pogo asked defiantly.

Government Crow looked expectantly at the golden cockroach, and then said, 'Pogo Alonka Forr, myself here and the golden cockroach have for the next few days the highest authority in the land! We do not need searching questions on OUR foundations! We are doing a report, which I will write with my beak when we finish commoting you and the others. Be patient, siabots, let your heart lie down!'

When Government Crow laughed, it was a cackle, its tongue held the laughter free, it licked the sound. Pogo remained sceptical, overusing his eyes on the sun and adoring it.

'We are with you here if you care to listen, Alonka Forr,' said the golden cee, correcting Pogo's eyes. 'Maybe if we tell you what we think, then we can help you answer our questions . . . One of the joys of being a judge is to grin ruefully at your own secret faults while you deal with the faults of others. I talk true. Now, with you, when I fly high and look down, I am not sure whether you are with the sun or with us! You say the oval carrots are for the war, but are you not in preparation for an ambitious assault on the sun . . .?'

'Do you want me to be meek or what?' Pogo interrupted irritably, his crossed legs doubling in the sideways glass.

'O no!' shouted the roach of the skies, 'With your absolute pride that will be impossible! But to go back to your carrots, we contend that your oval carrots golden or not should be used purely for defence in the war . . .'

Pogo broke in again, changing his piercing look to Crow

'Are you trying to tell me that you do not trust my weapons in attack? You want to limit me to defence so that you can control my power? How kwasia can we get? I have spent years developing my powers towards victory, and then you tell me I should be defensive! I know one person who will not like what you are saying, even though she is sometimes suspicious of me.'

'And who may this person be?' asked Government Crow with a wild frown.

Pogo hesitated, getting up and pacing up and down, basaaa. He replied, 'Nana Mai!'

Both the golden cockroach and old crow laughed hard.

130

'Nana Mai! This is richer than abenkwan! This old lady who considers your money-making suspicious? Ahhh!' Crow exclaimed.

'She may wrongly consider my economics suspicious, but not my politics,' Pogo retorted, his eyes back at the sun again, high, 'and I'm a hero! I don't need an elevated insect and a dirty crow questioning the very foundations of my life . . . besides, while on my golden horse I once saw the golden emblem now before us here surreptitiously eating Nana Mai's underwear washed out on the clothes-lines . . .'

There was an ominous silence as Mr Cee crawled out in its awesome anger between two lizards leaving its imprint on both, hard, as the lizards struggled to survive the terrible press of gold. It crawled back in laughing, with a threat in its laugh, saying, 'Pogo Forr! You and me, we have our gold in common, and I once tried to give you the power to defeat Torro swiftly, but it is this same powerpower that got in the way . . .'

'I have a photograph of what I'm saying,' Pogo declared with one hand on one thigh.

Government Crow, still angry about being called dirty, stiffened the government in its beak, and looked askance at the golden cockroach. Was Mr Cee a pioto eater true?

'Get the photo!' ordered Mister Gold the eternal crawler with all its ambition in its flying.

'What is he talking about, this Pogo?' asked old crow as Pogo stormed out with confidence to produce the said photo.

The fact that the cockroach gave no answer confused the crow more. They kept the silence cool for Pogo to return to; and outside the golden horse jumped about and reared in different directions, for it never had a golden mare.

'Go and ride my golden horse, you golden cockroach, gold crawl to gold gallop!' Pogo laughed, coming in holding the photograph.

No one saw Mr Cee give the photograph such an intense scrutiny with the eye and with the feelers that it started to feel hot in the hands of the unsuspecting Pogo. Pogo let it drop with a little shout, 'The sun has come on to the photo koraa!'

Pick it up and show it to us, let us see me the golden emblem eating the green lady's underwear! I believe for once you have me trapped, or so you think!' Mr Cee said slowly, its inner proboscis on fire with feeling.

Alonka Forr picked up the picture equally slowly, and then handed it over to Government Crow triumphantly. Old Crow gave a peck and a long look, looked up with bewilderment, took out its spectacles from under its wing, looked again, and then returned the triumph to Pogo by shouting, 'Pogo Alonka of Gari! You have defamed the character of the golden cockroach. Look! I see no cockroach in this picture! Look!' Alonka snatched the photograph.

His great gaze found no golden cockroach in the photograph either, this same photo that he himself had taken.

'Delali, Delaliiiiii!' Pogo called, 'Who has taken the golden cockroach from my picture here?'

Delali ambled in, expecting her husband to be riding his golden horse in the sitting-room as usual. But she just found him agitated. She transferred her quizzical look to her hands as she was given the photo to scrutinise. She kept the quizz in her face. Then sauntered back out to return to her sleep, without a word.

Pogo suddenly exclaimed, 'I hold your foot sir! Mr Golden Cock, I bow down to you! Your magic is definitely photographical! I beg bag bog beg you!'

'I do not accept your apology,' declared Mr Cee, looking immensely authoritative, smoking its sikadillos with its legs, 'I demand that you get on your knees first.'

Pogo the bewildered looked at it with a look that went further than what he was looking at. If he knew what the puzzle was he would keep the puzz in his face; but it changed to anger.

'What? Me the golden carrot hero kneel down to you? Never! How dare you come to my house to disgrace me immediately after my moments of triumph on the football park! I do not accept your mouth about making my gifts defensive. I will retain my ambition. You have intruded into my life, so now detrude!'

Old crow wanted a compromise, so he said to the thick thighs of Pogo, 'Why don't you give us half a kneel then? How can we upset you when we need you? The principle must be accepted: when you are wrong, you pay the price!'

'Shall we agree on a tenth of a kneel?' asked Mr Cee scornfully. 'Well . . . let's be going, this is the second time Pogo Forr is refusing to do something for me . . .'

Then, without any warning whatsoever, Delali walked in carrying her

132

sleep behind her, and knelt before Mr Cee, her hands in her hair. They all stared unbelieving, and she didn't say a word.

'Up, Delali, up!' screamed Pogo after he had recovered himself. But Delali couldn't get up: she had fallen asleep instantly, in her supplicatory kneel before the golden emblem. In his rush to pick her up Pogo tripped over his side-table, sprawling prostrate before the golden cee.

'Ah!' roared Mr Cee. 'Now we have our apology full length! He didn't want to kneel, he only wanted to crawl on his belly to me for forgiveness! This is the time to leave. Pogo, think of our points, and contact me soon! Look at me, I am flying, kneeling Pogo! Your pretty wife can sleep peacefully in her genuflection! And one more thing: I am sure you don't want me to tell Nana Mai that you have a secret photo of her underwear . . . She would be furious, angrier than Allah in his righteousness!'

Golden cockroach and Government Crow flew off laughing, with the silver owl appearing from nowhere to join them, its toffee all finished. Pogo restood in his own anger. He took hold of the photo, lit a match and burned it. But he couldn't restrain a scream when he saw that the photo had reappeared. He burned it again; it reappeared again. Delali awoke to find Pogo screaming to the sun, 'O great sun, what am I to do with this difficult insect? What am I to do?' She held him and held him until he laughed at her stupor. Then he went to sleep on top of her, lungulungu.

Golden cockroach and Government Crow had already reached Nana Mai's straight-road residence. The crow had eaten a lizard to celebrate the involuntarily prostrate nature of Pogo Forr's last forgiveness. Nana Mai had finally released the physics-door, and the professors there had now been freed to copy her ideas anytime they wanted. She had also thrown Torro through her hole in the sky, for she promised she would do so to the loser of the duel. He had returned painfully covered with clouds, and was using powerful fans in his house to blow them off him.

'Nana we greet you-oooo, we adore your elevation to the eldership. We understand you have appropriated the ship of truth for two days with all the crabs in it and even sharks . . . We are just coming from Pogo Forr's house . . .' said the golden cockroach.

'And Pogo had a picture of . . .' began the garrulous crow.

'. . . of you in a lily field with young guava trees, looking wonderful,' completed Mr Cee, glaring at the crow as Nana Mai stroked her mathematical parrot.

133

'Akwaaba Mr Golden Cockroach, akwaaba Mr Crow. Do you like the sound of my cornmill? I believe the decibels are purely African. I am trying to marry . . .' began Grandmother Bomb.

'Marry who?' asked Mr Cee in consternation.

'. . . to marry the sound with the sound of my parrot at different octaves. What will you have to drink? We are entering a new era, are we not? Please sit on my rotating chairs, and go round the world in my sitting-room,' the old lady said, her voice even deeper this morning, 'and don't be surprised if you hear I have become a Double Grandmother Bomb, because I fear that my daughter will very soon have another child. I had the shock of my life when she came to tell me that my two ex-husbands had approached her to approach me to approach their love. Ewurade! They both want to come to me together! And since they have heard that I no longer have a physics-door, they have applied to be my door, my husbands want to be my doors, want to stand eternally and be opened and closed . . . well, that's life.'

Crow laughed.

What a fine ironic smile came from Double Grandmother Bomb-to-be, and she filled the pause with it, you solo smile; for her visitors didn't join her.

'Nana Mai, we know you are the newest elder, and that we must tread carefully with you,' began the golden cockroach, 'but we want to know why you have never made any money at all in these two wars . . .'

Nana Mai didn't hear a word, for she had gone into the dining-room to have a bite of cashew fruit fresh.

'Do not ask Grandmother Bomb this question, she will thunder with anger, and then send you to ask Mr Pogo the opposite,' warned the parrot, scrutinising an advanced book on mathematics. It pecked the theorems.

Government Crow nudged golden cockroach but the nudge went to the other elbow, for the latter insisted on asking a similar question when Nana Mai returned wiping her mouth, in her restrained blue cloth with its matching duku.

'Nana Mai Sir – Woman Why do you live alone like this? Don't you think that, with your new position, you need the softening influence of something more human than a parrot and a cornmill . . .?'

'Be quiet,' Nana Mai said in a quiet controlled voice, brushing the upper feathers of her parrot, and taping the music of the cornmill. She

134

had taken on a massive silence, silence so strong that Government Crow wanted to run away from it. The chairs rotated uselessly as the Grandmother Bomb Double stared absolutely still at Mr Cee. Mr Cee returned the stare with ease, so that the double staring looked like two spears touching points hard and never giving.

Government Crow looked at one set of eyes, then the other set. It asked, as Nana Mai's face broke into a benign smile, 'Nana Mai, please allow your parrot and me to share the staring that has come between you and the golden cockroach, so that you can both get on with the important business. And if the parrot were not the same sex as me I would have loved paa to mate with it across the barrier of species . . .'

The multiplication parrot jumped with disgust, buiei.

'I thought you had come to ask me about what I was doing, not how I live,' Nana Mai said still smiling, but with an indefinable threat in her smile. A frown of friendship took the face of Mr Cee. Poor Cee, he had tried so often to win Nana Mai that asking her questions now from a position of authority just felt uncomfortable; as if she had some knowledge about his rejected heart that she could use any time she wished. Nevertheless the frown was one of friendship.

'The biggest thing I'm worried about overseas – when will we ever remember the names of these places? – is the series of biological changes they are planning on themselves. My parrot is not as efficient as the golden cockroach, but when I sent it in spirit – I'm trying to perfect the science of sending the mind and keeping the body still – it brought me this news: it's a secret they keep even from their own people: they are working on making it impossible to refer to us all as one human species. They hope that very soon some races will not be able to mate with others. They are not satisfied with stealing intellectual energy to burst out of the galaxy; they want to press ahead with biological changes to augment the barriers they have put around themselves physically . . . it is these silly exclusivist and deadly games they play that keep me working. And you know where they have based most of their sensitive experiments?' Nana Mai spoke in a sort of slow sad voice.

'Of course I know!' Mr Cee replied impatiently, for Nana Mai was now talking about his special subject. 'That is why I am the emblem in the first place, I am the emblem of survival . . . they are doing their most dangerous experiments in the capital of Africa South . . . I confirm fully what you are saying.'

There was a small pause, during which Mr Cee's eyes became rather misty. He continued, 'And it is because of our expertise that I keep offering you love . . .'

Government Crow shot up, and shouted, 'The sooner they change themselves as human beings maybe the sooner they will leave us alone!'

The parrot snorted at the intelligence of the crow, but it couldn't be ironic about crows and cockroaches and parrots talking about the ultimate existence of all human beings, for the simple reason that animals and human beings and everything else had a perfect balance in Achimota City, had an almost perfect whole.

'Torro must be destroyed in the new strategies, for he and his masters are beginning to be more direct in their assaults and in their terrible assertions,' Grandmother Bomb declared, rising, and adding, 'I have talked enough now, I am going to work on a new gun. Mr Golden Cockroach, make more use of the major's lunar rooms, and make sure the children become more powerful! We are going to be so careful in battle that sometimes only one soldier will be sent to the battlefield to fight at a time. One soldier, one rabbit, according to Major Gentl. And I insist that the new man on the new land should be sent back to find more information for us. We have only got a few months to perfect our strategy!'

Government Crow and golden cockroach suddenly parted under Nana Mai's excitement, for they felt it was no longer necessary to be formally disestablishmentistic; relations were odd enough, euphoric enough in bits to meet the new strategies of the Second War of Existence.

ZONE FOURTEEN

The mighty battle

It was when Torro the Terrible installed tiny lights on his teeth to brighten his smile that Major Gentl became certain that he, Torro, was actually planning a conventional war with a normal invasion, the result of which was supposed to be this: Torro would win Achimota City at last, rule it cruelly and capriciously, and then, having thus reestablished his reputation overseas, would turn over the city, but still as some viceroy-bi, to his masters for a haven of nuclear survival, and for western fun with eastern backing or indifference. It was a cheap and tragic history that had stolen the people and the lands of this country, and Major Gentl would shake with anger and swear that they were not going to take what was left too. His anger was in his gentleness.

Gentl had to think faster than he was eating groundnuts, for he had been told to assume the formal post of Commander of the Armed Forces, as well as Minister of Defence: how could a man who had left the army so angrily, and who was not the least bit interested in posts and status be put in formal positions like these? he asked himself, shaking his small head to make the chewing more complex.

Some of the bamboo in aMofa Gentl's house of bamboo had taken root and was growing heartily, thus creating kinetic walls that gave strange patterns to the whole building. Some seasons he had to trim the house, other seasons he left the small sharp leaves to command the entire place, with new shoots strengthening the walls and giving them a future. Beyond the groundnuts he was eating was a plate of gari, sardine, and shitoh half-eaten, with the other half resembling the shape of his profile in thought. So his bites defined his face koraa.

There sat Major Gentl as helicopters cut the sky round, with the sparse clouds bearding them. The heavens were crowded with missiles being sent somewhere beyond the moon, since it had been mutually agreed that they were not needed in a conventional war with extenuating magic. All these weapons of death being ferried across the sky were getting smaller and smaller and yet more potent, small to such an extent that very soon a child could carry the biggest bomb in one hand, and vindicate Nana Mai's heroic science for survival, sardonic weapons that were never used. Ama Three had continued to be solicitous, even beyond the stew in the evenings, when she used to rush to polish Torro's boots for the wars of the morning. Now she stayed, polishing Gentl's boots instead, sometimes one in the morning, and one in the evening; and she would even polish the undersoles, so that people could see her goodness as her major stepped off the earth with each raised foot. Once the poor major had to wear darkglasses against his own boots, both under and over. Gentl was wondering whether it was possible to plan at all against an enemy that was once necessarily one's Defence Minister . . . but stopped himself by reiterating that the strategies that went before were necessary too. When you treated your enemy's children for malaria, you certainly found out something about him; and realised your moral position vis-à-vis his as well. In a time of indirect but lethal war, sympathy at the right time was an attack, especially when it was sincere. But since the major himself knew that he could be sincere with almost anything, from bananas to camels, he decided that the only way he could carry out his new functions successfully was to break up this sympathy – so powerful against the subtleties of the first war – into minute grains that came out for people, things, or animals, without changing the thrust of the strategy needed for victory in the conventional war. Thus his mildness did not negate his anger for victory; nor did it negate his vast need for boiled groundnuts this particular day, and one nut devoured could be equal to one soldier in a platoon. Nuts and guns walai.

The major had thus become more aggressive, especially in style if not in heart. His deputy remained Commander Zero, now at his side, his shadow pungent with nothing. Zero had advanced one step, even though he was disappointed that he was not appointed a substantive minister: he actually had an independent shadow now, his substance could cast shadows, except of course for his popylonkwe which had remained the last tip of insubstantiality, for the simple reasons that the right women kept rejecting him for the wrong reasons. One of the first things aMofa Gentl did was to dismiss one thousand rabbits from the army for indolence; they had done nothing but eat carrots since the Second War of Existence began, and were banished just beyond

Government House to a new honeyhood . . . with a chance to return to the front once each had carried one hundred kilos of honey on its back.

When General Jolloff was transferred from the children's war to a battalion, he joyfully announced, with his moustache fully starched and fully grown again, that he had added another item to his obsession with rice: beans. Everybody in the batallion had to be able to spell, eat, and grow rice and: beans. *But don't get the general wrong.* He had worked out a series of astounding manoeuvres which involved marching diagonally uphill, flanking the entire military unit with anthills as a camouflage, and then having the whole armoured unit disappear miraculously inside a huge swamp, vehicles and all, with breathing made possible by thousands of plastic bags with air, emptied of their contents: beans.

Pogo Forr had been overjoyed to be given an entire brigade, which made him only slightly lower in status than Major Gentl. He was a member of the army council, and he counselled everybody, and cancelled little strategies at will; but he was smart enough to consult the major at every twist and turn. Government Crow had been more or less anointed and appointed the commander of a platoon of crows for being able to destroy, merely by pecking, several brain machines of Torro's, machines that were so sophisticated that it would sometimes be possible to destroy them by extremely simple means. Simple pecks of the century that made several Achimota City brains freer.

The platoon of crows could be deadly for another reason: they caused the first deaths of the war by attacking and pulling out the eyes of twenty of Torro's soldiers. Major Gentl had stood there stunned as the crows brought the eyes back, all forty of them, white Azanian eyes with the hate and contempt still glaring through; and you could tell by their eyes that they died more or less still racist.

The Gentl commander of the armed forces was appalled at the brutality of the deaths, but he immediately promoted the crows concerned, and warned them that there was always a humane way of reaching victory. The crows had accepted the promotion, but had risen to the skies in revolt against the admonition from their commander about brutality.

'Major, Major,' cackled the crows, 'do you want us to win the war or don't you? There are rumours that Torro is going to perpetrate some atrocities by killing a child and a rabbit with one knife just to warn us. Major beware-Ooo, beware!'

Poor Gentl: sometimes his mildness led to the assumption that he had no history of success, as if he couldn't deal with camels that rode him in return for being ridden, or with the wild people overseas that wanted his destruction. He rose from his cane chair and ambled over to that small board leaning against the garden hedge, on which he had written something for the education of the marauding crows: humanity and cunning equalled peace, invention, and pineapples. The crows had laughed and laughed, bisecting each other's beaks in great mirth, and asking of the major, 'Major, would you like us to peck out their balls instead, shuashua! Hahaha!'

Gentl had thought that they wanted to test his eyes against the horizon. He had risen and had suddenly given the crows concerned duties in the stores, much to their anger, for it was intolerable that the stores were on the moon . . . crowded in a crater at that. And the neems threw their shades at the pines, and all the branches fitted better in shadow than in substance. It could be Zero's soul in the trees.

The major suddenly dashed to the nearest hill to signal to Pogo to signal to Zero who had equally quickly rushed to the battlefield, for they had all heard the sound of planes. Their own aeroplanes were to exercise discipline by flying AWAY from their targets as often as possible, not only to draw the enemy out, but also to have a strategy of wings that was the opposite of the opposite of what the enemy expected instantly. Twenty crows were to make the shapes of aeroplanes, and were to whine like jets, to bamboozle the enemy; but at the same time, real planes were to be mixed with them. And Government Crow and its subordinate feathers were so good at their metal mimicking that Torro couldn't even tell the difference. He just said to himself with scornful laughter: 'How stupid of Gentl and Nana Mai to make some planes softer than others'. As for his radar, it just kept presenting figures of crabs, because that was precisely what preceded the aeroplanes; crabs joined claw to claw also in the shapes of aeroplanes, with taped drones so false that Torro was sure that such an elementary trick would not have any reality behind it. But it was precisely this trick that led to the death of Torro's fourth-favourite rat when Gentl's bombs dropped. Torro raged and roared, and buried the rat, with revenge written under its name. This could be the beak and claw war with diagonal movements of winning grace, ampa.

The next move was contributed by trees. aMofa the major planned to extend very quietly the branches and twigs of selected trees, with strong cardboard, right into enemy territory. Each cardboard, attached to its branch by invisible joints, was to take the shape of the attachment, the only difference being that it tapered off smoothly into nothing, just as a real branch would; and weapons and rabbits were hidden inside the cardboards, so that when the trees thus eventually groped to Torro's camp, it wouldn't be difficult for the rabbits to destroy hundreds of Torro's men with the bullet trees. Some crows perched on the extendable cardboard just for authenticity. One tree lost its bearings and ended up groping the moon with its cardboard, but that was also another type of authenticity, anything to trick Torro into chopping his beef as if nothing odd was happening, some obvious beef arrogance sparkling in the wrong way to the right of the fire. Sobolo! As far as Torro was concerned the war could be one hundred thousand chews, with dry red wine following, for in spite of the numerous setbacks, he never doubted that victory would be his.

But hundreds of his men perished when the branches opened fire, with the perching crows joining in and shooting with the small guns hidden in their beaks. Two dead men propped each other upright. Torro rushed about hacking the branches and shooting the crows, with a peculiar merriment in his helmet, for he was glad that at last people were dying; and that he could play with the conventional war easyeasy. And there was no holding back his children, especially Commander Carlo, who continued to whine after his father that he didn't want to fight on his side, and that after he had killed a few men, he would rush back to Commander mMo, whom he loved so much that he would like to fight on the same side as he fought, even if it meant facing his own father in war.

'So you want me keeled?' asked Torro of his son, aghast. Carlo gave silence back as an answer; and in any case Torro's attention had already been won by three consecutive bombs exploding at the same pitch as the deepest notes of Commander Zero's saxophone. And Torro became extremely angry when he realised that it was brass music with bombs in the instruments that was killing his men and his rats. He smoked sideways when he was angry, butterflies coming out of his anus again with warm abandon. Bullets of branch caught some of his soldiers when they stared at him amazed, owuo.

But regardless, Torro decided on a bold step that could put Major

141

Gentl's strategy off balance. He would run through the evening to Gentl's camp to persuade him to do two things of importance: first, to persuade Bianca to stop seeing General Jolloff behind the lines, and, second, to ask permission to bury his dead soldiers on the land of Achimota City, since the new land given to him was too small and too occupied with farming beef for it to be used as a cemetery. After taping a small white flag to his septic neck, Torro the Terrible set out with his rats and his new deputy, a man so like Commander Zero that the only visible difference was colour and saxophone. Even shadows weren't a difference since he also claimed he materialised in Palermo from mafia shadows, shadows of dead mafia families, whose spirits had ended up in Azania . . . but had picked up some Nazi souls on the way to fortify the evil there. Torro was proud of his new deputy whom he was going to spring as a surprise on Gentl.

Torro had two other trumps: he was going to run stark naked to unsettle Gentl, and then while Gentl's army was preoccupied with his nakedness, a brigade of his army would sneak up north behind the home army, and make a brutal surprise attack.

'What a clever accordo we have,' beamed a Tall Alberto the deputy to his boss, 'I worship you and you worship yourself! Maraviglioso! We shall defeat the pride of that old Grandmother Bomb . . .'

'Ah, shut up Alberto you fool, concentrate on watching me run, no!' screamed Torro flaunting his belly to the universe.

Run, run! There was Torro dodging between the evening mosquitoes with his rats and deputy following, and his flag of neck truce blowing up one nostril. Through the swamps, round the neems, across the pines, astride the bananas, jumping the pineapples, went Torro. He was decorated with bulbs as another sign of temporary truce . . . and the socket was in his mouth koraa. The Torro was so confident that when he reached a fine termite bridge he went under it, with his popylonkwe floating menacingly and majestically on the stream.

'Avanto, look at the majesty of Torro the supreme commander, maraviglioso more!' shouted Tall Alberto, so busy staring at his boss that he crashed into a banana tree, and annoyed the former the more.

'Separate yourself from the bananas, and let us proceed,' growled Torro. The joy of the rush to Gentl's camp was getting too much for Torro. He just stood in the stream and cried and cried.

'O supreme commander,' wailed Tall Alberto, 'your tears have made this beautiful corrente too mucho, and thees excess aqua so bizarro has already keelled one of the fat rats, I say mama mia it drown in your eyes!'

Torro looked at Alberto, a fish crawled between the gazing. And it was when his master released a tall kwee that Tallberto realised that another rat had drowned, this time with the speed of the stream rushing faster with Torro's farts.

It was immediately after the three elders of government – minus Nana Mai, and lost in their beards in the twilight – left Major Gentl's table that the crows brought the news ahead of the radar of The Torro's second coming. He was twice because he had been almost electrocuted in the stream with his bulbs, his show-off electricity; and thus had to return to reset the light and travel over the bridge in an orthodox manner. Tallberto had perfected the act of laughing while appearing to be groaning, and the rats had looked suspiciously at him while he laughed in groans at his master's plight. The only way Torro could reprimand the universe was to bellow at the stars to bunch together in the same pattern as his bodybulbs, so that he could at least articulate some sympathy from the neutral heavens. When he spat it was so electric that it reached the moon.

Gentl was amused at Torro's flamboyance, and climbed Commander Zero's saxophone mound to receive him. He had just been discussing the matter of the golden cockroach with the elders of government who'd just gone. The golden cockroach was inexplicably trapped in orbit above the city by a force that no one understood, not even itself; and there too was the silver mosquito equally trapped in a corresponding orbit. And if the golden cockroach would laugh at all in its new plight, it would be a laugh against the silver mosq, which, in spite of its betrayal, its desertion from the role of golden cockroach worship, was now caught in a similarly strange fate. It looked as if the silver owl was not quite sophisticated enough to be trapped at all, for all it was doing was constantly trying to fly in a hopeless manner to the orbiting cockroach. The diamond whistle had been retrieved by Torro who promised the owl that it would one evening wake up and find its head cut off.

At first the entire city panicked when it saw the golden Mr Cee tied in the sky with golden string; but things calmed down a little when the Grandmother Bomb announced that she had at last received a weak message from the golden master that the trapping force was from the skies abroad, and that though it was a terrible force that made it difficult to breathe, it was working out a formula to defeat it. If it did not defeat the force soon, it would die, with the silver malaria duplicating its death. Achimota City wailed for the emblem, especially Pogo the golden master number two who, in spite of not working with Mr Cee, received a vast and golden confidence from the crawling embodiment. Gentl had never doubted the power of Mr Cee to see beyond the stars but this time he showed his worry by deciding on a series of fast intuitions that he hoped would reflect the subtleties of Mr Cee's brain. Gentl had to crawl to think, sharing the ground with frogs, lizards, crow dung, cricket droppings, the shit of wise sparrows, and worm tunnels.

This evening aMofa Gentl wore a bofrot at each shoulder to emphasise the perishability of man and woman. The intuition he had as he waited for Torro was that whole platoons of soldiers would be ironing dead cockroaches when Torro arrived. Real cockroaches. Thus the army ironed insects with verve. This ironing was another way for a deflected intensity to pass, another wile for attacking the target by looking away from it. How old would you want your war to be before you won it? thought Gentl, with one foot lower on the mound than the other, and the camel with the eyes of effrontery leaning against him nonchalantly. He caught sight of Torro weaving in and out of horizons, with his bobbie-stand bulbs made translucent by vapour and distance. Sometimes when the rats gathered thickly in front of him, they hid him altogether. His deputy's head continued to sail over the trees talltall, and laughing into the spaces that his master was not looking in.

'He's coming-Oooo!' screamed the crows, under the authority of Government Crow with new perfume under its wingpits.

Everybody stood at a guarded attention except those planning and those ironing the cockroaches. There was a grave clap of thunder that the war drums, fontomfrom among the warware, echoed.

As Torro and his band approached, there was a complete silence. You could hear only the sound of bulbs hitting each other on him, and you could smell the small singe of rats that got too close to the lights. Torro saluted with a snort, holding his white flag in his mouth now, and ordering Tallberto and the rats to kneel down immediately in order to pacify the enemy small, this enemy that was always that bit cleverer than he thought.

'Hail to Torro!' said the rats, as Torro crushed one in anger, for he

144

wanted completed silence so that his snorts to Major Gentl could be heard through his tiny nasal microphone, Allah.

While his master and Gentl exchanged salutes and stared at each other, Tallberto couldn't stay still at all. He was moving about in disjointed abandon, looking for Commander Zero, and trying to put his footsteps in his shadow's footprints. Eventually Torro looked at him with an amplified contempt: he was doing little dances, and rushing into obscure corners to search for Zero.

'Why you iron cockroaches, no?' asked Torro suspiciously from behind his bulbs, his white flag in his hand now and being used to blow his nose and to receive a sneeze.

aMofa didn't say a word, he just pointed to Government Crow, which sneezed to answer Torro's. Torro was confused, but was absolutely confident that his army was now crawling right behind Gentl's to prepare itself for the surprise attack. You could see the rats gnawing each other in anticipation, little spurts of blood coming out in the shape of: rats. When Torro saluted for the hundredth time, he was met with salutes from a whole company. With a sudden signal from Gentl to Pogo Forr who had just arrived and was strangely silent – silent with the anger of the need to win, Pogo took a small bugle to his lips. The heat in the irons was suddenly increased, the cockroaches went up in smoke.

This was the sign for the home army crawling round the back of the back-crawling southern army of Torro's to attack. Hundreds of yoyi seeds were thrown up by Gentl's army a mile away, as a diversion: as soon as Torro's army looked up, many of them were shot down. All this went on while Gentl and Torro exchanged polite smiles and vigorous salutes. Torro's rats had rushed away to join the shooting. He suddenly removed two of his bulbs so that he wouldn't crush them when he sat on them. Gentl offered him palm-wine as the war raged.

'Geev me beef, geev me beef!' bellowed Torro, flaunting his nakedness. 'Now Major Gentl, you don't agree that my peeenis is a very fine thing, eet goes weeth my new title of Supreme Commander . . .'

Gentl's snakes rolled among the pockets of war. He himself nodded in rhythm to the swing of Torro's popylonkwe.

'You are short of clothes?' he asked Torro.

Then Gentl had to restrain a pack of commando crows that wanted to destroy Torro's popy. But the latter was quite undisturbed himself. He just pointed triumphantly to the orbiting golden cockroach, and asked

Gentl in a sardonic voice, 'Where ees your elementary power now, Major? I am beginning to tame all your sources of power one by one, ahhh! And I now put my fine white flag on my greatttt peeenis, to show you how much I reeespect your peace, pronto!'

Pogo, seated on his golden horse, stared with disdain at Torro with his pig-bull naked trunk, the treacherous truce flag arranged mockingly on his erect popylonkwe. Before anything could be said Commander Zero jumped into the scene, holding hands with his near-double Tallberto, saying, 'I have decided that this stupid western man-shadow-man Tallberto standing with me here could be an asset to the home army. He could mislead a whole army by his hesitations and his angular bending. He bends when he has to fire, and he fires when he has to bend. I am holding his hand, because it's the safest thing to do to a stupid enemy. Also I have persuaded him that it will be in his interest to resign as Torro's deputy . . .'

Tallberto looked furtively in the direction of his Supreme Commander. There was a silence as Torro growled and fingered three of his returned rats.

'You seelly Alberto, tall fool that you are, this is now the real war, and the days of fighting on the wrong side are past. I weel destroy you with the rest of them. Come and adjust the flag on my peeenis immediately!'

Deputy Tallberto hesitated, and had just started to inch towards his master when Zero pounced on him, shouting, 'Have you no sense being afraid of that mad naked man before us, just because you are both from the same country, and just because he is your boss! He will destroy you whether you are on his side or not . . .'

Tallberto didn't fight back. He extricated himself from the twelve-foot-eight-inch heap of two tall deputies, and continued to inch towards his master. He was crying with the contradiction of loving the home army and yet fearing for his life if he were to desert Torro the Terrible.

'I will serve you till I die, Supreme Commander!' he declared with a sorrow that disappeared with the overstress in his voice.

The evening leaves took the light of the camp over but not under, high but not low.

Torro ignored the menacing staring of Pogo, went over and gave Tallberto a hard kick in the shin to teach him the price of hesitations of loyalty, and then went up to Major Gentl with his flag still erect at his

146

pole, saying, 'Major, congratulations for foiling my surprise attack! I will defeat you soon, haha. My mission begeens with thees request: shoot General Jolloff straight away, for he entertains my wife. And what annoys meee ees that he has never touched her once. Does he not find her attracteeve? How dare he tell Bianca that he finds her fine but that he cannot do anything about hees attraction until after the war! Thees ees an insult to me! Hee doesn't want to do any fikifiki weeth her until I'm out of the way. Hee ees a coward!'

Torro turned round to see where the large growl came from. It was General Jolloff himself, thin before the wind, twirling his moustache in anger, walking east and west, and tossing rice and beans in the air and catching them. Bianca was totally vulnerable behind him, saying constantly to his back, 'Love meee, love meee!'

'You Torro, I am a fierce gentleman, and I was fighting before you were born. I order you not to speak about me like that. I warn you that I will attack you immediately with my sword from the children's war, if you continue to annoy me!'

'Love mee!' wailed Bianca, disregarding Torro completely.

Torro quietly asked three rats to cover his nakedness, for though he tried to hide it, he always felt overawed in the presence of the general. What did you do with a man who seemed so straight that his equally straight moustache made a clean cross out of him? And a man so stiff that his obsession with rice and beans appeared to be mysterious rather than ridiculous; grains of openness that allowed him to admire heroes like Gentl, but simultaneously created a compensatory irony with the likes of Captain Owusu.

'C'mon, move out of my way you Torro before I slice your membership with my sword!' General Jolloff screamed, with a post-anger salute at Major Gentl, and a push of impatience at Captain Owusu his permanent assistant.

There was a look of recognition in the face of Torro who blurted out, 'Ah, now I know where all thees rice and beans, thees riso fagliolino, come from. I find rice and beans in my best computers, I find them in my mathematics, I find them under my pillow! General Jolloff, you are a dangerous man! You try to spoil all my sophisticated machines with your feelthy rice! I even find rice in the river that I cross. Oooo.'

General Jolloff stormed off with the pleading Bianca in tow, as Torro sat on the bare ground with his head in his hands before the impassive Gentl.

'Major,' he began, 'I came to ask you to geev me more land to bury my dead. You people don't want me to love you, eh? Now you are killing the soldiers of your favourite enemeee. Major, I promise you that I will soon show you my full power! I weel blow this whole city apart . . . because I love you so mech, I must teach you a lesson!'

'There's extra land on the moon,' Gentl said without even looking at Torro.

'What! You make me nervoso! Bury my dead on the moon? You insult their memory!' Torro exclaimed in one breath, trying to pick out Pogo Forr from the military crowd; but he couldn't: Pogo was high in the sky with his helicopter, and his golden horse was piloting beside him.

Torro adjusted his bulbs in the pause. 'I can offer you unlimited wealth if you help me not to disappoint my bosses, Major Genteeel!' he whispered to Gentl, and then rose quickly before he could digest the look of extreme aversion on Gentl's face. The bofrots shook on the major's epaulettes. He knew that simple intelligence simple fruit could defeat anything.

The breeze carried aMofa Gentl's anger to the moon and back, leaving it in one eye as Torro stormed off, his mission unaccomplished. Tallberto made a secret sign to Commander Zero that he would be back, and then followed his master back reluctantly. The rats hailed Torro's name, writing it with their dung and in their blood. They bit their own backs to glorify his name, a name that had lost massively in the battle beyond, but which still had supreme confidence in its ability to win. Yet that strange and dangerous love that Torro continued to have for Achimota City, while at the same time wanting to destroy it, polluted the bolas and enriched the sewers. Major Gentl had moved on to the path that led to the GOAT OF MERCY, that bronze goat that took the suffering of those wounded in war. Gentl bathed some of the soldiers and rabbits and crows himself. Nana Mai had received another weak message from the golden cockroach: keep flying at a tangent to the enemy, bury all the real cockroaches sacrificed in the ironing strategy, continue to have that masterful sympathy that won you the First War of Existence; and Pogo is trying to rescue me with a golden carrot, but watch the terrible new onslaught that Torro will launch at lunch one

148

day. Major Gentl had cried at the first deaths in the children's war, and had almost lost his own son Adu with a big wound in the arm. Yet more land arrived as Gentl steeled himself for the bigger push of the war, push, push, push.

Hand-to-hand fighting

The sea washed them apart as they fought in the war, by the firing armies, Gentl and Torro. Torro punched through a fish to the major's jaw; and waves powered the whole punch. Major Gentl bit the sea as he struggled to get a better blow at his favourite enemy. The joy of his hair, trapping the waves and releasing sand instead, tore the deeps and augmented the storm, as the two stalwarts sought their heroism in salt . . . but aMofa Gentl's was a modest salt, more rolls in his heart than the waves.

The tides attacked the tear in Torro's pioto, revealing the great popylonkwe with the ludicrous flag of truce still tied to it. The flag had torn into the flesh and made it misshapen, the tip broadening into the sprays of moonlight in misplaced incandescence. Torro breathed in sea-water and coughed the waves away angrily, his belly getting lost under two waves and being found in a stormy third. The watching ship of truth danced to the punches; it had escaped from Nana Mai's experiments. Torro's neck turned like a bull's in water, in lines of septic pain with a boil to the east of it, and butted Gentl's mouth. Blood came to and from the major as that bit of sea reddened with a shellfish caught in the red. Major Gentl was strong enough, even with his small head, to change the colour of the sea with his blood. He dived with a curse and slid hard on Torro's boil with his boots still on. The sad pus lanced Gentl's fingers, as he rolled angling for the angle of victory. Torro winced but wasn't troubled at all, for he was using a wet computer during this wet fight in the sea: he had arranged just with a press of button, two hundred kenkeys and more banku to surround Gentl in menacing corn to confuse him; for every punch and every lunge of the major ended up in banku ke kommi, some quick fermented deep-sea rolls of corn.

And Major Gentl gave the most amazing historical blow ever seen in the sea, a punch made circular by necessity, and right through the entire banku and kenkey so aggressively surrounding him, with more than a score stuck up to his elbow. There was Gentl with his arms raised, tasting and pushing away the kenkey at the same time, rising with shrimps on his epaulettes, and shouting with a volume over the sea that he didn't usually create, 'If it is shitoh that you want to cover the sea with next time, I will punch at it, I will slap all the pepper off the sea!' Torro laughed and then peed on his computer. He laughed into the high and peppered foam.

And the storm continued over the sea, sending lightning to brighten the intensity of the fight between the two rival panting commanders. Atinga was perched on a stationary wave, waiting to see whether it would be necessary to rescue his master. Torro's rats tore at the jumping fish, standing on their rodent stilts as they looked hungrily at their master. They could eat history if necessary. The ship of truth was moving in somersaults, and as Gentl turned to look at this miracle, Torro gave him a punch that was raw and went through no fish. BOOF! The major reeled, cartwheeling in patterns of wet Adinkra, as the rats stiffened to attack him, and Atinga stiffened to defend. The faithful snakes slid so easily over the waves, rushing to Gentl's side, and swallowing two close rats as a warning to Torro.

'I will geev you a blow with my peeenis right now!' roared Torro trying to outroar the sea.

The lighthouse challenged the moon in the biggest sweeps of light. Torro was holding his popylonkwe ampa, and was aiming it at Gentl, who was still dazed. He, The Torro, now had motorised buttocks from an instant machine installed in his anus, and he was racing towards Gentl, with his flag-bedecked popylonkwe – held so straight and so tight – rushing at Gentl like the newest pink personal torpedo. Six snakes wrapped themselves immediately round Major Gentl as the massive popylo blasted against him, sending him yards across the waves with the impact. Atinga rose from a sudden sleep, and gave a warning shot; his wave was getting tired remaining stationary, for it was the stillest wave in the world, and was even prepared for gunshots over the tides.

'After I have keelled the tides I weel keel you too pronto! I have got you in the sea, I weel deestroy you now!' sang Torro discarding talking as a medium not intense enough for this aspect of the War of Existence.

When the major smiled, the snakes smiled, for the snakes knew they had to help his smiling: his jaw had been broken by that last punch of

Torro's; and so smiling was a military tactic. Sharks brushed against his jaw as he screamed in pain all of a sudden, screaming in rhythm to the sound of Torro's fast laughter. The snakes attacked the last shark by the broken jaw, wrapping themselves round it, and crushing it with a tremendously compressed strength. As the shark fell to the deeps it took one of the snakes with it, with the exhausted aMofa Gentl crying at the death of his second-strongest snake, with the most faithful crawl in the universe, ooooooooooooooooo.

The tears of Major Gentl made no difference to the sea, salt to salt. Torro too was exhausted now, with his festering neck under siege with Gentl's blows, and with small biting fish that did not respect the status of the one who wanted to be the Commander of The Universe. There was now a slow-motion quality to the fight, Gentl almost crawling among the arrogant waves that moved him off course, crawling in desperation to give the last blow . . . but how could you have the strength to give the last punch when the second-last blow itself was waiting for delivery? The ship of truth, still a wreck, but moving magnificently through all the wrecks of the sea in acts of divination and inner memoriam, went round and round the fighting two, the two friends who were eternally enemies. Wet enemies with very little punching left. The ship blew its rusty horn.

'ONNNNNN!' screamed the major to himself, as he wiped the blood on his lips against the blood on his left eye. The motorised tooshies had run out of fuel. Then Torro got a sharp hold of Gentl's balls, shua bet, and he pulled and pulled, as the major screamed in agony. There was nothing Atinga could do, nor the snakes; for both the major and Torro had sunk to the bottom of the sea, and were bouncing about the gasping sand. Gentl's boots were wrapped round Torro's neck in a hard hold; but this could not break Torro's hold on aMofa's ex-military scrotum. The two men were screaming under the sea with no sound coming out. The lungs would burst if there were no future to receive them. And the only future Gentl had was an extremely powerful spit into the eye of Torro – it was like an underwater arrow in the eye.

Torro now screamed uselessly, letting go of Gentl's shua, but holding on tenaciously to his own, as if in terrible compensation for all the suffering he had caused, in and out of the sea. Whether the suffering was wet or whether it was historical, Gentl did not let go of Torro's neck, not even after a passionate appeal from the ship of truth, which had continued to make circles all the way through the fight and down to the deeps. The butterflies had in desperation pushed the small engine out of Torro's anus, and were coming out in a great and wet profusion. Out came the butterflies again in the Second War of Existence! And it was only the final touch of a drowning snake that saved Gentl's life: the dying snake just rushed Gentl out of the sea, as the other snakes and Atinga followed in consternation, with the rats in disarray, OOoooo!

Torro just managed to climb out of the bottom of the sea on a long thin ladder improvised by the devoted rats that were drowning one by one with the effort of the rescue. Tallberto stood there hard, reluctantly, balanced on two rats on two waves, smoking a pipe whose smoke when released disappeared back into his mouth, never to come out again. His inner expansion of smoke let him balance better in some sikadillo levitation. He was dying to betray his master, and those parts of his body that were shadow were on fire with the desire for his master's death. Commander Zero, however, in his desperation to revive Major Gentl fully used two helicopters to fly him faster towards medicine; and he was so tall that he had one leg in each, with the camel humping over the major in worry.

The armies below continued to fight in patterned bulleting, salvos of shot in the east, salvos of shot in the west; and sometimes whole platoons couldn't move towards each other for the vast areas of ripening, pricking pineapples. And no one seemed to stop the termites from starting to make their massive new walls all over the battlefields. Often you had to lean over a red wall to spy your enemy.

When the major groaned, the propellers moved faster, and the moon gave more light in medicinal compensation. The major groaned again long distance into the craters, groans and light corresponding in sympathy across the skies. And there was Ama enthusiastically sorrowful as she prepared to tend her husband, for she had been used to the self-sufficiency of his health, and not the ministering of his sickness. The children stood stiff and worried, as the doctor arrived in a Mercedes Benz driven by Government Crow, with Government Goat in tow, complaining bitterly about the increasing authority of crows; a Mercedes Benz with stylish but raucous feathers at the wheels was too much. What they should have done was to anoint the bleating, instead of creating a dumb rival in the form of THE GOAT OF MERCY, bronze and all . . . a goat that couldn't even have the dignity of being on heat with some marvellous mounting, ebei! ebei!

But Torro was insistent, for after falling off the ladder of life ten times, he finally staggered to the house of the sick Gentl while being carried by Tallberto and the marauding rats – rats so free now that their master was wounded more seriously than usual . . . as if they were prepared to increase their freedom over his incapacity, for they adored him when they hated him, but did not hate him when they were not adoring. For after all the last rat that tried to show a surfeit of love for its master in its innocence ended up being sliced into two by this same master Torro, who growled that as soon as rats started to show too much love they became dangerous koraa; and Torro did this while in great pain with his neck, with the marks of the major's boots on his pus.

Torro's voice was shaking with pain as he held his waist instead of his neck, 'Major, you are always tougher than I theenk! Now, to show you how serious I am, I am pronto breenging you your coffin in advance, for you to taste how nice death is before I keeel you, no!'

Then he collapsed off the unwilling back of Tallberto, and it took all the strength of the rats to put him back. And beside Torro indeed was a shapely mahogany coffin, not in the usual flamboyant shapes of vulture and trotro. Commander Carlo raged at the exhausted form of his father, and then set fire to this coffin meant for Major Gentl. And Torro wasn't even conscious enough to witness what he would almost certainly have killed his son for if it were possible.

When the major finally woke up under the gaze of Ama Three, his gaze couldn't focus on the latter but went straight through the ceiling through the bamboo apertures to the suspended golden cockroach shining in the cool night. From what he could see of the expression of the trapped Mr Cee, his face wasn't in Achimota City at all; it seemed to be far away fighting a distant battle. The silver mosquito was obviously in great pain, and it wasn't helped by the constant irony that the golden cee piled on it for its desertion to Elder Amos Kittoe. The major heard faintly the voice of the golden emblem.

'Major, are we not in the same wounded state now? I am now fighting the bosses of Torro direct. They are very thin beings spiritually, for when you want to get through to them, you have to do much posturing, you have to break through that silly code that they have built around themselves . . . and the most disgusting thing I've seen since I have been up here looking far into the cities abroad is their greedy contemplation of discarded brain energy – they had suddenly decided that they needed less than was originally calculated, and highly sanitary scientists were busy poking about the flesh. Yes real flesh was the great surprise, Torro had been stealing real flesh with his brain machines, including his own, without his knowledge of the reality of this flesh! It seemed that everybody except one or two now had smaller heads than before! And there was this great fraud again against Torro himself: they needed him less and less as time went on. So there he is now caught in a process that has become habit, has become a taste for power. And this power wasn't even wanted intrinsically by the bosses; all this power was for processes that led beyond the earth. Can you put such a massively sick spirit back on course? We are fighting something very near an eternity of loaded dices! . . .'

The voice of the golden cockroach went lower and lower, until Gentl couldn't hear it. And it was replaced by the loud horn of the ship of truth, which had torn its way through land right to the bedside of Major Gentl.

'See the truth in my stern!' the horn roared, 'I am the wrecked sister of the golden cockroach, now caught up there fighting for the lives of everybody in this city. I am more interested at this stage in the fish that rub themselves innocently against my useless anchors, but I feel I have some responsibility towards my suffering brother up there. We were both born human beings, but chose to be emblems of the crawling earth and the tidy sea, so that this great city could survive. I became a wreck because the white bosses of Azania thought I was too beautiful an emblem to exist. The potential they have destroyed these last hundred years! Now, I want to remind my brother cockroach that the overseas cities have now become so powerful that they believe they can win wars without fighting at all; and even if they must fight, it must be through ludicrous and messy agencies like Torro's . . . but I am fighting because I believe that the universe is democratic! We in this city have reached a state where we believe that further so-called development is at present unnecessary, and it is our happiness they want! In their boredom, through which they taste only the recurring substance of their own tongues, they want to push us to our very limits: even though we passed images of famine long ago, they want us to enter the new century with

155

new and highly contrived images of suffering and degradation. I will remain rusty just long enough for the truth to come out!'

It was terrifying to see the golden cockroach shudder with the truth of its sister.

'Sister!' it screamed, 'Let your wet truth reach my height up here, for the dry war that I'm fighting here is a very hard warrr! For while I'm busy generating attacking waves against the enemy, the enemy is aware also that I am having to generate defensive waves to defend our history. There is something wonderful about a subjugated people, so long falsely put under the pile of history, now rising in a subtle and dignified defence of its very existence, and without bitterness that can't be got rid of in two decades either! They said we couldn't think and we thought, they said we couldn't make and we made, they said we couldn't worship and we did, and now they say we can't exist and we do! My dear rusty sister, as for me I'm only a golden cockroach. You and me, we lost our humanity long ago! And at first our people couldn't appreciate this: they forgot us, they lived over us and under us. But now that they are fighting to exist, they have remembered us! Pity to the silver mosquito, for it used to receive all my anger, and now that it has deserted me it is suffering it! I wish my feelers could touch your stern now as we used to play at hugging when we were children in another time . . . and talking about love, do you know that Nana Mai the Grandmother Bomb has warned me never to mention her heart again? And she has only visited me once up here in the sky, since her elevation to elderhood . . .'

The ship spun in circles on this dry land, out of sympathetic agony, as Mr Cee continued panting, '. . . and the worst thing is that apart from this Torro here, we are fighting people who are not even interested enough to seek more knowledge of us beyond that old knowledge that they themselves created of us for the benefit of their cursory glances!'

Major Gentl prostrate there blinked with the wet truth and the dry truth, as Ama hovered over him, wondering whether she did take her strategy too seriously, and whether she should have fought on Torro's side at all. What if her major were to die and leave her with the awesome knowledge of near-betrayal on her part? She shuddered for him in his fever, and wiped his brow more often than necessary. The ship of truth had made the room smell of crabs, and the children cleaned it fast, anxious for greater sanitation to let the major recover more rapidly.

aMofa Gentl had discovered something useful among the punching

156

waves: when you snorted the sea moved for you. He was just about to move to the other side to sleep when, quite suddenly, Nana Mai landed right by the bedroom door in her helicopter, administered some new medicine through the Goat of Mercy, gave Ama Three a perfuntory nod – she didn't trust Ama koraa – and then flew out again through the wide, wide bedroom window. All she had said to the major was that she loved graves no more, and that she thought it was silly of her to ride among the stars paying visits to the dead in an astronomy of necrophilia, that she knew the golden cockroach and her ex-husbands would find unbearably jealous. She had been eating atadwe with her mouth shaped for war, and her hands gentle for Gentl. The major was somebody that she felt she could have had much spirit in common with, but didn't. She admired the simplicity that he brought to complex things, his showless success.

Ama Three was snorting at Nana Mai's absence, wondering aloud whether it would be possible for the old lady to find more sense in her new elevation. aMofa looked away, his eyes sore. The bamboo walls moved quietly with the soft cries of the concerned sparrows, sparrows in the bedroom sympathising with the major in a military manner, with the snakes and the camel watching-aaaaaaaa until a tear dropped from each eye, big tears from aMofa simulating rain.

In his fever born of the punching within the sea, Major Gentl saw Torro in changing visions that moved in and out of the War of Existence, and which seemed to reflect reality for Torro himself; for whenever Gentl saw these visions, The Torro felt them. First of all Torro demanded a share of the rain, so that it might fall harder on his soldiers; for he insisted that his profusely sweating shoogly army fought better when wet, and that Major Gentl was being too selfish with water from the sky: the home army got sufficient rain in its barracks and in its corn fields, but the Roman army of Torro's Azania was disgracefully dry.

When Major Gentl sneezed in his sleep, it changed his vision. He saw Torro rushing to the most magnificent carpenter in Achimota City, Paa Dua, and demanding that he make the most military chair ever seen anywhere: legs for guns, stands for helicopters, rests for bullets, and backs for wounds. But what Paa Dua did was to make The Torro himself into a chair immediately; and it was a hard spectacle seeing Torro bursting out of his own flesh with his sideways and frontal stand, and finally getting his own human shape back in a desperate run into the neems out of his chairhood . . . for three minutes he had a wooden popylonkwe, Ataame.

On with the visions went the major; Torro mouthed without sound in his deflected reality, that even in dreams now there was war. The major's third dream thinned down Torro; Torro was sick at the neck, and just about to eat the thinnest cow in the world, its bones fleshier than its meat. Torro rose in sweat the same sodium as Gentl's, with quinine in his mouth, and a rat shaving his moustache grown quite suddenly in the sea. But his belly hadn't thinned down at all, heaving there in gross contradiction to the bones. Torro the Terrible was lying there sick by his neat lawns – with Bianca appearing every two days to change a bandage from one sore to the same. At the same time The Torro was arranging with some acclimatised Roman women, part-time soldiers, to make a huge kenkey as big as an old discarded atom bomb kept in his equally huge chamber-pot for possible intimidation of Achimota City if things got truly out of control for him, some nuclear chamber-pot, finefine. The way Torro placed the kenkey carried by helicopters made it difficult for the elders of government to enter Government House without passing through this incredibly carnivorous kenkey: there was a roasted goat in the middle of it, which the adventurous could nibble at while plodding through the fermented boiled corn initially ground in rhythm to the pain of Torro. While still sleeping Major Gentl made it possible for the kenkey to be defeated by its own kyenam and moko. And then the Roman cooks and the Achimotan cooks met in a small culinary war that left only the kyenam and the spaghetti as the survivors. Then in a final attempt to be victorious in these military dreams, Torro arranged while holding his neck in pus-filled pain, to have some orchestrated burps and farts; d-r-m-f-s-l-t kweee, some low-note wind, some high, and each designed to make history: the first war to be won by carefully controlled farts. And the dreams continued in reckless abandon, until both Major Gentl and The Torro woke up at exactly the same time, both calling for lime with touches of honey. Torro was somehow desperate to use his runaway camel as a telephone to bamboozle Gentl, for the talking would deepen with the humps, and Gentl could be confused. And as both men slowly grew healthier, they arranged, again simultaneously, hundreds of snakes and rats to crawl and stalk the land, in preparation for the final battle coming now, now.

ZONE SIXTEEN

Travail

Major Gentl of course knew that fighting the enemy, even in a war of existence, was fighting yourself, provided you started from the footage, Ewurade, that humanity was one; and that those who dealt in outdated distinctions were merely thieves of conclusion and betrayers of premise. Torro had never uttered a racist word – or so it seemed – and had evidently built up a great and irrational love for Achimota City, and not necessarily the love of girls trapped on alternate days for his sad and bellyful embraces, when Bianca was busy looking at others. But rather a love that recognised the humanity of the enemy, but still wanted to control and power it. As if there was a ludicrously superior existence to be maintained; as if it was all a question of power, and not Achimota at all. So even though Torro had become more human but in a childlike, selfish manner, he had begun a stupid process that was a slave to itself, power, and which took the reduction of the Achimotan as a series of false and obsessive stereotypes. The Torro's bosses were far narrower than he was, and that was why they were using him, and that was why he was using himself. After studying Major Gentl with his reduced mind and with his computers, Torro had come to the conclusion, thief that he was, that the sympathy of Gentl was a large South African sandwich that he could bite out of existence quite easily. Torro would chew into the centuries, and bury a whole people in false graves.

At first Torro had thought that he would be accepted freely by the free Achimotans, merely by the fact that he fraternised with everybody, and ate social groundnuts among the termites, bananas, and pineapples. But he constantly forgot that Achimota City had advanced beyond even the keeping of missiles as necklaces worn casually and ironically at parties and in sanitary toilets. And no one knew that Nana Mai's biggest love was the passing on of her inventions to the next generation: her daughter could be as crabbit as she was, but was prepared to carry on her mother's work, and even to take over elements of the now nonexistent

159

children's war, so that existence for Achimota City was not merely a series of hiccups between generations, but rather a number of extremely hard joins pressed from mother to daughter, from father to son with the metal as unbreakable as anywhere else. Thus Achimota City had achieved something harder than the ancestors could offer at that time . . . but the ancestors too were learning, were changing.

Major Gentl had recovered completely, unlike Torro's septic neck – which his bosses were refusing to heal, even though they knew how to do so; and which the Achimotan herbalists wanted to heal on condition that he accepted defeat and then joined the city as a faithful and forgiven citizen. But poor Torro was lost, and was rather preparing for the last and massive battle that he knew he would triumph in. Gentl, in his everexpanding aggression, had sent a vast number of hiccups in envelopes to Torro. Nana Mai had retrieved most of the brain energy, including some of Torro's even, partly as a strategy of victory, and partly as a moral gesture, so that the war would be as even as possible, even if the bosses could cheat independently and through Torro at the same time.

All of the home army was now either motorised or on horseback, with that dynamic general Pogo Forr resplendent on his golden horse. Even the Air Force and the Navy were on horseback, with sophisticated equipment cantering above the hooves, letting Torro think they were being stupid when they were rather being clever. The Navy rode its shippy horses in the sea. The Air Force flew into the moon for nothing, with the horses holding on desperately; and that too was an important part of the strategy for the war.

Ama had smiled into her saddle when aMofa Gentl had said with force to her that it was just this intellectual flexibility that the enemy was afraid of. She rode her smile and she was about to say, 'and that was why I fought on Torro's side for some time' but she didn't. Another thought had come to her: the war of Achimota City was the war of Azania, for they were fighting for the same existence; and what made the bosses so angry was that they saw no increase in bitterness, for after all, as soon as there was an all-consuming bitterness instead of a cold and strategic humanity, direct attacks could be contemplated, and even Torro could possibly win something against Gentl.

All the saddles of the home army were made of oval carrots, with gold at the circumference. Pogo had gone in ecstasy because he was now made the governor of the newly arriving lands, and he managed this with his generalship and deputy ministership too. His ambition, for now, fitted perfectly into the structure created for it, OOoooo. Things had never been clearer as the last battle approached, as Achimota polished its thinking even through many of its citizens who did not do any. And in the distance you could see that The Torro had given each group of Gentl's mailed hiccups the lights he used to smile before Bianca put off the electricity, this Bianca who was now getting more and more courage against her husband, and she now even knew her date and place of birth.

Major Gentl was stiff on his camel, with a horse nearby for equestrian planning. Beside him was Alonka Forr, Commander Zero, the sergeant shadow riding on the shadow of the camel, Atinga with a new haircut to free his brains for greater bodyguarding in the final war, the snakes, the children, including Torro's, and his favourite helicopter which had a horse of its own. Commander Zero, even though he was missing Tallberto, had his saxophone beside him, for he wanted to dance into battle, playing above the playing of the bugle and the drums. His inner shadow felt extremely tough to Gentl's touch this evening: he usually asked the major to toughen his shadows with his touch, on occasions of importance. And he was truly set for the conventional war, with his one secret that he didn't even tell Tallberto: for every shadow he would kill in battle, double the substances behind them would die. Pogo was looking militarily smooth in his new golden glasses, and he was dying for the sun to rise in the morning so that he could worship it, and then get his final answer about the solar hotel rooms therein. All the tension showed in the shanks of the horses, and in the writhing of the snakes. The children chattered ceaselessly.

The golden cockroach above was actually glowing over the evening, and even Nana Mai didn't know whether it was a glow of strength or a glow of alarm, for no message was coming at all; and the silver mosquito was so still that you would think it was dead. And nobody knew that but for the golden cee devouring one hundred altered deadly organisms from its aerial prison – released by Torro's bosses from the Azanian cities and from East and West – the whole of Achimota City would be wailing for the thousands dead and dying. But Gentl felt a strange vigour in spite of the travail of the golden cockroach and the silver malaria.

161

The evening was scattering with a sudden shower that managed still to avoid the lands Torro and his army stood on, some sideways home-army rain; and the jubilant Zero now blew wet music, trying to impress some of the female soldiers, in case some pre-battle romance was possible. Pogo Forr, having become slightly quieter with the judicious assuaging of his ambition, now looked with great pride at the glow of the oval carrots . . . It was not only the Grandmother Bomb who fed the city with useful inventions, and they would soon see the power of the roundish carrots. But still, Pogo wasn't beyond doing the outrageous thing at aaawl: he just stood on his golden horse in the full view of the entire army, and urinated to the rhythm of the bugle. This was the type of thing that Abomu Kwame loved. He rose too, but with his akpeteshie angles all gone – he couldn't find the key to his spiritual cupboard – and he chorused Pogo's peeing, the difference being that he had neither the dignity nor the golden horse to embellish the urine.

The war drums rose in the night. The camel was so long that the major could pace up and down on it, sometimes staggering against his own strategies; and when he was about to walk and fall off the end of the camel out of preoccupation, the snakes would rush in touching lines against the camel, and provide an instant zoological bridge for the major to step on. This silly Abomu Kwame was in charge of the bugle and he was dying to misuse it. What was saving him was that he blew his notes so short that before the brain could interpret it, the ear had already rejected it. The armed forces were thus full of musical suspension. *You hear the notes, you no hear the notes.*

Several Pogo-trained horses galloped 440, but they had only one space to gallop in; for on his way to the sun and to the oval carrots, Pogo had solved simultaneous speed and stillness . . . the horses galloped on the same spot, thus fooling the beefy beef-eating Torro who never failed to eat when he was worried, and who was now eating his breakfast this evening: on unusual occasions Torro ate his breakfasts the previous evening. Allah: the moon was wearing a fine cloud of darkgrey, and you could see home beetles flying provisions to the soldiers, under the supervision of Government Crow, which was so excited that it cackled off-key, to the utter delight of Government Goat standing there in its ministerial erection . . .

Torro sent a telegram at midnight to Major Gentl asking if the battle could be postponed please, since he was feeling so lonely without his children, and saying that his deputy Tallberto couldn't be found anywhere either. The telegram asked, 'How can you defeeet a desolate enemy?'

Major Gentl, with a snort of disbelief, nodded to Pogo nodding to Commander Zero: they had decided to postpone the chaaaarge, but half the army would be up trees, so that Torro's ground-hugging bullets wouldn't take them by surprise. The other half was to sleep near the new lands whose original gentleman, considering himself the century's best been-to, had welcomed the presence of Torro there, for the smell of spaghetti had reminded him of apartheid and Europe together always. He was even dressed to fight in Torro's army.

Hundreds of different types of snoring told Gentl that his army was exhausted with doing nothing, boof. There was absolute silence from Torro's camp, as Gentl prepared for the surprise attack that never came at aaawl. So Pogo was up before the sun next morning, and then later the sun was up before Pogo when he took a quick nap. And what secrets did the sun bring with its rays? All the sun told Pogo was that the answering oval carrots, answering without fail to the power of the sun, had now become more than one substance: they could be eaten, they could be fought with, they could decorate heroes, and they could change the future ten minutes ahead. Pogo raised his hands high in triumph as Gentl stood beside him. But he had to drop his hands again, for the sun insisted that this power could only be used if Torro and his bosses cheated, and when the sun itself was shining directly on the golden cockroach.

At midnight Major Gentl cleared security with Pogo Forr, beside whom stood General Jolloff busy counting the grains of rice in his waakyi, trying to make sure that the rice did not cheat the beans. His cook was Bianca, who between bouts of cooking and infatuation with him, had gone and forged the general's signature without his knowledge, for a marriage certificate between him and her. How happy Bianca was over the forged marriage, until he found out, and had threatened to tell Torro. It was a most painful thing for Bianca to tear up the love-sick certificate before the angry eyes of the general; even Captain Owusu became angry, rushing around to see whether he would be called to save falling rice from the general's epaulettes of beans and rice beyond beans.

Gentl cleared the security because he knew he had to pay a last visit to the moon before the deciding battle. His reconstructed lunar road was

163

held up by innumerable particles of dust, and there were ingrained skids on it from the motor-bikes of the children rushing up to the moon during the duel. He was hoping to get a lunar wavelength on the cities abroad, in case he could get a secret message to Torro that the beleaguered golden cockroach would not detect to distract it. He lay relaxed in the craters, his small bright head challenging the width of the moon. After thirty minutes of gazing, with recurring thoughts about whether Torro was getting ready to attack or not, Gentl saw shapes and heard sounds coming through his cracked binoculars from the frosty lands: first of all any vision or any perception could have its opposite uselessly presented straight to the brain without the perceiver willing it at aaawl; secondly, different types of metal had become the rather ludicrous manifestations of immortality; thirdly, humanity was declared as something truly belonging to another century altogether, something completely out of date; and then next, the outer had completely displaced the inner, the mind had become absolutely external, with a curious paradox that they thought they had solved. It had turned out that all the outer stimulus that they were busy creating was for a mythical inner that no longer existed there; so that all the vast impetus being created to make the outer something like a thing in itself had nothing to perceive it; and after this Gentl saw that a few of them had seen that the world was something like a jigsaw puzzle: let only a section of humanity push out towards the galaxies, EVEN WHEN ALL THE OTHERS WERE READY TO JOIN THEM, and you would get a travesty of that very humanity that they hungered for, you would get truncated human beings – half-puzzles – wishing they were more whole than they were, yet travelling all the same, as if brains were everything and the truest and broadest intelligence was nothing.

Don't mind them! thought aMofa Gentl, for residues of the true African drum, of the subtleties of true African movements, width and intelligence, would follow them like obsessive ghosts that would haunt the universe forever, if they insisted on exclusively developing that insane urge to make THAT great road to the universe as narrow as possible. Their subject will never meet their object, assuming the former would even exist at aaawl in a few years' time. Major Gentl found himself crying on the moon; he was wetting the craters with humanity. There was no steel in his tears koraaa. The more they planned for a narrow freedom, the more like ants they would become!

O you aMofa! the major thought to himself, don't live, even if for moments, in the historical concepts they have manufactured for you! For, after all, Achimota City was a being of its own, with an acute sense of what the twenty-first century was all about; and this sense had been so successfully developed that the likes of Torro had to come to invade it. But O no you don't: this was not the same colonial situation that the first invaders met, for here the Achimotans had mastered the type of living that had sympathy, power and creation as well as harmony. And thus the anger that the Achimotans had was purely an anger of survial! As soon as the war was over, they would lose interest in the cities abroad again . . . what were their names did you say? . . . There seemed to be a sound coming through the binoculars, but Gentl ignored it and went on with his half-dream, half-waking thinking from his favourite sweet crater on the moon. Surely the first intelligence was a wise and powerful reverence before existence; and the second intelligence was the sympathy that grew from this; and the third was, both consciously and unconsciously, to keep in rhythm body and soul with the first two; and the fourth view, after allowing for natural attachments to known people and places, was to retain that sort of global subtlety that allowed you to move in and out of cultures, without shouting the greatness of your own throughout time; and next, the type of power and wealth that existed in the icicle cities now was self-perpetuating in such a way that even though there was a mad rush to some so-called modernity, everything – especially states of mind in a white cultural rest that was both terrible and silly – had a deep conservatism that narrowed everything down to nothing; and last but not all, wasn't it an elementary intelligence that the more mindlessly you transformed the outer, surely the more difficult it became to: one, sustain a relationship with it in any profound way; and two, to go beyond that disappearing space between what is being created and who is doing the creating?

Having forgotten his sotto voce, Major Gentl caught himself shouting to the moon, 'How much more greed and degradation will it take to realise that there are other ways equally intelligent or even more so, that look down with pity and contempt on a people that claim that every universal quality is theirs!'

Suddenly the moon was mean with its light, for that type of passion didn't fit up there. An old hoarse voice WAS coming through the

165

binoculars from the frozen cities, and Gentl was struck by its absolute neutrality, its lack of commitment to anything except perhaps fads and some strident perfectionism that let every inflection in the voice be pre-planned, as if the voice said: 'Freedom was planning the planner out of existence.'

Gentl was now listening intently, but all he heard was 'code code code x y z, give them the edge of the fight, the earth can't wait.' Since the compromised binoculars were as usual self-translating, what Gentl heard, with one ear still cocked listening for Torro's attack below, was this: 'We no longer believe in communicating with those we are about to destroy . . . The best way for us to maintain a morality is to keep the consequence of our actions away from our direct senses . . . If we steal your brain energy or put mysterious germs in your atmosphere, surely we are doing this in the interest of a higher civilisation that is reaching beyond the stars . . . We have decided that conceptually there is no difference between existence and nonexistence, hence we do not consider anything wrong when you no longer exist . . . We have not only solved all paradoxes, but have also retained their separate elements of contradiction . . . You people over there have become absolutely marginal to our existence . . . Happiness is a luxury, but good fun isn't . . . In a position of absolute power conscience is out of date, irrelevant . . .'

Major aMofa Gentl threw the binoculars away in disgust and raced on his lunar road towards the earth, and what the major's speed said to him was that even when we've taken elements of their culture to survive, as they themselves have done with other cultures for centuries, we cannot quite break through their codes, nor erase the sly comments of colour said behind our backs; they are going to end up in the one-way streets of the universe, and then they may need our help! It's not envy that lets us criticise this culture, it's sanity! Indeed the major believed that Achimota was more balanced than anything else he had seen or heard of, with its vast openness and toilet missiles that could yet protect . . . and with its many Baby Samas that could pee free while presidents preached.

By the time Gentl landed, the battle was on paaa, and Torro, so confident and thinking he, Gentl, had finally run away leaving things to Pogo Forr, was drinking medium red wine all over his medium height. And when he finally saw Gentl rushing off on his motor-bike he spewed some of the wine over his soldiers, out of a surprise tarter than than the wine.

'Today be today!' said the smiling major to Torro, who replied, 'Noooo, I deeefer, I say tomorrow eees tomorrow! I weel crush you by tomorrow!'

The battlefield was crowded with jot-ends from the thousands of cigarettes smoked by the Roman soldiers there on behalf of France, Germany, Japan, America, Britain and South Africa. This was seen when the morning came, and Torro's army had advanced half a kilometre.

Amassed on the home army's side were the thousands of fighting men and women, the sparrows, the crows, the camel's six cousins that had suddenly appeared, goats, hundreds of rabbits, termites, the train engines, the snakes, two rivers diverted into the army with their intelligent water power, belligerent bananas, pineapples, the essences of the northern part of the world that had become rotten in the bottle with their long-distance cheating, the chamber-pots now free of these essences, making the city itself freer, and then the suffering presences of the golden cockroach, still busy on another dimension of the Second War of Existence, and the silver mosquito.

The silver owl was in the advance rat-catching party headed by Government Crow. Torro on the other side had rats and Romans, elephants and lizards, computers and . . . Tallberto was nowhere in sight: he had entered an anthill by mistake in his quest to run away from Torro, and had met the following to the west of the battlefield: Ant A crawling in a space reserved for innocence, and as far from the queen as possible, and thus offering nothing in courage to help in the desertion of Torro – Ant B was of course the real occupant of the termite hill that was called the anthill, and it had bitten so many dead bodies in the past that it hardly respected human beings anymore; Ant C saw nothing, and was the special pet of the vigorous soldier termites that guarded the one maa; and finally Ant Z thought it could give Tallberto all the encouragement he needed to fight on the home side, simply because it conceived the war as an explosion of two different-coloured galaxies, and then it bit Tallberto who raced out of the anthill with a scream expressed at the reddening bite.

Tallberto rushed past his own army so fast that not even the computers saw him. He ended up near the cooking Bianca who, as a compromise, had been authorised to cook for both armies with some marvellously fast cookers that could cook tonnes in a few minutes. There was thus the yoo ke gari army, and the macaroni army, with rice in between.

ZONE SEVENTEEN

The last battle

And so the battle was on fast, judged much like the speed of the tail of a snake. Torro had begun by slyly capturing Professor Dolla the second ex-husband of Nana Mai the Grandmother Bomb. He did this by simulating Nana Mai's voice, and of course when Dolla heard it, he rushed from the suburbs straight into Torro's trap. Torro killed him by putting him right in the middle of a bullet and then firing it – the first man to die within rather than without a bullet. Jollo Gyan her second ex-husband thought this was the chance for him to assert the past of his husbandry. But he too fell into a trap, and only managed to crawl out wounded from the jaws of a hundred rats when he blew his trumpet to scare them off.

People never forgot the massive and suspect indifference of Nana Mai the Grandmother Bomb at Dolla's funeral, which lasted only ten minutes so that the battle could proceed. 'You can bury his heart first if you like,' was all Nana Mai said, while the wounded Gyan scoured her face for any inordinate signs of grief for the newly dead, as the bullets and bombs whistled by. And Torro chose the funeral to exhume the bodies of hundreds of his Roman soldiers, and he scattered these bodies in the home cemeteries, in the markets, even in the fruit bars. There was at first pandemonium, and nobody ate kyinkyinga for hours; but Torro made matters worse by rushing around away from the battlefield and eating beef in a disgusting manner calculated to make the city vomit. There was a great roar of anger against him for Dolla's death, and for this scattering of putrid flesh over the streets and plains.

Torro continued unabated by stealing one of Gentl's snakes and slashing it into ten pieces, sending the pieces one by one to Gentl, through hungry rats that devoured half the pieces on the way to the major's camp; rats that met their deaths at the jaws of the waiting brother snakes of Commander Gentl, with a double 'C' from ever-increasing authority.

CCommander Gentl, the major had just prevented Torro's men from capturing the renegade camel, WHILE HE, GENTL, WAS STILL SITTING ON IT, Ewurade.

So this was at present Torro's strategy: dashing around creating different levels of tragedy while the main battle raged, so fiercely that for two breakfasts in a row, food could be shot away from the mouth by bullets from both armies.

CCCommander Gentl, with his 'Cs' trebled ludicrously in the rain by silly admirers, had one afternoon gone to the battlefront in his pioto, having forgotten his trousers, with Ama Three too busy admiring his legs to tell him. The mad Torro had immediately taken a close-up of Gentl's legs and tiny tooshies, and then had enlarged the photographs considerably, and placed innumerable copies throughout the city: hoping that both citizens and home soldiers would be so outraged at the thinness of the legs that they would – how unbelievable! – withdraw their support from the major, through leg resolutions passed through the four elders of government. Major Gentl just laughed without his trousers on for the second time, and acknowledged the cheers of thousands of his countrymen of the city . . . cheers that were given just when Pogo was passing in a most general-like manner, and thought they were for him. He had reared his golden horse in selfish salutation, but then he smiled through a snort when he rememberd that he had been given more power than previously, and thus no longer needed to stress his compensatory showmanship. Hurray CCCommander Gentl!

The battle continued with or without underpants – Torro had immediately removed his in an insane pioto jealousy – and had heated up considerably with the crashing in mid-air of two of The Torro's helicopters rushing to occupy the same space, simply because the computers had ordered them to do so. The sergeant shadow had just returned from the sky with some fresh okros for the golden cockroach, one of whose feelers was missing with the great pressure; and the military shadow came back with the fear that up there the silver mosquito was so still that it feared it was dead. No silver funeral, no silver funeral, Pogo had roared, for he had wanted to check up there himself, to reinforce gold cockroach with gold Pogo. For six minutes things were so furious in pace that the guns travelled faster than the bullets . . . and Torro roared in anger when two rifles killed his men, with the bullets still in the hands of those who fired, and the guns themselves stuck grotesquely in Torro's men . . . Torro hadn't computed that in wars of existence bullets could fire their guns.

Bianca continued to cook, moving from oven to oven in a stylish wheelbarrow.

The aromatic war continued with soldiers, especially of Torro's side, choosing to die in many different kinds of spice and incense, with guava perfume still subtler, deeper in the nose. Things had become a little pessimistic for the Romans of Rome and Azania, for many of them had brought their own coffins right on to the battlefield. As soon as they were shot, they dived in, almost as frisky as the dives of dolphins, with the perfumes copious on their skins. They hated Torro's neck of pus, but fought faithfully, because they believed they were fighting for a higher cause. Also, they were dying to get the missiles used to save them dying, but with half THEIR brain energy gone, all they did was what millions of advanced people did all over the world: obey the boss!

'Hear me!' roared the chief dog of war sent over from Torro's side to augment the work of the rats, some of whom were so frightened of Gentl's army that they spent most of their time nibbling at their own dead.

The ground was lush with dead Romans. Torro searched every shadow for Tallberto, but the latter had been clever enough to have switched to that type of shadowhood that could not be traced on computers or radar koraa. Torro moved angrily out of the afternoon and waited for the evening to hide all his losses. He looked at his children chatting to Major Gentl, and wept as the weather changed inexplicably, the air in the military pocket being far colder than the air over it, frozen fingers just when you put your hands in for your handkerchief to wipe sweat or blood. The dogs of war jumped over the cold pockets.

'Hear me!' repeated the chief dog hot under the moon, 'I have come to attack you, whether you are good or bad! I do not care for your goals, I do not care whether Africans have properly entered the consciousness of other peoples or not, I am here to bite, so present your skins to me, I am prepared to bite skins of any colour, for even I, a dog, know that colour is dead, and it is only primitive things like me that will keep it going for profit, with all its incomprehensible distinctions! Allow me to bite you all! I know Torro the Terrible arranged for my presence – he promised us a million bones after victory – but I am even prepared to bite HIM, if it will mean that my teeth will feel free and distinguished. Hurrah to all the bites of the world, even those with a history behind them!'

Tallberto was now there openly on the side of Achimota City, ducking under his own height several times and then reaching it again. With his special manual radar given to him by Nana Mai he had so far managed to direct six aeroplanes with their Afrikaans wings right into the sea, some wet crashes, these wings fashioned in the forgotten rich cities of the world.

'The real world has no morality!' screamed the dogs with their barks on fire from the bombs.

Tallberto couldn't find Commander Zero, but still loved directing aeroplanes into the sea, and he had felt so confident doing this that he allowed one plane to pass through him, in sudden shadow metamorphosis, before splashing forlornly into the sea.

The ship of truth blew its ancient horn in encouragement, and the moon flipped like a coin in the sky, and it couldn't be caught until five minutes later by the silver owl looking useful for once. But immediately after the silver owl threw the moon back up into the clouds, Torro leapt up very high, his pus in pain, and cruelly beheaded it, seizing the diamond whistle just then back again at the beak of poor owl, and blowing the whistle into its blood. The moon was red for the same number of minutes that it took silver owl's blood to finish. And Tallberto was full of remorse, for he thought that if he hadn't had the success of enticing the aeroplanes into the sea, the moon wouldn't have slipped in joy, for old owl to catch it and have its throat cut. And, as Tallberto's last tear dropped, Commander Zero appeared and doubled the shadows of the crying, refusing to wipe the tears until the shadow for each had been formed distinctly. What was Torro doing? Going round still, killing the periphery until the centre was left helpless? Zero and Tallberto linked arms and braced the horizon; they arranged their muscles against the skyline, ready for anything that Torro would try.

Being so obsessed with victory Torro had started a new habit that took Bianca even further away from him: he would take out his popylonkwe minutes before he urinated – a clever form of advance planning – and then forget completely that it was out. He would thus walk about with great authority, reinforcing his strategies with his forefinger . . . not knowing, mewuo, that the great gratuitous forefinger

172

between his legs was doing even more pointing than its cousin above. And Major Gentl, seeing the suppressed smiling that some of Torro's soldiers were doing, decided to speed up the home strategy; so that some of the enemy soldiers were shot before they could change their smiles to grimaces.

The termites of Government House had now been sent on a serious crawling mission to do as much biting of the enemy as possible, but more important, to bite through Torro's walls and defences, and get through to the new communicatons and computer rooms, and bite everything there as well. But near Torro's house, the termites met a massive steel wall. They sent a quick message back to Gentl that it would take three days to bite through it.

'Go on!' Gentl replied after a quick call through to the elders of government, with Pogo Forr standing beside him.

The termites ravaged the steel with their pinching. The three days were to be used to watch an instant video of the war, both armies seeing each other at work, and releasing shouts of ridicule at little trips and little scratches, but not caring at all for the way this man died or the way that man held his own wound.

Even though he was perfectly healthy, Major Gentl went back on to his sick bed, to reteach himself the humility of his body. And as he lay down with Ama Three polishing his toenails out of an intense desire to get back to the ambiguities of the battlefield – perhaps even to cook for Torro's computers, god forbid – he remembered the recent history out of which Achimota City swallowed Accra and Tema; out of which the white South Africans, more or less driven to occupy a bleak piece of territory in their country, had scattered to Europe, America and even other parts of Africa, just like Torro now, holding destructive agencies for their bosses, and hoping to be given Azania back later. aMofa Gentl was remembering, in the calm of the work of the termite jaws, how easily the people used to be arrested in Accra, Kumasi, Takoradi, Ho and Bolgatanga; was remembering the open gutters that the British built, building closed ones in places that they thought they would spend much longer at; during those days, political leaders were the real and absolute masters, and the papers and the radios and the televisions were crowded with control; creativity was regarded as alien or aberrant; and there were enormous marches in the wrong direction, with everybody knowing this was the wrong direction, but going all the same, because that seemed to be the only way to survive: for as soon as a person chose to go in a different direction, he or she was either starved by having no access to resources at all, or cut down immediately.

Those days were extremely bad, for those who had made themselves into oppositions were largely opportunists, hoping to jump in to chop their share and be welcomed as heroes on top; and you should have had a look at the churches and other groups at that time: big status-stuffed men and women with plenty fineries outside, but with insides so hollow that the echoes of a lost righteousness were heard three times three score there. You should have seen the utter complacency about the dangers of the future from the lost villages – now stolen, land and all, precisely because of the weak and mad floating before the vigorous waterfalls of history – right on to the noisy towns where people were creative in deals and tricks and lavender, but never suffered real creation in their lives: you either copied or imported everything, even though you ate home food, buried your dead with tradition, did your naming ceremonies, in other words all the easy authenticities you could do, but when it came to the last large ones, you just floated and encased yourself in the everlasting movements of fine dancing and fine ritual, *Ewurade Nyanko-pon! Dream, dream, Major!* You can at last afford to laugh at the past, for the new toughness and resilient width of Achimota City was something for revelation, joy and ritual suffering.

Major Gentl woke up to the consternation on Pogo's face: all the termites had been electrocuted in the computer rooms.

'I now know we should have attached the oval carrots to the termites!' screamed Pogo, rearing about on his golden horse right in Gentl's bedroom.

The major rose up with a start, as if the old feeling of oracles that he had in childhood was coming back: he gave one heavy salute, and twenty men fell down dead in Torro's army. He gave another salute, and fifty men perished. There was a huge cheer from the home army as the saluting continued. And simultaneously the oval carrots had become like sharp saucers, slicing through Torro's army with ease.

The foolish ones among the home army, like the bugle-minded drunkard Abomu Kwame, were already celebrating victory, but it was too early: the golden cockroach was getting weaker and weaker in the skies, and the silver mosquito did nothing but twitch. A weak and desperate message now came from the golden cee: the more successful

174

the home army fought below, the easier it would be to defeat the golden cockroach above, and once Mr Cee had been defeated, the War of Existence would be lost to Torro.

This terrible move from the bosses was faced with great agitation by the elders, Gentl and Pogo, with Nana Mai holding her parrot in worry so hard that it screamed out its mathematics.

'Did you not say that you did not want to solve paradoxes! Well, here's one for you NOT to solve, ha!' came a huge voice over the battlefield and spreading to the entire city.

For the first time the citizens of Achimota had heard the rotten voices of the bosses abroad, voices of neutral horror that Gentl recognised instantly from his lunar binoculars. But no one was frightened by the triple-taped voice at awwwl, not even the children; no one but Torro, who, in spite of all the interaction through their mutual code and through their sophisticated communications systems, had never heard the voices of his bosses. Rome, yes, some years back, but this terrible voice of war was something quite different. And the bosses, being human beings trying to be gods, made a mistake: they forgot to inform Torro that they were going to broadcast direct to Achimota City. The confused Torro started to send a whole series of contradictory messages to his army. With one message, a thousand men buried themselves out of a terrible loyalty that they did not really understand. And they buried their own doubts with them. Why did Torro's wife and children go over to the other side? Why did Torro lose Tallberto his deputy, again to the other side? Why was there so much humanity of such an advanced type in Achimota City? Why did the golden cockroach and ship of truth, and so many other strange animals and presences, support the home army? Why were the moon and the sun supporters of this city? They died with their questions, as the bananas and the pineapples ripened together.

Perhaps the biggest favour that the enemy did to Achimota was to make the new road to a new life easier by stealing vast areas of people and land. The emptiness seemed to make the new way easier; but now with the city stable in its originality and humanity, it was ready to receive its land back, to TURN THE NEW on its own returning citizens. And there was another paradox: all the rest of the returning people didn't seem to know that they had travelled at all: all they did was to marvel at the changes they were seeing now, and to ask why these changes were made without their knowledge. The first gentleman to

175

return never failed to reject his origins, but in the end he rejected Torro too, standing on the new land that Pogo ruled, standing with a big frown against the city, and avoiding Pogo at all costs. Pogo lived on the adoration of the new lands, but he never failed to go to Major Gentl for humility. Was the real future now coming for the entire country?

It was the snakes that finally transformed the paradox and saved the golden cockroach, this cockroach that had absorbed dangerous genetic engineering, had fought against toxic wastes thrown at it, had slapped at bacteria released at it, had defeated chemical poisoning, had rejected inferior drugs and other goods, and had squashed bamboozlement. The snakes transformed the paradox of victory below, and defeat above, transformed it but did not solve it: all the snakes did was to grind one of their number and then offer another paradox in this chess of survival: speed and crawl crawl and speed, life and death, and they just cut the thought waves by crawling over them, just at the point when Nana Mai's brain-restoring machines had added that little bit extra to the city's full brain power. Big brain waves saved the golden cockroach. The ship of truth too had helped its brother cockroach by constantly blasting its life-giving horn both upwards and downwards.

Major Gentl and Pogo Forr had masterminded the battle on the ground, and the battle of the wings, with the support of the children, Commander Zero, Tallberto, General Jolloff and the taciturn Captain Owusu. And when victory finally came with the destruction of The Torro's hub of computers and communications, it was the crows and the sparrows that carried the minute bombs to blow it up. Torro's house rose in fire, with the laughing servants scattering like hens; a fire so big that it changed the colour of waves nearby.

The low plaintive sirens sounded for a whole day, augmented by the drums. They sounded for both the dead and the living, and for both armies. The rabbits dug the graves, and the large beetles carried the dead into them after libation. And the crows cried for everybody, with priests and herbalists working in the background. The electrocuted termites were buried too.

One thousand soldiers of Torro's army survived, and Pogo Forr accepted them into the new lands with a showy and irrepressible wish to rule them fairly, so that they adored him in return. Pogo, of course was still, like Major Gentl, under the elders of government, but his enthusiasm couldn't be stopped. He had the whole populace dancing and shouting for joy . . . until aMofa Gentl whispered into his ear that Torro the Terrible was yet to be found.

'Torro?' asked Pogo quizzically. 'Let Torro wait small till I dance a bit more . . .' Pogo danced ten more drums before following the major to search for Torro.

And the elders had decided that Torro should be given a chance to reform, and to stay in Achimota City, for after all wasn't he misled by his bosses . . . But it wasn't a decision that was popular. They argued and argued as they danced and sang and helped the surviving termites to rebuild the termite architecture of the city.

General Jolloff had taken out an injunction against the presence of Bianca, and had ordered her to return to her disappeared husband.

'How can I return to him when he has disappeared?' she asked petulantly.

Eventually Ama Three and Delali took Bianca in, in turns, and they promised her that if she truly didn't love Torro anymore, they would crouch with her on the horizon looking for a husband for her soonest.

Commander Zero and Tallberto had immediately married a fine dark maiden each, even before the end of hostilities had started to cool. Zero had committed the doubtful woman before she had had the chance to change her mind. He and Tallberto were so adventurous that they promised each other that they would keep on trying to live next door to each other, even if it meant living on the moon – being semi-shadows, they felt it philosophically important to keep moving around to try and live as close to each other as possible. But now they were helping Major Gentl and Pogo Forr to look for Torro.

'TORROOOOOO!' Tallberto shouted into the universe, but got no reply koraa. There was Commander Carlo holding the hand of Commander mMo, both rushing up to Major Gentl and his searching group, and pleading, 'Please, don't keel my papaaa, just send heem to Rome.'

mMo had remained silent, but agreed with his eyes. Gentl just nodded and went on, as the children turned back. They searched inside neemberries, pine cones, microchips, the tanks of tanks, the fingernails of dead soldiers about to be buried; they searched under the ship of truth, they went to the convalescing golden cockroach, all to no avail. Until, deep in a valley where the Goat of Mercy lived, they heard the amplified voice of Torro. The voice was coming from underground.

'You weel never find me, gentlmen,' Torro said weakly but loudly. 'I have buried myself in a coffeeen that moves. I am a bad man, I geev you much trouble. My bosses they betray me. Do not deeg for me. Eef you dig for me in one place, I weel disappear into another. I tell you my coffeeen moves. And I have only leetle breeathing left. Look after my wife and cheeldren as you deed even during the war . . . but let me tell you that I am a bad man: I have set off a bigbig bomb to destroy your city, after I am dead! I love you all, so I would like you to die weeeth me . . .'

Pogo Alonka Forr turned round in desperation to Major Gentl, the question-mark of the bomb written on his face. Major Gentl just smiled and pointed up at the sky: there was Nana Mai the Grandmother Bomb dragging a huge defused missile behind her helicopter. She had seen Torro's trick far earlier and had phoned Gentl to tell him.

Before they could start digging to bring Torro to justice, they heard a last cry from him: the rats that he had buried with him to service him – fetching food in and out of the coffin, transferring his toilet and his spit to the earth, wiping his sweating face, and keeping the large store of beef fresh in the coffin by pouring their own blood on it – had finally turned on him in the confined space. They tore him apart, starting with those hands of his that had torn so many rats apart themselves, and then working up to his large and terrified eyes . . . Pogo snorted a benediction, as Zero and Tallberto stood impassive, massive with justice, their shadow parts appearing and disappearing, the sergeant shadow joining them without their knowing. Atinga had walked up with the camel and a helicopter for Gentl to make a choice as to how he would return to his bamboo house. The major preferred to walk, some walk-bi.

All bombs and guns were now taken to the underground vaults, and it was hoped that they would only be used when absolutely necessary. The squirrels swept the city with their tails, as the Goat of Mercy walked from house to house, giving sympathy where needed; at times of crisis, it shed its bronze and took on hide. Government Goat never failed to look at it with sarcastic eyes. For a whole week there was consternation in spite of the celebrations, for Nana Mai the Grandmother Bomb had resigned her eldership, insisting that she would only serve in times of crisis, and that she was too busy with her research, her grandchildren and her cornmills, not forgetting her house, and parrot. Her resignation was refused, and she tendered it again, with Jojo Digi exploding with

178

anger that the old lady was doing something too mech and that 'did she consider that she was greater than Yaa Asantewaa or what?' Amos Kittoe was quite happy to have silver mosquito alive, even though it had remained with the golden cockroach, and visited the elder only once a week. He gave Nana Mai several precedents of Achimotan history, explaining why she should not resign in the moment of triumph. Chairman Kot, having resumed his marriage ceremonies with Mrs Wife, was feeling vigorous with a tremendous release of energy brought on by the new atmosphere of peace. The rabbits were back at Government House carrying honey sullenly again.

'Try Mrs Wife in my place,' retorted Nana Mai, when Chairman Kot tried once again to persuade her to remain in the Elders' Council.

Kot shook his head, walking round her in disagreement.

'Besides,' she continued, 'I am training my grandchildren to be scientists.'

Delegation after delegation was rebuffed by the Grandmother Bomb, until she finally agreed to . . . think about it for two years. That was that. The system of rotating power was to be tried again, but Chairman Kot's suggestion that the elders of government too should be rotated was rejected absolutely. Baby Sama as usual peed through the public meeting, feeding fat on his mother's breast when no one was looking, not even his mother.

Pogo had suddenly proposed that Major Gentl should be made an elder for his continuing victories. Gentl just laughed, boof. How could he who had for years been trying to drop the major in his name, to reflect the day that he left the Armed Forces, how could he now agree to further elevations? He had given Alonka Forr a severe look after the laughter, and declared that he had already resigned as Commander-in-Chief, and Minister of Defence.

'My way is downwards, not upwards,' he had told Pogo at the latter's glass house, which he was still using to administer the new lands.

The oval and golden carrots were put away with the weapons, and Pogo had never felt happier.

aMofa Gentl, so lonely in victory, was walking down the neem avenues of Achimota City. In the past as he strolled around, he could always see traces of Accra and Tema; but now they had completely disappeared under the historical wheels of Achimota. And now that South Africa was free, and had established true links with cities of all sorts in Africa, it was seen clearly that Achimota City was the standard that they all had to follow, a place where power was the last resort, and humanity and invention allowed even the smallest human being to open out into the trees and into the universe, to see the whole, to touch the inner.

The camel and the trains walked beside Gentl, with his snakes crawling around the waist. Ama Three and Delali had ceased to talk about each other's husbands inordinately, and had in a bold move taken Bianca to Nana Mai who had surprisingly agreed to look after her until all her love for poor General Jolloff had finished. There was aMofa with his small face dotting the streets and the fruit, satisfied that this city had all the consciousness it needed, and that they were more than prepared to face anybody who wanted to steal any. It was as if the names of the rich cities were coming back to him again, but he put them out of his mind and walked on.

'Give me twenty cedis' worth of boiled groundnuts, please,' Gentl said to the seller in the bamboo kiosk.

As he walked off, the seller asked herself: 'How can such a simple man save us so often, and what will we do in this city when he dies . . .?'

She had her answer, for also following Gentl, and eating the same boiled groundnuts, were his children, Torro's children, and so many other children that loved the way he moved, with or without his discarded major of the name. Ewurade, look at the way he moved in the year 2020 in Achimota City, so surrounded by fruit, animals and children . . .

keteke train
kobolo truant
koko porridge
Kokompe large workshop area
komi ke kenan kenkey and fried fish
koobi dried tilapia
kosee bean tart
koraa at all, completely
kosee bean tart
kote genital
kuraba chamber pot
kuse-kuse sorry, how sad
Kwahu area in Ghana
kwankwaa crow
kwasia fool, foolish
kwee wind
kyenam fried fish
kyinkyinga khebab
labalabalibilibi not to be trusted
lalat like that
logologo intercourse
logorligi not straight
lonkwe genital
lungulungu tortuous
makola a famous market
mewuo an exclamation
mogya blood
moko pepper
momoni dried fish
neem a large tree
nemico enemy (Italian)
nkonkonsa trouble making
nkwasiasem nonsense
nonally non-ally
ntefi spit
ntokwa quarrel
nyamanyama rubbish
odo love

odododiodo war cry

odolontous (also 'odolont' elsewhere) to do with love

oseee yeee a war cry

osode a type of music

oware a game

owuo death

oxter armpit (Scottish word)

paa much, a lot

papaapa very much

patapaa quarrelsome

pesewas pennies

pioto pants

pona a type of yam

popylonkwe male organ

portello a mineral drink

quartic mathematical term

sakoa nana an exclamation

samia an expletive

sankofa symbol of how past and future affect present

sapele a type of wood

sapo sponge

sculacciare to spank (Italian)

shitoh pepper (ground and fried)

shrow a herbal substance

shuashua a play on 'sure' and on 'shua', a word for testicle

siabots be patient

sikadillo an invented cigar brand

sikapoo rich

sobolo an exclamation

sunsum soul

tafla tse excuse-me-to-say

tama waist beads

tilapia fish

tintiintin very long

tooshies buttocks

topo mouse (Italian)

trotro passenger vehicle

tulipano tulip (Italian)

waakye a meal made of rice and beans
walai! an exclamation
wusa a herb
yewura sir
yoo ke gari gari and beans
yoyi fruit